Praise

"Beware. *Froze...*

New Yo... author

"Gripping, atm... ...ggers,

New Yo... ...y bestselling
author of *Saint's Gate*

"Watterson's evocative prose brings to life a Wisconsin winter where the most dangerous threat isn't the cold but a cunning killer who will leave you chilled to the bone." —CJ Lyons,
New York Times and *USA Today*
bestselling author

"A tale of psychological suspense that builds to a chilling ending . . . will keep you turning the pages late into the evening." —Jamie Freveletti,
international bestselling author

"Taut, tense, and completely original—I couldn't put it down! Kate Watterson is a terrific storyteller and this compelling page-turner will wrap you in gripping suspense until the very last page."

—Hank Phillippi Ryan,
Anthony, Agatha, and Macavity
Award–winning author

TOR BOOKS BY KATE WATTERSON

Frozen
Charred
Buried (forthcoming)

CHARRED

Kate Watterson

TOR®

A TOM DOHERTY ASSOCIATES BOOK • NEW YORK

This is a work of fiction. All of the characters, organizations, and events portrayed in this novel are either products of the author's imagination or are used fictitiously.

CHARRED

Copyright © 2013 by Katherine Smith

A Tor Book
Published by Tom Doherty Associates, LLC
175 Fifth Avenue
New York, NY 10010

www.tor-forge.com

Tor® is a registered trademark of Tom Doherty Associates, LLC.

ISBN 978-0-7653-6961-1

Tor books may be purchased for educational, business, or promotional use. For information on bulk purchases, please contact Macmillan Corporate and Premium Sales Department at 1-800-221-7945 extension 5442 or write specialmarkets@macmillan.com.

First Edition: June 2013

Printed in the United States of America

0 9 8 7 6 5 4 3 2 1

For Suzanne Smith-Reh,
who is very much a friend as well as a sister-in-law.

Prologue

It was one of those evenings. Quiet. Too quiet, really. All dark woods, with the occasional flicker of a firefly, and lightning spiking to the west. The air was heavy, the scent of rain visceral and immediate.

Rain could be a problem.

I had it planned, but you could never count on the weather. My father, descended from generations of pessimistic farmers, always told me that. At this moment, though I discounted anything else he thought mattered and reiterated time and again, that one line I believed.

A storm was moving in at the worst time possible.

The hay bales, hauled from the barn, were still dry as tinder right now. I'd had to walk three miles to the convenience store for the matches, because they'd taken it all away. Lighters, kindling, even turned off the pilot on the stove . . .

It came down to just that.

Me or them.

They'd known, and I'd known, and when we both realized it, the inevitability was like being set free. They *were afraid, but still didn't believe. The possibility was there, like the fly buzzing at the window, an unpleasant sound but part of the landscape.*

That was about to change.

Bending down, I struck the first match and it flared and went out.

Son of a bitch.

The second I shielded from the breeze with my palm and it caught right away. Just a light blaze and I warmed my hands, because they were cold and clammy from nervousness.

Surely everyone was nervous their first time.

Chapter 1

The world shimmered.

It was that damn hot.

Detective Ellie MacIntosh said an obscene word under her breath as she slid out of the car and the humidity rolled over her like a tidal wave.

With a grimace, she said, "Sorry I'm late. Long story. Okay, why am I here?"

Not her usual greeting, but it had already been one hell of a day. Never mind that the arch of sky was a glowing blue and the air thick enough that when she took in a sharp breath she got a lungful of acrid smoke.

"One victim," a young patrol officer said, pointing toward the still-smoldering building. "We've been waiting on you, and the ME is on his way, Detective."

Santiago, her new partner, was already on the scene, his wavy blond hair looking like he'd just got out of bed. It was almost noon. She didn't want to know if that was true or not for myriad reasons. He nodded as she walked up toward the house and remarked sarcastically, "Nice of you to show up."

"First of all, I took a vacation day to visit my sister for the holiday weekend and so I'm technically not on duty. Second, I was headed out of town when the call came and had to turn around, then there was an accident on 94, and my cell phone went dead. You know how hot it is to sit in stopped traffic today?"

He lifted his hands. "Hey, I was joking. No need to get hostile. I've an ex-Marine buddy who lives in New Orleans. He sent me a text telling me how he felt sorry for us up here in Milwaukee, that's how bad it is. I think I heard it hit a hundred in International Falls, Minnesota, for Christ's sake. It's the jet stream or something. Even the Canadians are roasting, but forget the heat."

"Easier said than done."

"Wait until you see this, MacIntosh."

Wait until I see . . .

No good conversation ever started that way.

"See what?" she asked sharply, glad she wore a sleeveless summer blouse with her slacks, her jacket back in the car. Maybe she didn't look as much like a homicide detective, but neither was she going to be covered with an instant sheen of sweat.

Santiago shook his head. He had intense blue eyes and was around her age she'd guess, early thirties, his attitude slightly cocky, which she found abrasive. He was smart according to her boss, and she thought that was true with a few reservations, though this would be their first interaction on a case outside of the station.

It was probably wrong because she didn't know him well enough, but there was a bit of an issue. She didn't *dislike* him precisely, but he had an edginess that made her wary. If she didn't operate on her instincts she wouldn't be good at her job, and he rubbed her the wrong way, plain and simple.

He handed her his notepad, but his writing was inde-cipherable, like graffiti on a tenement wall, some of it in capitals and other words too small to read. Apparently he'd never written a college term paper, which was some-thing else she'd heard. He'd worked his way up through the law-enforcement ranks without higher education. She gave it back. "Give me a vocal thumbnail. I rarely do notes anyway."

For a second he looked annoyed, but it was just a flicker across his face. "Fine. The fire apparently came out of nowhere, and because almost everyone in this neigh-borhood works, no one noticed the blaze until the place was too far gone to save. The fire department answered, but there was no going inside. It was flames up to the roof. They didn't decide to call us until they went in and discovered the victim."

"Owner?" Ellie squinted at the house through the haze of smoke.

"Not our deceased."

"Oh? You know that how?"

"A couple named Tobias owns the house. A neighbor called them to tell them about the fire. She was at work all morning like just about everyone else. He had a job interview and went to get one of the tires replaced on his car. He was still in the waiting room when the fire was called in, and had been for over an hour."

"Sounds like they can back up their stories?" she an-swered, wiping her brow with the back of her hand. "Why does it have to be one hundred and ten degrees on the day we investigate a fire? Okay, so not them. Who do they think it is and why is this a case for homicide?"

"They have no idea who it could be." He walked next to her toward the house, which no doubt had resembled the other houses in the neighborhood, single-story, neat and square, with a small front yard with a cement walk and bushes along the foundation. Now the sprawl of hoses, the smoke still hanging in the air, the gaping hole in one corner, and the broken roof made it a one of a kind.

She looked at him sharply. "None? Are you serious?"

"Nope, none. And when you get inside, you'll see why we're here. There is no doubt this fire was set."

He had the assurance of a seasoned homicide detective and she wasn't quite there yet.

Fine. This was not an exact science. It was more like an acquired skill, something you might have apprenticed to if this was the Middle Ages, but it was right now and she was a fast learner.

"Accelerant?"

"The arson squad can tell you for sure, but let's just say I am making an educated guess and I'll say yes."

The ambulance pulled up then, quiet, no lights revolving, no siren. That was never a good sign, but then again, if there had been any need for speed, she wouldn't be there.

Too little, too late . . .

She nodded. "Let's go in and take a look if we're clear."

"The fire department guys say to step carefully, but they've got it out. The place is one hot fucking mess."

It might have been okay if he didn't laugh.

She shot him another sidelong glance as they walked up the cracked steps to the smoldering building. Billows of smoke still eddied out to mar the cloudless summer afternoon. Jason Santiago had what she thought of as a Renaissance face. A slightly Roman nose, his eyebrows darker gold than his hair, his chin almost too square to make him attractive, but almost was almost. He was good-looking, not that it mattered to her one way or the other really, but his personality so far was a bit of a problem. She said deliberately and meant it, "None of this is funny."

"Lighten up. I just pointed out I wasn't trying to be funny." Like her he wasn't wearing a suit coat, but wore a button-up with a collar in deference to the job, and there was a hint of wet rings under his armpits, his white shirt stuck to his torso, his sidearm prominent in the shoulder holster.

The front door was warped, the glass glazed by dark streaks, the handle wrapped in protective police tape. She asked, "Where are the homeowners?"

"They're waiting next door with a neighbor. Both of them are in shock, or doing a very good imitation of it if they aren't, and it is too hot to expect them to stand outside. I thought the wife was going to pass out in the driveway."

"I might too if my house burned down with a person inside it who wasn't supposed to be there. I'll go in and take a look and then go talk to them."

"Whatever you want. I've already done both."

The tone irritated her, but then again, she *had* been late.

"Once again, sorry."

It was grudging, and if he noticed he didn't show it as he swept the door open. "Let me let you into the candy store."

She'd been warned he was a wiseass.

She shot him another glance that said she didn't approve of the levity and he looked entirely unmoved, his gaze sardonic.

Whatever.

The real problem was she knew cops and he wanted

to see her reaction to the scene, so it must really be bad. *Great.* She was new to the department and this was no doubt some sort of stupid male test . . . She could practically hear him thinking *Let's see if she barfs . . .*

Because Jason Santiago would use the word "barf." She was sure of it.

Well, she hated to break it to him, but after the serial murder case in northern Wisconsin last year, she didn't rattle all that easy.

It took her a moment before she stepped across the blackened space, lifted in place over her face the mask one of the firemen had given her, and then registered the unnatural odor and *saw* the body.

Yeah, at that moment she could see why they were there.

It was displayed on what looked like the coffee table, set on the hearth, no doubt about it, raised as if an offering on a makeshift altar, the rest of the room in ashes, part of the ceiling down, the couch still smoldering, the carpet soaked from the rescue attempt. The remains resembled a forgotten rack of ribs on a grill, blackened flesh, bones poking through like spines on a fin, teeth startlingly white against the macabre background of what used to be a face. Open windows made no difference; the smell was there even with the smoke, a faint hint of cooked meat.

It was gruesome as hell.

But this was her job, what she'd signed on for when offered the position. In northern Wisconsin, when working with the county sheriff's department, she'd been a detective handling all sorts of cases. Now that she was a homicide detective in a fairly big city, dead bodies were going to be part of the scenery.

Still, she didn't like this aspect of her job and doubted anyone would. The hunt, yes, but not the reason for it.

One foot in front of the other. That was how this worked, right? The carpet squished under her shoes and fixtures from the ceiling hung like stripped skeletons, naked and useless. The room was close with death; steaming, wet, and at the moment could be the most unpleasant place on the planet.

"Jesus, it's hot in here." Santiago mopped his brow with his sleeve, his voice muffled by the mask.

Ellie had to agree with that. "This is staged. Victim was dead before the place was torched."

"Oh, yeah. Hell yes. My thoughts exactly. Victim torched before the fire. Look at the table, it really isn't all that burned, not nearly as much as Mr. or Ms. Crispy."

She was really going to have to learn to ignore the tasteless remarks.

They both stood very still, gazes roving over the topography of destruction; quiet, apart, thinking. She could see why even identifying the sex of the victim could be a problem. The body was nothing but a blackened outline suggestive of a human being.

Ellie went closer, though it wasn't particularly what she wanted to do. "The arms are crossed. No one dies that way."

"I have to agree with you on that one."

"Why is the body laid out and posed?" She pulled gloves out of her pocket from habit, and slipped them on.

"I'm thinking it's a statement."

"Maybe gang related? Can you tell?"

"Is that an inference because of my last name, Detective?" His smile was thin.

"No." For a second she was puzzled, but then caught

on. *Seriously?* She couldn't really care less about his background. He looked just as Scandinavian as she did. "I was asking if you have something to impart, so feel free. I've not been in Milwaukee that long, remember?"

Truthfully, she was struggling more than a little not to gag because the scene was so disturbing, but there was no way she'd give him that satisfaction.

No. No gagging.

"I was in a little trouble when I was younger. Jesus, gossip in the department is as bad as a high school hallway."

His eyes were straightforward, not openly hostile, but it was there. He half unbuttoned his shirt, the material hanging open. "Leave the last name at the door. It wasn't gang related either."

"Actually, no one has mentioned to me anything about your juvenile activities until you did just now. You always this defensive? I merely wondered, since I agree it looks like a statement, if it was a signature you might recognize from your police experience as a *detective*."

"Nope." The word was flippant, but his whole attitude was flippant in her opinion.

"You do realize we are supposed to work as a team, right?"

Because of the mask she couldn't see his expression, but his eyes narrowed a fraction. "Yeah, I sure as hell realize that, Detective MacIntosh."

It wasn't that great a start to this case that they were already arguing.

MacIntosh didn't want to work with him. He got the vibe every single time she looked at him.

That was fine.

He wasn't thrilled either. Honey blond hair, wide hazel eyes . . . Normally he liked pretty women; he was quite a fan, actually, and though it sounded sexist, he really didn't want someone who looked like a high school cheerleader for a partner. Besides, though she'd worked a few homicides according to Chief Metzger, in Jason's opinion, she hadn't paid her dues. The only thing that had landed her the job was one high-profile serial-murder case up north and the fact that she'd helped recover the missing niece of a federal judge this past spring.

He'd worked dozens of cases and he was good at it, and he resented the idea he might have to baby-sit her. She'd gotten the job so easily, equal footing with him, equal money . . .

Jason adjusted his gloves, looked at what they had to work with, which wasn't much, and shrugged. "We have a few problems in this city with gangs. And no, this is not gang related. They like to leave a calling card. This might be a statement, but if it is, I have no idea what the motherfucker is saying."

The language bothered her. He could tell from the flicker of disapproval in her eyes, but he really didn't care and she was going to have to get used to it. Surely she'd heard worse. She'd gone a little pale too since they'd entered the nightmare, but otherwise she hadn't so much as flinched.

"*If* the message is intended for us in the first place. It seems to me the homeowners are the likely target." MacIntosh walked gingerly around the destruction of the room, her slender shoulders tense, her attention everywhere but the body. Couldn't blame her for that, he had to admit. They couldn't touch it, and until the scene was processed, anything else either. She said decisively, "Let's go ahead and do the interview now. The crime scene guys can let us know when they're done."

See now, *that* was another reason he didn't like her. He'd been with the department for twelve years. Busted his ass to get hired in the first place because of his juvenile record, worked his way up as a patrol officer, then paid his dues through vice and up to homicide. He looked younger than he was, he'd guess he was at least four years older than she was, and he sure as hell knew more about the Milwaukee crime map than she did.

No two ways: He didn't like her trying to take charge and she really, really needed to realize it or they were not going to get along. "I've already talked to them. I offered the notes on the interview, but you gave them back."

"*I* haven't talked to them," she responded, looking directly at him since the first time they had entered the stinking room. If she wore makeup it wasn't easy to tell. Natural lips, clear skin, hair straight and shining blond to her shoulders, eyes unadorned. Not married that he knew, but he'd heard a rumor she'd moved down from northern Wisconsin because her boyfriend lived in the area.

It was in him to argue, but he managed to contain it and not point out that she was being insulting, but then again, they really hadn't worked together yet except for a couple of cases that were mostly paperwork. So he said nonchalantly, "Go for it. I'll stay here with our overdone friend."

Maybe, just maybe, she caught the tone because she sent him a sharp look. "I might catch something you didn't during the interview, Santiago."

"You might." He hunched his shoulders and looked at the grisly corpse, then glanced out the window. Through the scarred glass and smears of soot, water still dripping from the frame, he saw the medical examiner's car had rolled up.

About time.

He didn't envy the guy this one. Dr. Reubens was young, fairly new to the job, not one of the gray-faced old guard that had seen it all. This might even rattle a seasoned ME.

MacIntosh looked at him. "Looks like the room is going to get crowded. I'm going next door to talk to the owners."

Chapter 2

I'd wondered once or twice about the basement. It was one of those things, a kid's nightmare that resurfaced, the closet that needed to be looked in because you just had to know, the growling beast under the bed, fangs bared and claws flexing.

But I was fascinated by that beast. Not repelled, but intrigued.

Instead it had proved to be just a small dank square, filled with junk like abandoned iron bedsteads, discarded folding chairs, an old kerosene tank, a bag of soccer balls and baseballs, all of them too torn to use, the broken washer that was supposed to go to the dump . . .

I was also fascinated by the mildewed boxes of pictures no one would ever look at again, the faces blurred and forgotten, the clothing out of date, their imprint on this world gone except for a musty container shoved into a dark corner, of no use, no value.

I took the box and hid it in my room. It was like having a secret cache of friends, an inner circle, my ownership of their images giving me power over their eventual *fate, for those photographs were their only link back to a world that had allowed them to pass unnoticed every day. All except for me, who studied their faces and gave them stories.*

But friendships can be good or bad.

In the end I made them pay for our time together. I burned the box and the faces curled and went black and then they were all gone.

It was a very beautiful moment.

The room was quintessential fifties décor: a faded once pale green couch with square legs, a hutch with wheat-patterned dishes, a worn rug, lace doilies on the end tables. But it was surprisingly comfortable, Ellie thought as she sat down, probably because it smelled a whole lot better than the house right next door.

She might never forget that smell. Of all the experiences in this life she would prefer to skip, the smell of roasted human flesh was in the top ten for sure. *Jesus.*

"Can I get you some lemonade, Detective?"

She glanced up at the elderly woman who hovered in the doorway, and then at the young couple that sat together on the couch by the unused fireplace with a hearth showcasing a vase full of plastic flowers. She shook her head. "I appreciate the offer, ma'am, but no thank you. I only have a few questions for Mr. and Mrs. Tobias and I'll be on my way. I know they already spoke with Detective Santiago, but sometimes details surface when you think it over a second time."

The young woman had obviously been crying, her puffy eyes and streaked face the epitome of misery, and having seen the inside of their home, Ellie could only predict her current state of unhappiness was not going to improve. She had no idea how diplomatic Santiago had been, and if she had to guess from their brief acquaintance, not very.

"I'm really sorry this all has happened." Ellie usually didn't take notes except mentally and this was no exception. That pad and pen made people nervous, and she'd never found if someone told her something important she didn't remember it. Later she'd type up her impressions in a file on the computer. "Can you explain to me the events of today? In your own words. For instance, did anything out of the ordinary happen before you left the house this morning?"

Mr. Tobias, thin, lanky, and faintly scarred from acne, shook his head. "I didn't notice anything. And I know I locked the door. I let the dog out right before I left."

Dog? Shit, she hadn't seen a dog . . .

"He isn't in the backyard. The firemen think he might have run off," the helpful elderly lady said, still hovering in the door. "My husband is out looking for him. He knows Bill."

These poor people couldn't catch a break. Ellie couldn't do much about the torched house or the strange corpse except to hopefully find out who did it, but she sure hoped Bill would find their dog.

The wife had started quietly crying again. Gently, Ellie asked, "Do you remember anything, Mrs. Tobias?"

The woman shook her head and sniffled. She might be pretty under other circumstances, almost fragile looking, with short brunette hair. She wore a beige skirt and light blue short-sleeved blouse, and a thin gold bracelet dangled from her limp wrist. "I work at the library about two blocks from here . . . I heard the fire engines go by and told my supervisor someone was having a bad day. I had no idea . . ." A choked sob ended the brief recital.

That was an ironic and unfortunate comment, Ellie had to agree.

"Who has keys to your house? Just the two of you?"

"And her father," Matthew Tobias interjected. His tan shirt was partially pulled out of the waistband of his pants and one bit of wispy blond hair stuck up at the back of his head. His wife stiffened. Almost immediately, he stammered, "Not . . . not that I think he would ever be involved in this."

"No, of course not. The keys could have been stolen and he doesn't even know it. We'd appreciate it if you'd check with him and see if they are still where he usually keeps them. With all the damage, we can't tell right away if there was forced entry, but the fire department said the front door was locked."

Mr. Tobias clasped his wife's hand. "We don't understand any of this. The other detective asked us if we keep our coffee table on top of the fireplace hearth. Of course we don't. It's in front of the couch."

Not at the moment. No one was ever going to prop his feet up on it or set down a diet soda while he watched television on that particular piece of furniture again. If it hadn't had a tile top and metal frame, it might have been gone altogether.

A cuckoo clock in the corner thrust out a fake bird and made the requisite sound. Ellie decided to try one more time. "What I'm looking for is any event out of the ordinary, not just this morning but recently. Anyone take your morning paper? You find a window unlatched? What about trouble at work? Either one of you?"

"Enough to kill someone in my house and burn it down?" Tobias laughed incredulously, but mirth was not associated with the hoarse sound. "No. *That* kind of a problem I'd remember. Besides, at the moment I'm . . . between jobs. Michelle has no idea why this happened either. We've been sitting here talking about it." He rubbed his face. "It's . . . surreal."

He wasn't going to feel the same way once the police left, the fire department pulled out, and what they were left with was one hell of a mess and their insurance company. It was also a crime scene until the Milwaukee PD was through with the house, and sometimes that took a little while. It was going to be all too real very soon.

His wife asked in a pitiful voice, "Why would anyone do this to us?"

What about the poor person who wasn't alive and well and drinking lemonade, but Ellie refrained from pointing that out. They were in shock; she would be too. "I don't know, but I am going to do my best to try and find out."

"It won't change what happened," Matthew Tobias whispered. "But I suppose we should thank you."

"Any idea where you are going to stay tonight?" Ellie was a cop, but she was also a human being. As of yet her stone and timber house up in the woods of Lincoln County hadn't sold, and she valued every single piece of furniture and anything else she owned in it. If someone had done to her what had just happened to them . . . she wasn't sure how she'd deal with it. There was always something that couldn't be replaced. Furniture for the most part was not a tragedy, but pictures and other keepsakes were just . . . lost.

Matthew put his arm firmly around his wife's shoulders, more effectual than he seemed on first impression. "We have friends and family. We'll make arrangements."

At this point it was futile to try to question them further, especially since they didn't seem to have any information to offer, or *wouldn't* offer. Ellie rose, nodded, and headed for the door.

Bad timing.

They happened to be bringing out the body from the still smoldering house, the quiet street crowded with spectators and a camera crew from a local station. Santiago stood at the fringe of the police tape, talking to one of the crime scene guys. One lean hand ran systematically through his already disheveled hair, and he shook his head emphatically.

She wished they connected better. Rick, her last partner in the investigation that had helped her get this job, had been a typical pigheaded male in some ways, but they had gotten along. He had never possessed a jagged edge like she felt with Jason Santiago.

Not that it really mattered. They *would* work together because that was what the department wanted, and as long as he was a good cop—everyone said he was—then it would have to be okay. Maybe he'd grow on her. Like a rash or something, she thought wryly.

She walked over, looking at Santiago, not the gurney being loaded into the ambulance. The body was zipped into a bag, but that didn't help; she'd seen it, and the image was burned into her brain. The doors closed with a final bang that rang out with a singular sound. Her partner glanced at her. "Well? Our lucky couple give you anything?"

"Not really." She blew out a short breath. "Let's talk to the neighbors, find out who was home at the time the fire started. Maybe someone saw something. Anything. If the fire was set, and it clearly was, it looks like two people broke into this house uninvited and only one of them left. Until we have more information and an ID of the victim, all we can do is go fishing."

"Let me guess, you'll cast and I'll reel them in."

That tone again. She looked at him. "What?"

He lifted one of his eyebrows and said, "Never mind. Fine, let's go."

Carl Grasso let himself into the foyer, welcoming the cool waft of the air-conditioning, dropping his keys into a crystal bowl. The faceted mirror his mother had bought in France hung above the marble table and he caught his reflection in the glass. He'd probably changed some in the past five years. A few more silver flecks in his hair, maybe some more lines at the corner of his eyes. He usually didn't pay much attention, but he had to shave every day, so he saw his reflection each morning; he just didn't really look at it. All the requisite parts were okay, eyes, nose, mouth, square chin . . . at least he wasn't losing his hair, not yet anyway, and he worked out like a religious fanatic and ran at least ten miles a week.

Anything to fill the time.

He discarded his tie over the back of a wing chair in the family room as he walked toward the kitchen, going into the butler's pantry and taking out a bottle of single malt scotch from the bar, and fishing a glass out of the cupboard above the small sink. Two fingers, some distilled water, and a couple of ice cubes, and he took a sip, thinking about the day.

About the murder in Bayview.

He still didn't know much, but he knew *enough*.

If he considered this too much he wouldn't do it. So he went back into the kitchen, set his glass on the marble counter, and got out his cell phone. He hadn't talked to her in two years so maybe her number had changed, but he tried it anyway.

Rachel answered on the third ring, her voice tentative. "Hello?"

"Hi. It's Carl."

"Oh." She sounded nonplussed. He could see her in his mind's eye, shapely, early forties now, auburn hair, or it had been that shade when they'd been involved and he could testify that it was genuine. Then her voice returned to the usual modulated professional tone he remembered. "Well, Lieutenant Grasso. I admit this is a surprise."

There were French doors that led outside to the patio and beyond that, the water in the pool shimmered blue-green in the slanting light. Not quite dusk yet, but it was coming. He took another sip of his drink before he said, "I think The Burner is back."

"No 'how are you'? I'm fine, by the way. I'm opening a bottle of a Willamette Valley chardonnay and I might drink every drop because I just took my mother to dinner—wait, excuse me, how could I make such a mistake. I meant supper. Dinner is at noon, supper in the evening. She corrected me when I invited her and there I went, slipping again."

He laughed quietly. He'd missed her. And yes, her mother, whom he'd met twice, was a woman who had her first child in middle age, so there was a more pronounced generation gap than usual.

"I'm sorry," he said. "You know me, always on the job. Besides your mother, how are you? How is the position at the university?"

"Being a professor of journalism is not nearly as exciting as being a reporter, but I like it." She sounded like she genuinely meant it. "I even agreed to teach summer classes this year."

He heard it in her voice. *Why not?* They always had too much in common. A restlessness and sense of purpose that should have brought them closer but instead made them drift apart.

"Good for you."

"It might be," she agreed, the audible sound of liquid splashing into a glass in the background. "Now, what's this about The Burner? Who is that?" Then she stopped and there was a momentary silence and her voice was remarkably different when she spoke again. "Wait. Are you talking about that homicide five years ago?"

"I am." He slowly swirled the ice in his glass. The sky was starting to turn an interesting shade of red streaked with indigo. "I think it might be the same person, and that's my affectionate nickname for the perpetrator in that particular case."

He'd worked it for months until he'd just reached one dead end after another, and Rachel, as an investigative reporter, had interviewed him about it, and that had been how they met. Essentially lust at first sight, but their relationship had gone nowhere, much like the investigation.

"Why?" She switched instantly to that professional reporter he remembered with the rapid-fire questions. "Hold on, I'm taking off my earring." A pause. "All right, go ahead. I woke up just the other night and was thinking about that case. What a coincidence. What makes you think there is a connection?"

"Body on a table and the whole place lit on fire."

She said something softly under her breath and then asked, "Are you serious?"

"Yes. Unfortunately, I'm not on this one."

He wasn't even homicide any longer. His fault. He knew it, but he missed the division, and this had once been *his* investigation.

The rustle in the background might have been her settling into a chair. She had a condo right across from the lake, modern, comfortable, perfect for a single woman, with spectacular views. He'd been there more than once, spent the night quite a few times actually, and he liked it. The place was opposite the house his parents had left him, which was anything but cozy and modern, but he hadn't seemed to be able to come to a decision about putting his home on the market.

Clinging to the past, he would guess a therapist would tell him, but he didn't see therapists—didn't really believe in them—and at the end of the day, it was just a place to live.

Rachel asked carefully, and he knew it was careful by the tone of her voice, "So, what are you going to do?"

The ice had melted in his drink, the liquid a beautiful pale gold. He considered it abstractly. "I might look into it on my own."

"Why did I know you were going to say that? Should you?"

"Have dinner with me." The suggestion was not exactly impulsive. The call had been a little impulsive maybe, but the question, no. He'd been thinking about it, about her, for some time. "Do you still have all your notes?"

"Burned bodies over dinner? That sounds romantic, Detective."

"We've done it before."

The double entendre made her laugh, though he hadn't particularly planned it. It made him laugh too. "I meant—"

"How about tomorrow night? I assume if you haven't changed considerably, you will want to discuss this as soon as possible. Pick me up at seven."

"Dinner tomorrow then."

"Supper," she corrected and ended the call.

Chapter 3

I drove along the rutted road about twice a year. In the spring the apple trees bloomed, tiny white flowers exploding like a frost of fallen snow, and later in the fall, the apples would weigh the branches almost to the ground. The deer would come at dusk, shadows in the dying light, and eat the fallen fruit, the big bucks heavy with their racks, the does small and graceful. One year my father shot a ten pointer, out of season, and bragged about it for years.

The barn had started to fall in on itself a long time ago, rotted timbers collapsing slowly, sagging like an old woman's tits, showing its age, no longer useful.

Parking the car, I got out and slammed the door, the sound echoing in the quiet. My shoes crushed the overgrown vegetation, instantly damp in the evening dew.

It was unnaturally quiet, as if my invasion was a personal affront to nature, even the birds silent at the presence of an interloper. It was almost eerie.

Ellie parked her car and sat for a moment, looking at the house. The Land Rover was in the garage no doubt, parked in the clean, neat interior, the shelves holding only a few necessary tools, the lawn mower in the other bay. The exterior of the split level was brick, the lawn had some nice mature trees, and the neighborhood was upscale middle class, into the 25 percent tax bracket. Down the street there were some kids playing basketball in a driveway; she could hear the smack of the ball on the pavement and the resulting shouts when someone sent it up.

She'd forgotten to pick up the bottle of merlot she'd offered to bring. *Damn.* He'd better have some, she thought as she slid out of the car. Luckily, Bryce was a more talented cook than she was, so she could at least count on a nice dinner.

The glass door was shut, but the door was open, and she didn't knock but just twisted the knob and stepped into the flagstone entryway. It was high, two stories, with a modern chandelier made of pendant lights—her suggestion—and ivory walls. More grand than her usual taste, but she had to admit the place was finally coming together, the furnishings in the living room masculine with leather couches and mahogany tables, a couple of lamps with stained glass shades scattered around and no television, which always impressed her. That was in the den, down the hallway, and Bryce didn't seem to use it too much, preferring his precious books. Not too surprising, since he had a Ph.D. in literature, but she was a lot more used to guys who watched ESPN like it was their job.

This was the most interesting relationship of her life and she really wished she was more convinced it would work out.

She was into it . . . into him, the sex was good—great even—but he was really laid back, and she just . . .

wasn't. Her job, what she did, was not conducive to being laid back.

Not to mention that they had met when she was working the serial murder case up north and he had been the main suspect. He'd been cleared, but one of their problems was that she was not anxious for any of her colleagues—particularly Santiago after today—to find out she was involved with someone she'd once investigated.

Bryce was in the kitchen. She could smell the tantalizing aroma of garlic with a hint of soy. "Please tell me," she said by way of greeting as she walked in, "that you are cooking Chinese food. It smells like it and I am trying to not get my hopes up because this has, like I told you on the phone, been one hell of a day."

He glanced up from the counter, which was poured concrete in a rich brown color to match the tiled floor. A stray lock of dark hair routinely fell over his forehead and tonight was no exception. He had finely modeled features and a killer—if rare—smile, and a nice, lean build.

The smile flashed. "I might be. Your favorite. Garlic chicken."

Heaven.

"I canceled on my sister because I was almost out of the city when I got a call from work. And, by the way, I forgot the wine." She set her purse on the counter. "Sorry. Maybe that makes it two for two on my part. Jody is ticked at me and we have no wine."

"Relax. It wouldn't have gone with the food anyway. Have a glass of the Chablis I chilled earlier." He jerked his chin toward the refrigerator. "I wouldn't mind one either."

"Waiting for me?"

"Your text spoke volumes. Even before you called I'd decided you needed garlic chicken."

Bad day. Watch the news. Can we eat in?

Short and sweet and all too accurate. She took out two glasses, uncorked the wine, and he tossed the marinated chicken into the pan where it made a satisfying sizzle. The chopped vegetables on the cutting board also looked promising. For lunch she'd eaten a dry as dust doughnut left in the box in the break room at the station. On her day off, no less, and the beginning of a holiday weekend.

She set down his glass on the counter close to the stove, took her first oh-so-amazing sip, braced her hip, and said, "We have an interesting case."

"Sure sounded like it." He scooped up onions and tossed them into the mix. "Or I got that impression."

"Arson and murder."

"Match made in heaven." Some ginger went in, the pungent aroma instantly wafting out.

He had the most perfect profile. Great tousled ebony hair, straight nose, a nice mouth, masculine chin. This evening he wore just a T-shirt and khaki shorts, his feet bare, and he moved with athletic grace, efficient and quick.

The chemistry was definitely there in a physical way.

"What?" She blinked, the glass halfway to her mouth.

"Setting something on fire to obliterate the clues?" He paused, the knife poised over the pan, what looked like chopped garlic on the blade, his gaze inquiring. "I assume a fire, and the resulting effort to put it out, makes quite a mess for an investigator. What doesn't burn is then sprayed with water, right?"

Actually, he was right. One hundred percent.

He wasn't a cop. That was one of the best things

about him besides that he was intelligent, nice to look
at, and a really good cook. Ellie unfortunately remembered the inside of the Tobias house and nodded, taking
a swift hit from her wineglass. "Yeah, a mess. You could
say that."

Besides being literate to the nth degree, Bryce was
fairly intuitive for someone who wrote computer software for a living. The garlic slid in, but he was still looking at her. "How bad was it? You look . . . well, you
have a certain *look*. I've seen it before and it isn't good."

"Thanks. I take it I shouldn't be flattered."

"I didn't mean it *that* way."

She knew exactly what he meant. Midway to intensely
focused, and flirting with grimness. "If the stage hadn't
been set up like it was, I might not have even seen it as a
homicide. That speaks of someone who doesn't mind
having the police involved. Do you want me to chop the
green onions for the garnish?"

He stopped, his dark eyes narrowing. "Stage?"

"As in the body displayed in a theatrical manner, a
message that was really unmistakable, never mind how
wasted the inside of the house might have been. What
about the green onions?"

At that point he stepped back and nodded, passing
her the knife. It was something she really, *really* liked
about him. He was one of the few people she'd ever met
that knew when to let things go.

Except, the problem was, she wasn't. She didn't ever
let things go until they were entirely resolved. A personal flaw.

"The killer wants us to feel him out there." Neatly she
severed the white part of the root from the onions and
the scent was clean and almost sweet. Outside the window over the sink, the street was peaceful and serene as

the evening faded in a molten slide into the heavy dusk. There was a barbecue going on somewhere, maybe at the house two doors down, because a man and a woman carrying covered dishes got out of a minivan, both of them laughing.

This was, after all, the day before the Fourth of July. Somehow, after a stint in that house with the dead body, she didn't feel all that festive.

Bryce picked up his glass of wine and lifted it to his mouth to take a quick drink as he stirred the chicken. "Okay. If you can't tell me I understand, but I'm naturally curious. Maybe it was the word 'stage.' How so?"

She could never do that. Cooking for her required a single-minded concentration, but their personalities were certainly very different.

Maybe too much so. She couldn't decide if that was good or bad.

"I won't give you the gruesome details because I know you don't want them, but the victim was definitely placed in a position so we know they didn't die that way naturally, and then, it appears, set on fire."

"That's gruesome enough, thank you. No more details necessary."

"The medical examiner is hopefully going to tell us more." She said it in a meditative voice, more thinking out loud than anything. "Dead is dead and I would look for the killer either way, but it really feels like someone went to some trouble to make us investigate this one."

"Why the hell would anyone want to attract the attention of the homicide department of the Milwaukee Police?" He spoke with the conviction of a person who had once been under scrutiny.

She'd wondered that herself. Quite a lot in the past few hours. Ellie lifted a shoulder and lopped the top off another scallion. "Who knows? I agree, it sounds risky to make sure we know what happened wasn't an accident. However, my job is pretty straightforward. *Why* doesn't interest me all that much. *Who* really does. And he'd better watch it, for he really has my attention."

"Does he? And in a bad way. I can tell you from experience, he doesn't want that."

He was probably right, Ellie thought. The dark spot in his life might have shifted, but Bryce spoke with the resigned cynicism of someone in the aftermath of a bitter divorce and who had been suspected of being a serial killer.

Add: *You might just date a homicide detective.*

She needed to refocus. Oh sure, he stood there in the kitchen just a few feet away, but he'd faded and gone blank as she looked at the diamond-patterned backsplash and remembered things she wished would never be imbedded in her psyche, like blackened corpses.

She mused out loud, "You're on the right track, of course. That part I don't get. Who would seek to deliberately draw our notice? Maybe, when we find out the identity of the victim, we'll be able to at least speculate."

But she was speculating now, wine in hand, mind busy, the shiny knife turning the onions into tiny white and green rounds . . .

"How did they get the body there?"

She appreciated the effort. He knew that engaging her this way would make her run through it out loud instead of doing it abstractly as they ate, trying to keep from him that she wasn't really part of the conversation.

"He." She finished chopping and settled on a bar stool. "I doubt this could be a conspiracy."

"Why?" Bryce had told her once he found this part of her fascinating. It was different from how his mind worked but a little like brainstorming a book . . . he rejected out of hand violence and the motivation for it, but then again, it was her job, and the what if scenario intrigued him? Human motivation usually did.

"It doesn't feel like it but it is too early to know."

"I, for the record, never want to feel a crime scene," he said in a subdued tone.

"There could have been forced entry, but I don't think so, and the crime scene team couldn't find anything to indicate it, but I think he knew the house." She eyed him over the rim of her glass, her gaze still no doubt speculative. She'd been mulling it over all afternoon.

"A friend then? Neighbor?"

She shook her head. "It doesn't really fit. Not this one."

"Okay, you know better than I do."

"This is what I know. I know that this person killed someone and took their body into that nice, middle-class home, and burned the structure practically to the ground in broad daylight. What does that say to you?"

"The guy is off the grid," he supplied easily, checking the rice, fluffing it with a fork. "I'm no expert, but that isn't sane in terms of what he did and how he did it."

She laughed. "You've been very helpful, Dr. Grantham."

"Hey, my job isn't analyzing the psyches of those you deal with every day. But okay, if you want, I'll give it a shot."

Her glass of wine hovered near her mouth. "Go for it."

It was difficult to remember, but on the other hand, all too real. Charred body, dripping ceiling, the reek of it all . . . She'd not been too specific, but specific enough that maybe he could imagine it. She hoped that as a would be-novelist he had a good imagination.

A part of her wanted this to be the single romance of her life, the others fading into a background of memory with no regrets. He'd failed at marriage once before, but she was starting to think it was worth it to try. Whether or not she was willing to admit it, she'd come down to Milwaukee for him. Sure, the job opportunity was better than a small northern county could offer, but she'd been happy enough up there.

They really needed to talk about it, but instead she wanted to discuss a corpse found in a burned house.

That said something. Bryce would meet her halfway, she knew that about him, but she was only about a third of the way there. And it wasn't just his previous marriage; she had some trust issues that involved, if she had to put a finger on it, the loss of her father, whom she had adored.

Why was life so complicated? She didn't know, but the case was an easy way out.

Once again, homicide detective. But she was also a woman, and luckily Bryce got the message that she just wasn't ready for the commitment conversation yet because he didn't push it.

"He's playing a game." He moved the pan off the flame.

"So far it isn't a fun one." She regarded him in a way she knew would spark a more meaningful discussion, inquiring but slightly mocking. "Tell me more."

"You give me too much credit." He carefully laid down the fork. "But I'll try. You've got someone who feels this sense of display resonates with him in some way. You are the one who told me all killers have signatures. We just don't get what they are right away."

"So . . ."—her eyebrows lifted in question—"the signature is?"

"You're a lot better at this than me, but the table maybe?"

"I don't know." Ellie thought about it. "Yes, the table, I agree with that, but that's not all of it. There's a chance it was just convenient." She shook her head. "I don't know if I'm better than you at this or not. At least tonight. Maybe I'm just tired."

"You are." He sounded far too sure. "You're damn good at it."

She sighed, ruffling her hair with her fingers. "What about the scene stood out to me? I keep asking myself that question. What was *different*?"

"I'm happy to not be able to answer because I didn't see it, and am happy about *that* because it sounds more than awful." Bryce, as usual, was prosaic and sensitive.

Sensitive. Since when did she go for sensitive?

Since him, she supposed.

It took her a moment where she blinked and then frowned. "Nothing . . . I mean the place was trashed as you said, by the fire department and the first cops on the scene, who had to make sure no one was still alive in there. Sloppy but effective, that's us."

"Were they really sloppy?" Bryce eyed her, a box of chicken stock in hand. "Usually you're calm, but tonight you're wound up."

"No. Yes. I'm not sure." She hunched up one shoulder in a characteristic mannerism that meant she was thinking. "What choice did they have? The answer is none. If they were sloppy, we all were. How could they possibly preserve evidence under those circumstances? They did their job, but it is frustrating."

"Who are we talking about? You need to keep me in the loop if this is the topic of evening. Doubts about the way the investigation is being handled?"

That was a valid point.

"I don't think so, and I was at least half an hour late to respond so I didn't hear Santiago interview the Tobias couple the first time. The scene was impossible to process. Enough said."

He said mildly, "Your sister knows what you do for a living. She'll get over it that you canceled."

"I know." She reached across the counter, took a green onion, dabbed it in salt on the cutting board, ate it, and elaborated. "I just think something was *there*. I can't put my finger on it right now and it has me upside down."

He scooped the garlic chicken from the pan, poured it over the steaming rice in a wide-sided deep blue bowl, and sprinkled the green onions on top. "Like what?"

"Something was different."

Bryce opened the cabinet, with efficient economy took out two plates, and set them on the counter. "Different how?"

"I want to say he's done this before. I think this was not a call for attention, but a private ritual he needed. And so he did it, and did it in broad daylight and walked away, so that says something for his sense of empowerment. He could have been seen. He *should* have been seen. But he wasn't, or if he was, no one we've talked to yet noticed him. By the way, this smells fantastic."

The house had a formal dining room—she still wasn't sure why he'd seen the need to buy such a large house except he'd told her he liked the quiet street and she knew he could afford it, but most of the time they just ate in the kitchen. Ellie didn't mind the informality, and when he took the bowl to the table in the corner near a big window overlooking the backyard, she got out two place mats and napkins with the ease of someone who knew the house well.

They ate, quiet together, letting the case subside into the background.

After dinner she debated whether or not to stay as they cleaned up the dishes together. If she left it wouldn't surprise him all that much. Bryce wasn't blind to her doubts, he was far too intuitive for that; besides, the day she had would hardly put anyone in a romantic mood.

On the other hand, she wasn't positive she wanted to be alone either.

"Stay."

She realized she was standing there, and the inner debate must have shown on her face, for he took the dish towel from her hand. "Just stay. Not only have you had two glasses of wine, but you really do look tired. We can sleep together without sex, Ellie. When you aren't interested, why not just tell me?"

But usually they did make love. Part of it was that she was very attracted to him physically, but she was afraid part of it was something else. It had occurred to her more than once that she used physical intimacy as a substitute for emotional intimacy.

That was her problem, not his.

Maybe she *was* tired, because she looked him in the eye. "I'm afraid of you."

It took him aback, his expression incredulous. "What?"

"Not physically, of course, don't look at me like that, Bryce." She took in a deep breath. "I'm not positive I really know you yet and it throws me off. Let's face it, neither one of us is good about talking about our feelings. It scares me a little. No, make that more than a little. The deeper we get into this, the more of a problem it could be."

It took him a minute to respond, which didn't surprise her, so at least she knew him well enough to discern he'd weigh his response. Then he said quietly, "Ellie, you don't *want* me to tell you I'm in love with you."

On that score she found he was absolutely right.

Chapter 4

There was no question I'd slipped once. Not a hard fall, jarring, knocking the breath from my lungs, but I'd stumbled and hit the ground in a figurative sense. A tumble from grace; a mistake even . . .

But they hadn't caught me. It might have been better if they had.

I was in high school. If you want to call it a school . . . a cut-rate community institution with painted brick walls and linoleum floors, the echoing halls filled with the sound of slamming lockers, the bell herding us like obedient sheep to our respective classrooms where bored, uninspired teachers offered whatever knowledge they possessed on subjects society had decided we needed to function in a productive way.

I wasn't expecting it, but no one ever does, do they?

But I hated for the first time.

The bitch had drawn my attention when she had laughed. At me. Her mistake. My mission crystalized then into a solid carbon mass of intent, of cause and effect.

Really, none of it was my fault.
As far as I know, they have never found her.

JULY 4

The place smelled like shit. Not literally, but to him, *shit*. Like obscure antiseptics and formaldehyde and other bizarre preservatives to stop human decomposition.

Really, the morgue was not his favorite.

Jason let the door shut behind him, blew out the breath he didn't realize he'd been holding, and put his hands in his back pockets to show he was comfortable, which he wasn't really. Ironic, for dead bodies were crucial to his chosen profession. The difference was while he was extremely interested in finding out how they died and who was responsible, he had no desire to cut them up and peer at their internal organs. Luckily for him, someone did, and he hoped the autopsy would produce some sort of clue.

"Detective Santiago."

He turned. Dr. Reubens smiled at him, wiping his hands and lifting his brows. He was young, if midthirties was still young and because that was *his* age, he thought so; forty seemed younger all the time. The medical examiner had a compelling smile and deep-set blue eyes. Light brown hair, thick and curling, and a small dimple in his left cheek gave him the appearance of an insurance agent or a high school athletic coach, something much more wholesome than his vocation. His scrubs had some suspicious stains on the front, and though Jason never had thought of himself as squeamish, he'd just as soon not know what they were from. "I'm here for the autopsy report."

"Nice outfit."

He glanced down at his shorts and flip-flops. "I'm off-duty and I'm supposed to go to some sort of cookout later. Hey, it's the Fourth."

Though, if he were honest about it, charred meat was not at the top of his list of desired foods right now, so the cookout didn't sound all that appealing. He hadn't been looking forward to the party all that much in the first place, as it was being given by someone he didn't even know, but Kate had accepted for both of them.

Kate. She'd been pissed at him for coming home so late last night and he could have earned a few points if he'd explained why, but he hadn't. He wasn't even sure *why* he hadn't explained.

Maybe so she would stay pissed? He might have to think that over later.

"Let's go through it." The medical examiner walked to a stainless steel table where several clipboards sat in neat rows, and picked one up. "The burn victim from yesterday. Interesting, I must say."

"Like interesting, how?" Jason glanced around the white, cold walls and then narrowed his gaze back on the other man. Really, this place gave him the creeps. "What did you find?"

Reubens shook his head. "Not much. I can tell you the victim is female, give an approximate age—it's in my notations—but I really have no idea how she died. There is no obvious trauma. If I had to speculate, she was decomposing before she was set on fire. There are traces of some sort of substance on what skin is left, but I assume the fire department will determine the accelerant and that is probably what it is. She must have been thoroughly dosed with it from the consistent nature of the burns. In short she went up in flames and very quickly. I know for certain she was dead before the fire started, or at least not breathing. No smoke damage to her lungs."

"No manner of death?"

Reubens cocked his head to the side. "No one ends up on a coffee table in front of a fireplace without some pretty iffy individuals being involved. I'll put suspicious circumstances in the opinion when I have it written up."

"Iffy? That's a scientific term, right?"

The doctor laughed and rubbed his jaw. "What do you prefer? Unsavory? Makes me sound like my grandmother."

Jason tried again. "No blunt-force trauma or . . ."

"Sorry to disappoint. Like I said, I can't tell you how she died, just that beyond a shadow of a doubt, she's dead."

Fuck.

"You aren't disappointing me." Jason wasn't an asshole, or didn't think he was—MacIntosh might disagree—he just needed a lead. "I don't want people out there killing other people any more than you do, but I was sort of hoping you were going to give me *something*. Anything helpful?"

"I do my best, but this one wasn't easy. My job is to give you information." Reubens dropped the clipboard onto the table with an audible clatter. "Given the circumstances I could guess at manner of death, but we don't do that here, or at least *I* don't. So, cause of death unknown, but it wasn't the fire, and manner of death can be labeled suspicious, but I am not comfortable saying it was homicide with any degree of certainty. There's no evidence to prove it."

Son of a bitch. He'd been hoping they'd get something definitive from the autopsy.

"The body was posed." Jason would just as soon not argue the point, write up the report, and be on his way, but that image unfortunately stuck in his head. "You say the victim was already dead . . . how in the fuck—er, sorry, but how *can't* it be murder?"

"It could be." Dr. Reubens slightly spread his hands. "I'm not saying it isn't. I'm saying when this person"—he pointed to a drawer in the wall—"was set on fire she was already not breathing and I can't tell if she died of natural causes or someone, for instance, stuck a pillow over her face, a method that, by the way, leaves hardly any trace, especially if you incinerate the remains."

"I'll keep that in mind, just in case I want to get rid of someone. Okay, well, approximate age?"

"Past puberty. Height and my guess at her weight are right here." He handed over a single sheet of paper. "When you have an idea who she is, dental records will have to be utilized. No one could possibly recognize her. Toxicology might help, but those results will take a few days."

That was the ugly truth. He'd have nightmares about that blackened corpse and that macabre, grinning faceless skull. He'd seen gunshot victims, stabbings, even a couple of hangings, which were no picnic, but this one was horrific. If he were at all interested in making a horror film, he would definitely include that scene where he walked into the dripping room and saw that particular corpse. Death wasn't ever pretty, but this one had been really bad. The intertwined clawlike fingers missing every bit of flesh would simply not leave his conscious thoughts.

Let it go.

"Thanks," he said, and left the morgue, happy enough to get the hell out of there. He checked out with the secretary, scribbling his name on the log, and then went outside to find that the temperature had escalated about five more degrees, the wall of heat like a battering ram.

"Holy crap." He sucked in a breath, plucked at his lightweight T-shirt, and then made his way across the parking lot to where he'd left his car. The asphalt reflected heat like a stovetop burner and he thought idly as he took out his keys to unlock the Mustang that this sort of temperature was fine if there was a beach nearby, a cold beer in your hand, and bikini-clad women everywhere.

But for Milwaukee in the middle of July? It really sucked. It got hot enough here . . . it was the Midwest after all. Ice cold in the winter, hot in the summer, but not *this* damn hot. The unusual weather had everyone on edge.

His phone vibrated in his pocket and he fished it out before sliding into the car, which was like a preheated oven. MacIntosh, he saw as he glanced at the display. He pushed a button. "Yeah?"

Not a charming greeting, but hey, that wasn't part of his job requirement. He'd just left the morgue. He didn't feel all that charming at the moment. Maybe he wasn't ever charming.

"What did Reubens have to say?"

"Nothing worthwhile to us, except it looks like she died somewhere else. He thinks maybe the body was already decomposing."

"That's strange. So he carried her inside?"

"I thought so too. Ballsy, isn't it?"

"I like that though, it gives us something."

A pause. Awkward. Why the hell couldn't the chief have given him Simmons as a partner? They played basketball together. Simmons he could handle. Goddamn it. He asked, because he couldn't think of a single other thing to say, "Where are you?"

"West Allis right now, following the slimmest lead on earth, but it is better than nothing."

Even though they didn't jibe, he had to grudgingly admit that she seemed to be a smart cop. Not big-city street smart particularly—he doubted if the woods of northern Wisconsin groomed you that way, but intellectually savvy. "Mind telling me just what kind of lead?"

We are supposed to be working on this together.

He didn't say it out loud. She had, so he refused to repeat it.

"Matthew Tobias has a sister who lives here and I thought it was worth a shot to talk to her. Remember the neighbor who mentioned she stayed with them for a couple of months not all that long ago? When I started thinking about that, I wondered if she might know something. I have no idea what that could be, but I did manage to get her number, and she's actually at home today."

He started his car and said over the growl of the engine. "Give me the address. I'll meet you there."

"Matthew called me." The woman set down a glass of iced tea, and put two fingers to her forehead. "It's unbelievable. He and Michelle stayed with her parents last night. They are devastated. I don't know how else to put it."

The efficiency apartment was spare, with a few scattered chairs and a battered coffee table, the rug patterned in bold geometrics and the only new item. Since Matthew Tobias' sister was a student and self-professed slob, it was fairly cluttered.

"I would be too." Ellie picked up the glass and condensation dripped on her leg. She wore a skirt today instead of slacks—it was just too damn hot for the latter, and she rubbed the moisture away with her palm. "That's exactly why we are here. Your brother and his wife were really in shock yesterday and found it hard to answer questions. We were wondering if you could remember anything that might link the fire to the body."

"Me?" Pretty, but as colorless as her brother, she looked perplexed. "Why would I know anything?"

"You stayed with them for several months. That means you know the house, the neighborhood, at least a little, and of course, you know them."

Santiago leaned forward, which really caught the young woman's attention. It wasn't hard to figure out why. This afternoon he wore a thin T-shirt with a rock band insignia of some kind on the front, loose shorts that would be more at home at a fraternity party, and flip-flops. In his defense they were both supposed to be off-duty, but he looked like a surfer, not a cop. He had nice biceps, which meant he probably worked out, and his eyes were that almost startling shade of blue.

Fine with her if their interview went better because he came across as a macho cop, and on short acquaintance, he was good-looking and a little funny.

In Ellie's experience that wore off pretty fast.

"Anything can be helpful. You'd be surprised." He smiled, very friendly—and falsely so—his gaze as razor sharp as ever. He didn't mean that smile. Ellie had seen it before; case in point, the day she'd met him when they were assigned together. He'd acted as if he was just fine with it, and she now knew he wasn't. The dilemma was whether or not to take it personally. Was it that she was a woman, or was it *her*? Actually, she thought it was more complicated than either of those things.

Santiago asked, "When did you last visit your brother?"

"I . . . I don't know. How is that important?"

"It probably isn't," Ellie interjected. "But we are trying to make a connection between who the victim could be and your brother's house. You have to admit it is an interesting situation."

"Oh." Her weak chin was more pronounced when her mouth fell open slightly. "Yes, it is. I guess I wish I knew something. I wasn't there much, to be honest. The lease was up on my place and I was still taking classes, so I just slept there really. Spent most of my time at the library. The neighborhood is pretty quiet. Lots of older people. They would have preferred a house in the suburbs or something—you know, something newer, but they couldn't afford that. Matt has switched jobs a couple of times."

That was interesting. "Why?"

"A few years ago he got hurt on the job. His back. He was on disability for a while but it ran out. When it flares up he misses work. He can't help it."

She'd never thought this would lead to anything anyway, so Ellie rose and handed Matthew's sister a card. "Thanks. We are just checking out any possibilities. It never hurts to ask. If you think of anything, please call me."

Nancy Tobias folded her fingers around her glass. "Wait. I hadn't thought of this before but Mr. Helton might be able to help."

Santiago had risen also in one impatient movement, his eyes narrowing. "And he is?"

"They don't own the house. They're buying it on contract. He lived there before them. The housing market has been so lousy that he went ahead and took an offer without a bank loan. I don't know if it will help, but I suppose it is possible."

Not much, but better than nothing. Worth a trip to

West Allis? Maybe. Ellie doubted it would be a big breakthrough though; nothing was that easy. How the hell did they not know that already? "Thanks," she said, her overall feeling that this was a dead end easing at least a little bit. If this Mr. Helton could give them any sort of lead, then maybe it was worth it.

They left, walking out onto a sidewalk that radiated heat like a blast furnace. Her partner drove an old muscle car of some sort, a Mustang, she noted, sleek and shiny, the dark blue color more than a little showy. It was parked at the curb of the busy street. She pointed. "That thing have air-conditioning?"

"Built in." He gestured at the convertible top. "Though I got to admit it is a pain to take the top down. Should we go shake down the Tobiases for Helton's address?"

"They've been fairly cooperative so far. I think a phone call will do it."

"I'll take care of it." He fished his keys from his pocket, tossed them in the air, and caught them in a whiplike swoop of his hand.

"Ask them if they found their dog, will you?"

"Why, you going to interview it?"

Smartass. She said, "It bothers me to think they not only lost their house, but maybe even their pet too."

"Ever think you might be in the wrong profession, MacIntosh?"

"The day they assigned me to partner with you it occurred to me," she responded dryly.

He laughed. "Kind of brought that on myself. Fine, but don't worry about the dog."

Ellie turned in the act of stepping out onto the street. "Why not? Did they find it?"

"Yeah, they got it back. Remember the old guy next door was looking for it?"

How she didn't know that the dog had been found and he did was a mystery, but it was good news. "I remember. Good for him."

She and Bryce were supposed to go to his parents' for dinner and fireworks and she needed to go to her apartment and change. Unlike Santiago, she liked to look like a detective when doing an interview.

Of course, maybe she was being too hard on the guy. After all, here it was a holiday weekend and he'd taken the time to drop by the morgue, never her favorite chore, and if he was dressed for beach volleyball, it could be argued he wasn't officially on the clock.

"If I can get ahold of the Tobiases, and get that number, I'll call you. Everyone I know is doing something this weekend. How about you? Plans?"

"Yes." She didn't elaborate. "You obviously have some."

"I do." He unlocked the door to the car. "Speaking of which, I'm late. Kate's going to kill me."

Kate. Girlfriend? Not wife; she knew he wasn't married. No wonder. He left without so much as a good-bye or even a cursory wave, and Ellie watched him drive away a shade too fast for the speed limit. This Kate had to be an interesting person to want to put up with him.

Ellie crossed the street, slipped into her car, and punched on the AC, taking out her cell phone. She called and left a message for Bryce, told him where she was, and pulled out a moment later, still thinking about the case.

It was good to be working a true homicide again, not just wading through paperwork because some junkie overdosed in a back alley, or two street kids got into a brawl that ended badly. That wasn't murder, that was cleanup duty. Back up north she'd been assigned all sorts of cases, but so had all of the other detectives.

Fourth of July weekend.

Fireworks. Hot dogs. Murder?

She pondered as she drove down the main street, brow furrowed, almost inattentive to traffic. Did that have any significance? Was the date a catalyst? Probably not. The fire had happened the day before.

But it was a possibility it had something to do with the holiday.

Like what?

She had rented a small condo when she moved several months ago, not a permanent solution by any means, but until her house in Lincoln County sold, it was comfortable enough. Then she'd have to make a decision about moving in with Bryce, an option they hadn't thoroughly discussed yet. His place was certainly big enough, but that was part of the problem. It was *his* place. She liked the house and the neighborhood, but it was what he'd selected after his divorce, and why the hell that mattered she wasn't sure, but on some psychological level it did. She equated the house to his former marriage, which added another layer to the problem she had of how to approach their relationship.

As she pulled into her neat little driveway, her phone rang. She glanced at the number and pushed a button. "MacIntosh."

"You aren't going to believe this one," Santiago told her. "Chief Metzger just called me. Matthew Tobias killed himself about an hour ago by jumping off a parking garage downtown. No wonder he wouldn't answer his cell. The guy kind of did me a favor. I didn't want to go to that damned cookout anyway."

Chapter 5

I clearly remember the day my grandmother died.

The unnatural quiet when I came home from school, the scorched scent of the cake she'd been baking when it happened, the sight of her crumpled body on the floor, the hem of her dress hiked up enough to show the top of her stocking on one leg, the pool of urine soaking her clothes and on the worn linoleum . . .

I didn't run outside, or panic, or do anything really but stand there with my book bag dangling from one hand and assess exactly what this was going to mean to me. In vivid clarity I remember no sense of grief, though I suppose I really was sorry, but that wasn't what resonated through my soul.

Grief? How is that defined? A sincere regret and sense of loss?

It felt more like a resignation over the whims of fate that even at that tender age I recognized as being out of my control. I tried to cry. I really did. I stood there and told myself I probably should. I should cry. Wouldn't an average kid cry? She'd been, all in all, very good to me.

Stepping over her body carefully, I can clearly recall switching off the oven. The house smelled and there was smoke drifting from the still-closed door of the old range.

Smoke and death.

I knelt down and touched her hand.

It was already stiff and cold.

I was fascinated.

Carl picked up the crate and went to set it on the desk. It took a few minutes to find the file he wanted, but it finally fit into his hand and he had to wonder in a moment of wry introspection just how often he'd handled it.

Dozens of times? A hundred?

Probably. You'd think he'd have a better way to spend the Fourth of July, but at least he was having dinner with Rachel later, though Italian food wasn't hamburgers, grilled corn, and ice cream. Thank God. He had to admit to an aversion to celebrations that involved families and laughter. He'd lost his parents in a car accident when he was twenty. No siblings. One ailing grandfather left in Seattle he saw maybe once a year.

The accident had happened on Thanksgiving. Maybe it was why he disliked any holiday. No turkey for him. He usually grilled a steak and watched television.

His own name jumped out at him first, the initial report dated over five years ago. He pulled it off the top of the stack and set it down, adjusting the desk light. By pulling a few strings he'd gotten the ME report on the current burning/homicide almost the minute it hit the desks of the two detectives investigating the case. In the department it was always who you know, and he had been around a lot longer than the pretty little blonde and that hotshot Santiago, who reportedly liked to think with his dick now and then but somehow still wasn't thrilled about the assignment with MacIntosh. Carl would have thought she was just his type.

Office politics aside, he was damned curious to see what the ME report had to offer.

Half an hour later, he experienced a familiar elation that he had missed like hell. The case *was* suspiciously the same . . . not exactly, nothing could be that easy, but the coffee table, that was unusual . . . the burning, the house lit up afterward . . .

"What are you doing here, Lieutenant?"

He glanced up to see Chief Metzger propped in the doorway, his eyebrows slightly raised in inquiry. The chief was probably a little young for the job, five years or so older than his forty-two years, stocky but fit, his arms right now folded across his chest. His hair had thinned prematurely and he'd decided to go with it, trimming it to almost nothing, but once upon a time, he'd been a marine, so it seemed to suit him. On a weekend he wore jeans and a golf shirt, but he looked good in a suit, knew how to handle his authority without being too much of a prick, and basically, Carl liked him. He wasn't sure he could accurately say they were old friends any longer, but they were long-term acquaintances on cautious good terms, even after their differences on the case that had gotten him reassigned.

"I'm going through an old case file." He patted the papers on his desk casually.

"Today?"

"Why are *you* here, Joe?"

His boss just chuckled. "Okay, point taken, but my list is a must-do, not a volunteer project. What file brought you here?" He put up a hand. "No, wait, let me guess. The homicide yesterday. Am I right?"

There was a disadvantage to working with someone for years. He might just know you a little too well. Carl sat back in his chair. "It caught my eye."

"I figured it would."

Damn Metzger. He remembered everything. Carl set aside the file and folded his hands on his desk. "Why is that?"

The other man's gaze was razor sharp. "You had a case . . . years ago; how long was it? When I got the call and heard the murder included arson I wondered about it, and I suspect that's the file right there on your desk. Look, Carl, I've assigned detectives to this case already."

Oh, he knew it. He knew it all too well. "I could do it better," he said evenly. "Come on, Joe, I know it and *you* know it. I've got more experience."

"Don't sell Santiago or MacIntosh short. He's better at breaking down a witness than any cop I know, including you, by the way, and she's got that special edge I've been looking for since I had to move you to vice."

That wasn't easy to hear. Demoted was bad enough, but replaced was worse. "It really could be the same person that did that burning five years ago, and this is my case."

"*Was* your case, but I'm listening. Come into my office."

This wasn't exactly a coup, but then again, Metzger was at least *listening*.

Carl followed him down the hall and took a chair by a desk that was cluttered with paperwork, but he knew he was organized, just no one but Metzger could find anything in that daunting pile. The chief sat down behind his desk and rubbed his chin. "Why do you think there is a connection?"

"I feel it."

"Well crap, Carl, I'm not one to discount instincts in police work, but give me a fact or two, will you?"

His smile was tight. "I can do that. There are some dissimilarities. The latest victim, for instance was a woman and the first was a local reverend. A pastor. Middle-aged. There's no connection between them. Not that I can see anyway, except that table."

Metzger folded his hands and stared at him. "The table? It is apparently enough for you to come in on your day off when you could be lying by the pool with a cold beer in your hand. You go ahead, convince me this is pertinent."

With confidence, Carl said, "I can do that."

"Can't be a different perp." Fingering a glass of scotch, his gaze intent on the face of the woman across from him, Carl spoke slowly but surely. "He's the same one."

Rachel gave him one of *those* smiles. The kind he hadn't ever been able to decipher, even after sex, even when they were sweating and breathless in the aftermath, because it always felt like she was on camera, even now, after she'd left television for academia.

He hated that. This wasn't a production. It was an investigation.

"Maybe, but you couldn't find him the first time, so what makes you think you'll have any success now?"

The restaurant was noisy, which was good. Though their conversation wasn't necessarily secret, he was not interested in anyone overhearing them either. "I went over my notes. I went over *your* notes from when you were following it. All of it has a purpose and the presentation is the same. Exactly."

"How can you tell? Has the body been identified?"

His sources in the department had said no. Now that

he was no longer a homicide detective he wouldn't get the real reports unless he really called in some favors, and it wasn't to that point yet.

He leaned back and shook his head. "No. But we have the table, and a fire."

"There are some similarities, I agree." She had ordered white wine and sipped it, her long elegant fingers curling around the stem of her glass.

Rachel looked good, he thought. Older by a few years, but then again, they *were* older, undeniably. Still fresh, her auburn hair suited her fair complexion though it was cut shorter than he liked, but she wasn't on television any longer, and maybe it was easier; he had no idea. She wore it brushed back from a face that had character; high cheekbones and a full mouth and large blue eyes. Her lipstick was a little dark, but then again she'd been on the dramatic side her entire life. Nice breasts and rounded hips completed the picture, along with a shimmery indigo dress and a silver bracelet on her wrist. She was cool and sophisticated and driven.

He knew her life inside out. Lesson one: Never date a detective because he's going to investigate your past.

Hers was fairly interesting, at least from the standpoint that she was not necessarily television material, but she'd made it work.

Farm girl from Indiana, majoring in telecommunications in college, which was a pretty innocuous degree for most, but she'd had every intention of using it all along, because Rachel was exactly like that. She had a plan, always, and it included television journalism from the very beginning. She had the looks, the poise, and had gone back to graduate school and was now a professor at the University of Wisconsin.

Impressive.

He hadn't fared nearly as well and should have done much better.

Ivy League background. Made detective when he was still fairly young . . .

After fifteen years on the force there had been an incident that resulted in an investigation by internal affairs, a stinging slap on the wrist in the form of a temporary suspension, then the demotion. He'd been a little out of line maybe . . . it would be better if he could remember that particular evening more clearly. When a detective is called out, even if the charge is dropped, it really hurts his career.

Still, obviously the burning was one of the cases that had been open when he was reprimanded, and he'd always regretted it. Like unfinished business, that loose thread left dangling, the door you weren't sure latched securely behind you and nagged at you until you picked up the phone to get one of the neighbors to check . . .

Gambolli's was busy, which didn't surprise him, even on a holiday when so many people were doing the great American cookout. It was easily one of the best restaurants in town. He'd ordered rigatoni with sausage and a marinara sauce, and predictably Rachel had gotten broiled fish and a salad. There was a reason her figure was still trim. The food arrived, whisked into place by an efficient waiter who actually had an Italian accent, and Carl picked up his fork before saying, "The last time the neighborhood was different. I wonder why."

"You aren't assigned this case, Grasso."

The pasta was good, spicy but not too much. He really wasn't fond of green peppers if they were cooked, but like this, they tasted good. "The chief thinks maybe I can help."

"Does he?" Her eyes took on a speculative glint he recognized. "Metzger wants you on this?"

"Not officially."

"What does that mean? So . . . in your spare time you want to do extra police work?"

He thought about that big, spacious house he'd inherited. The swimming pool in the backyard with the brick patio, how he'd had all the windows replaced last year, the kitchen remodeled; the lawn care service that came twice a week. But it was, essentially, empty except for him rattling around in it in the evenings and on his days off. Most people would be envious, but in truth, it just all bored him. A personal flaw probably, but he had others that were worse. He said succinctly, "Yes."

Her dress had thin straps and her shoulders were bare and dappled with freckles. He liked women who didn't need to lather themselves in cosmetics, and her natural beauty had always appealed to him.

"You know what," she said quietly, giving him a level look. "I've never been sure if this case drew me, or if it was more how you might handle it."

"What does that mean exactly?"

"It's always interesting having dinner with a killer." Her eyes were steady across the table.

Even more so sleeping with one?

He'd always wondered. They'd never really talked about this outright before.

"Feel free to clarify." He took a bite of pasta and tried to ignore that she'd struck a nerve. He thought about it as they ate, remembering how she was in bed, wondering if he had scared her a little at times, not that he'd been rough with her, but he was . . . "forceful" might be the right word. Maybe he made love with an agenda, like he did everything else. Some women liked it, some did not. She sure seemed to at the time.

"It was neat and clean," Rachel murmured, "and no one could prove a damn thing. But I covered it, and we both know that what happened that night wasn't self-defense."

He took a sip of wine before he responded, the movement deliberate, before he said pleasantly, "Prove it."

"I'm not interested in proving it. And lucky for you, neither was Metzger, most probably because you are an extremely talented investigator. Tell me, were the consequences worth it?"

Were there regrets? Not on his side. But he'd never admitted it, not to anyone, and he doubted he ever would, not even to Rachel. He picked up his napkin, touched it to his mouth, and then smiled. "Everything we do in this life has repercussions, you know that as well as I do. I can't change what happened that night. It happened, it's over, and dwelling on whether I was right or in the wrong is pointless. I was not charged with a crime, which I'm sure you remember because as you just said, you covered that media circus."

Sometimes death was meaningless, like what had happened to his parents. And sometimes death was perfect, symbolic, and just.

He liked the latter scenario much better.

She leaned forward and spoke softly, just loud enough he could hear her over the bustle of the busy restaurant. "I could never find it, but there's a connection between you and that girl who was attacked. The truth is, once I met you, I didn't look very hard because I was so sure of it. If I found it, I'd have to make a pretty difficult decision and so it was an easier path to set aside the reporter for the woman."

"I happen to like the woman," he said in the same low tone, a slow smile surfacing. There had been the chance, all along, that someone would put two and two together, but he'd known it going in, and Rachel was the most likely to dig deep enough. She was very good at her job. It wasn't why he started sleeping with her, but it was part of the equation.

However it had all gone down, he'd been right, in his mind.

It still made him a killer, and what bothered him a little about the entire thing was that she liked it, liked the edge, liked that he was dangerous. He'd gotten that from their first meeting.

What did that say about *her*?

Jason loathed the party.

It didn't really surprise him, as he hadn't expected to like it, but it was worse than he expected. Of course, it didn't help he was underdressed. He'd expected maybe a little beach volleyball and some beer on ice when he heard it was going to be on the lake, not white cloth-covered tables and waiters with trays of drinks in a high-rise condo that had a rooftop deck overlooking the water.

The view was stunning. The company was not, but that was just his opinion.

Kate naturally looked great in a sundress and glittering sandals, but her casual was apparently not his casual, her dark hair shining, her expression outwardly serene, but he could tell she was annoyed.

Very reasonably, or so he thought, he said, "You could have told me."

They stood by a row of tropical plants that must take someone hours to water in the heat of this record-breaking summer, looking out over the downtown skyline and the spectacular sunset. She said almost under her breath, "I believe I did say a party at the home of a dean who did his graduate work at Cambridge, England, and who was a Fulbright scholar."

"You said a party by the lake." He looked down at his flip-flops. "And I dressed accordingly."

"God, Jason, you can be so—"

"I spent part of my afternoon in the morgue discussing with the medical examiner the finer points of a murder victim's anatomy," he interrupted, not inclined to apologize. He had his faults, but being underdressed seemed like a minor matter to worry about when he thought about that blackened corpse. "I could always leave."

She sent him a withering look, but then relented. "No, of course not. I'm to blame. I forget sometimes how literal you are."

Somehow, and he wasn't the one doing a doctorate in psychology, that made it still sound like his fault. He took a sip of wine, grimaced, because who the hell served white wine on the Fourth of July at a party, and said, "Yeah, well, my job deals with facts. The Milwaukee Police Department prefers that I'm literal. Please tell me there's a beer here somewhere."

Kate was, essentially, a great girl. She laughed and took the wineglass from his hand and gestured with it toward a corner of the rooftop. "You are such a philistine. Over there. Go."

He did, still thinking about the case, even as he took out a dripping bottle of Bud Light—thankfully it was all on ice—and popped it open.

A philistine. Yes, well, maybe. He could make a comment or two about her snobbish friends and their academic society gatherings. As for his background, she had no idea. He'd been suitably vague about his past . . .

maybe mentioned that his parents had split when he was young—that meant his mother had walked out when he was five, leaving him with a bewildered father who worked about twelve hours a day at a blue-collar job and had very little patience with the turn of events. In the end they'd managed by virtue of a mutual truce. If Jason didn't make trouble, he was fed, if peanut butter and jelly counted, and his father was content.

However, when he got into high school the dynamics changed. He'd done it to himself, he knew it—he'd known it at the time. Started drinking, smoking a little weed, nothing big, but just enough to annoy the shit out of his old man.

That had backfired in a big way. Looking back he thought it might have been a bid for some attention, but at the time he told himself he was just having a good time. Skipping so much school meant he was called in to the principal's office one time too many, he graduated at the lower end of his class, and his father had kicked him out that very day.

He'd learned a thing or two on the street, so the experience actually helped now that he was a police officer, but it had been a hard way to earn it.

"So you're Kate's cop."

He was in the act of taking a long drink and he turned to see a man standing a few feet away. Young, late twenties maybe, dressed in a polo shirt, tailored slacks, and what looked like Italian loafers at a swift assessment, with brown hair swept back in a fashionable cut. Perfect teeth bared in a smile.

Jason really despised people with perfect teeth. His past didn't include braces, but luckily he only had one really crooked tooth and he'd been told it gave his face character. He replied, "I kind of like to think of her as mine rather than the other way around, but whatever. Yeah, I'm Detective Santiago. And you are?"

"Not nearly as high on testosterone." The guy extended his hand, the other one cradling a glass of wine. "Brian Wilfong. Just wanted to say hello. I've never met a homicide detective before. Kate talks about you all the time."

All right. He'd concede he came off a little aggressive. Jason said, with more effort at politeness, "I take it you work together?"

"In the same graduate program." The other man took a sip of wine and regarded him with a bit of amusement, the light wind ruffling his hair. "From a psychological viewpoint, you don't seem her type."

"But you don't know me." *Asshole*. He didn't add it, but really wanted to, except he could tell Kate was already pissed off at him.

"Good point. I just meant the job. She's very cerebral."

Cerebral. Who the hell talks like that?

He pointed out in his most pleasant voice, "Police officers have to actually think, believe it or not. Solving crimes requires it."

Brian looked amused, but it didn't quite reach his eyes. "Point taken."

Competition? All at once, he thought so. Kate was attractive; if *he* didn't think so, they wouldn't be living together.

"Hey, nice to meet you." Wilfong—what kind of a name was that?—walked away.

Jason watched him go, thinking about how much he despised so-called intellectuals who thought they were superior just because of a few letters after their name. He and Kate were having a few problems . . . maybe Brian was one of them.

The lake was busy, lights on the boats sending glimmers over the water, and soon the fireworks would go off, and really, as much as he felt out of place, from this view, it was no doubt going to be spectacular.

All in all, Jason decided as he took a look at the well-dressed crowd, he'd rather be investigating the case. What did that say about him?

Maybe one day he'd ask Kate, the psychologist.

Except he was a little afraid to hear the answer.

Chapter 6

Almost dawn. That promising glimmer on the horizon. The subtle outline of the building next door taking shape was like a ghost, only a hint at first, but something was out there. The faint burned smell of coffee filled the room, the glowing light on the machine a red eye in the darkness. Coffee smelled good when it was brewed, but like crap when it sat there for hours.

My old man used to drink it morning, noon, and night.

For years I couldn't walk into a breakfast place without a twist in my stomach at that smell, like a belly punch. Needless to say, I don't like to be reminded of him. I've gotten over it, luckily, and so I poured myself another cup and went back to my window.

Resilience is a gift. A person can really adjust to almost anything, I've found.

Almost. Maybe adjust is the wrong word. Acclimate works better.

JULY 5

Ellie slowly stirred her cup of coffee, tasted it, and then added more sugar. Watching the fireworks had been nice the night before, but unfortunately she'd been late—too late for the cookout, but Bryce's parents had been gracious about that. As soon as she met them for the first time she could see where their son got his easygoing demeanor. That was all well and good, but she'd been starving. He'd made her a sandwich at about eleven o'clock, when he'd finally asked her if she'd had a chance to eat, and even though she'd stayed the night with him, she'd been way too tired for anything except falling asleep the minute she crawled into bed.

"You made coffee. Thanks." He wandered out into the kitchen, boxers only, his hair an unruly mess of midnight curls, opened the cupboard and took out a cup.

"I fell asleep on you," she said by way of apology.

"If only." He opened the refrigerator and rummaged for the milk, of which there was none—she already knew because she'd looked for it earlier. "*On* me would have been great, but next to me is still nice. Damn, no milk. This happens all the time."

It was impossible not to laugh at the disappointed mutter. "I'll go out and get some. Least I can do."

"No, I throw most of it out anyway because I only use it in coffee. You'd think I'd figure that out. It's more sensible economically to just never buy it. Half the time when I pour it out it's like cottage cheese." He filled his cup and came over to drop into an opposite chair at the kitchen table. "You're up early."

The neutral tone of his voice spoke volumes.

"I'd love to sleep in." She meant it. With all her heart. But then again, she was finally *working*. "The case . . . I don't know. I woke up and started to think about it and that was the end of that."

The air-conditioning hummed in the background. It was predicted to be another scorcher, highs in the nineties, humidity over the top. The heat wave was apparently determined to hang on. Bryce sat back, extended his long legs, and nodded. "It would keep me awake too if it was my problem."

She moodily stared at him across the oak surface between them. The question that had really woken her was on her mind. "Why the hell did he jump?"

"Matthew . . . Tobias, is it? Interesting question. Since you asked it, I'm going to guess you don't think he stuck a body in his house and burned it. Otherwise it would seem pretty clear. He was worried he was going to be arrested for murder."

"I don't think so. I really wouldn't have suspected, other than investigating in a routine way, that he had anything to do with it. Both he and his wife seemed so shocked."

"Good acting?"

"Superb, if it proves to be the case."

He took another sip of coffee. "If he was battling depression, the fire might have literally sent him over the edge."

That had occurred to her too, and Bryce had gone through a very acrimonious divorce so he knew a little about depression. She murmured, "Could be. He worked nearby before he was fired. He could have been thinking about it for a while. Maybe it sent him over the edge."

"But a good case of the blues isn't necessarily the fast track to suicide. Jumping, though. Not how I'd choose to go. Any chance he was pushed?"

Good question. She'd thought of that too, but it really

didn't make much sense. "A chance, I suppose. No witnesses. The medical examiner might be able to tell us something, but a push leaves no trace when you go splat on a sidewalk."

Bryce winced, his glass halfway to his mouth. "God, don't put it that way."

"That might have come off a little insensitive. Sorry. He was the one that jumped. Blame him." She regarded the window, the view of the backyard showing smooth grass and one large oak, shading almost the entire space. "But unless he's an idiot, why kill someone and put them in your own house and then set it on fire? Hello . . . you might just be who we look at first. At the least, you know we'll be all over your background, plus you just burned down your *own* house."

"One would think that would make no sense, but can I point out he jumped off a parking garage? Not a lot of rational thought going on."

"I'm not arguing that. He's clean at first glance anyway. No record, no history to make us think he's the one, and the insurance from the fire will probably only cover the balance of the mortgage they owe Helton since the market has tanked here like everywhere else. He isn't a bank, but the documents they signed are still legally binding." She shrugged, wishing it wasn't already in the eighties so she could go for a run to clear her head. "There's no motive. Opportunity, yes. We look at that first. Motive is more tricky."

"Sounds like a great way to pass the day."

"Versus writing computer software?"

"Is that a challenge, Detective?"

She regarded him directly. "No, you are one of the smartest men I know. That said, you use an entirely different part of your brain, so how the hell do I know how hard it is to do what you do? I couldn't walk around a program like what you design to save my life, but I do know how to find someone like the person who set that fire. More information would be good, but I can deal if it isn't going to be easy."

His mouth quirked into the reluctant smile she loved. Really rare, like a glimpse of a protected species, reserved by him for special occasions only. "I *know* you can find him."

Six simple words. It diffused her argumentative stance, set her back on her heels in a figurative sense and brought it all to a halt. "How do you know that?"

"You have something."

"Oh, that's specific."

"You have what I think is a pretty glaring clue that Tobias didn't do it."

It was impossible not to stare at him. In general Bryce was good to look at anyway, so it wasn't much of a chore. With a hint of a dark morning beard he resembled a pirate in a romance novel, bare-chested and surprisingly muscular for a man she knew didn't work out more than playing the occasional round of golf. Good genes were hard to beat. "I'm all ears," she told him, getting up to refill her cup. When she turned back around she caught him still faintly smiling and demanded, "What?"

"You love this . . . for the lack of a better phrase, the hunt."

"If you mean to imply that I like that there are people out there—"

"I don't," Bryce interrupted. "I mean that when something like this happens, you are exactly the right person who wants to find out who could have possibly done it. We need you, and I admire it."

Said that way, she wasn't sure how to respond. Maybe he had a point. Having a relationship with a woman like her had to be pretty interesting and she worried on a daily basis that he was going to get tired of her schedule, her constant abstraction . . . her. He didn't flatter himself that she'd taken the job with MPD solely just to be near him, she knew that . . . it had been a promotion and a chance to do more of what she was really good at, which was solving crimes like the one they were discussing at the moment.

This case was just what she needed to convince her she'd made the right move.

She said mildly, "There's no doubt that Tobias could be the one who torched his house, but I can't see it. Why do *you* doubt it?" Her eyes were narrowed over the rim of her cup, her back propped against the counter.

He set his elbows on the table and frowned. "It was clearly planned. The body was put there, the fire set . . . and if I were the one who had gone to all that trouble, I really would have left a note explaining myself if I'd decided to end it all. The sequence of the events seems to me his death is more a cause and effect. The insurance, as you said, will pay the mortgage off, but he and his wife lost whatever equity they might have had because they don't actually hold the mortgage. A blow like that is pretty brutal."

"But not enough to kill yourself over."

His smile was brief. "Not someone like you. Not even someone like me. But not everyone is resilient. If he thought it was the end of the world, then it was. You don't live in his reality. Didn't you say he'd moved from job to job?"

"Yes." She chewed briefly on her lower lip. "All right, I buy that well enough and overlook the implied inference that you are somehow more sensitive than I am because it might be true. I'm still not seeing your glaring clue."

"The suicide was impulsive. Your arsonist on the other hand is pretty damned methodical."

"I hate to break it to you, Dr. Grantham, but that is not a clue. It is a conclusion. For the record, we are not allowed to draw conclusions."

"But you do. You just call them hunches, or intuition."

It took her a moment, but she acquiesced. "True enough. If we only operated on facts we wouldn't ever get anywhere. The system is cumbersome enough as it is."

Outside the sky was a brilliant blue, cloudless, almost metallic. No doubt his last electric bill had been ridiculous, but this month promised to be worse. The air hadn't shut off in days. He crossed his ankles. "So what next?"

"We couldn't talk to his wife yesterday."

"She couldn't talk to homicide detectives?"

"Sedated, or so we were told. I suppose, given everything that happened, that makes sense. She was more than a little shook up over the house . . . we didn't push it. Her father's a doctor and he stood firm against us seeing her. It made for a difficult argument."

"You have to admit it was one hell of a day for her." He rose and went to dump out the last bit in his cup in the sink.

"I'm sorry I was late. Stood your parents up and then I missed dinner."

The change in her tone caught his attention and he turned, capturing her gaze. "I told you last night it was okay, Ellie."

"People tell other people all the time something is fine when it really isn't."

The insecurity wasn't her. But neither was dancing around a touchy subject.

Was he in love with her?

They had almost discussed it the night before, but not quite. She wasn't convinced she *wanted* to discuss it.

You don't want me to tell you I'm in love with you.

"I'm being honest." He said it in a prosaic tone. "My parents like you, they get your job, and they never have sweated the small stuff."

"I'm not worried about them."

"Oh? Then?"

"You." Now she was being really honest.

"Me how?"

"Cops don't have the greatest relationships. There's a reason for it." Her mouth lifted at the corner. "We're suspicious and don't usually think the best of people because too many of them are assholes, and have I mentioned we work long, irregular hours? I'm sure I wouldn't date a police officer if I was at all a normal person."

"I'd use ordinary if it was my choice. Abnormal implies something much worse than my possible inference of greater sensitivity."

"Okay." It was reluctant, but she laughed as she downed the last bit of her coffee. "I've got to go."

"Can we have dinner tonight?"

"Sure." Her voice went soft. "Absolutely." She could use a night out.

"Preference?"

"What do you think?"

"Lulu's it is."

She yawned. "I'm going to take a shower. Santiago is swinging by to pick me up in half an hour."

She knew he wasn't thrilled about Santiago. Cocky males weren't Bryce's favorite type. All he asked was, "Here?"

"I hope you don't mind."

"I prefer it, actually."

She padded over in bare feet and rose to kiss him very lightly on the lips, her breasts brushing his chest through the thin material of her shirt. "Possessive doesn't suit you at all, but it is cute in fleeting moments."

It was, and maybe even more so since it was out of character. She worked with men and that wasn't going to change.

He caught her as she went to turn away and gave her a much more satisfying version of a good morning kiss. He tasted like coffee with a hint of mint toothpaste and his lips were firm and warm. Afterward, when he received a quizzical look, he merely said, "I think I forgot yesterday to put a new bar of soap in the shower. You might want to check."

Half an hour. Not a lot of time, but . . .

She lightly touched his cheek. "Or you could just join me."

Chapter 7

There's a swamp in my brain. It sounds melodramatic put that way, but in a metaphorical sense it is accurate enough. Muddy and deep, opaque and dangerous. I can't see what's in there sometimes until it is just too late.

I dreamed my first fire.

It was magnificent . . . orange running into scarlet, licking upward, shadows leaping, the heat searing, destroying everything it touched. It was alive, rippling with power, devastatingly beautiful.

It singed me, washed me clean, took off every strip of skin, melted my bones into puddles of cells and atoms and crushed the blackened stumps. I was devoured, swallowed whole . . . and I woke screaming in the middle of the inferno, drowning in the boiling swamp.

My mother told me later my fever was 105 and that the flames licking up the walls and covering the bed were part of the delirium.

She was wrong. It was vivid and real, and I can prove it.

It left me irrevocably scarred.

The way I see it is if the saints can experience divine visions, why can't the sinners?

The prestigious neighborhood surprised him a little. He didn't know a lot about MacIntosh's personal life, but Jason was pretty sure on her salary she couldn't afford a house like the sprawling split-level Tudor with the neat if unimaginative big sloping lawn. Just the intricate etched-glass front door alone he was pretty sure cost more than his car. The department had its share of gossip—in any work environment people talked—and a little more than usual about her because of the circumstances that won her the job offer in the first place.

If he had to guess, the house belonged to the fairly infamous guy who had the misfortune of catching the attention of the serial killer she'd finally caught last fall. He was supposed to be some kind of brilliant computer guy and his house sure looked like he was brilliant, all right.

He pulled in, punched in her number. "I'm outside."

"Good morning to you too."

Damn. Kate had told him a hundred times he should at least say hello. He was going to have to work on that. "I thought you'd probably hear my car."

Luckily his partner didn't seem to take offense. "Be right there."

She was true to her word. Detective MacIntosh came out the front door, no nonsense as usual, hair loose around her shoulders, her hazel eyes direct as she opened the door of the Mustang and slid in. "Where are we going first? Helton or Mrs. Tobias?"

That was pretty gracious for her. Since he'd figured out she was a lot more used to running an investigation than accepting guidance, he appreciated the courtesy.

Jason adjusted his perception a notch in her favor and responded, "Helton can see us at ten. Mrs. Tobias isn't currently available, but I have it on good authority she can't avoid us forever. This your house?"

"No."

He lifted his brows in unspoken inquiry.

She just fastened her seat belt.

Fine. Her personal life was an I-don't-give-a-fuck situation anyway on his part, so he left it alone.

With a backward glance, he pulled the car out onto the street, his wrist negligently on the steering wheel. "Helton swears he has no idea who it could be. All right, on the phone I don't necessarily discount that, but I'd love to see his face when he says it."

"Why?"

She wore a light-colored blouse and chocolate-colored tailored slacks and her hair smelled really good. Jasmine? He had no idea, but it was floral and light and the heat made the fragrance permeate the interior of the car. It was stupid to even think about it, so he refocused. He was a guy, he'd noticed, and now dismissed it.

"Helton?" He drove down the sunny street—Jesus, it was hot again, the whole state needed rain—and braked for the stoplight. "He's what I call a white-collar scumbag. He doesn't break legs or crack heads, he doesn't even extort as far as I know, but Matthew and Michelle Tobias bought a house from him at a really high interest rate and it burned down. He was the bank, let's keep that in mind."

"We know the fire was set. We need to go over his finances with a fine-tooth comb."

"If it wasn't a holiday weekend that would be easier, but I checked him out and he doesn't have any outstanding warrants or a record. He lived in the house for almost twenty years and just made the deal with the Tobiases maybe a year ago."

"Okay. Interesting, and good work."

He'd actually spent hours on the computer, so she should appreciate it, but it didn't prove much.

He glanced over. She had a nice profile, pretty nice body too. Breasts not big, but firm and well shaped, a good balance for her slender body; whoever owned that really expensive house might be a lucky guy. Jason said in a contemplative tone, "He is a good possibility. And has a motive. Which up until now we don't have, but I'm not sure we aren't wasting our time. Insurance fraud would fly, except for one thing."

"The dead body. Insurance fraud . . . no." She settled back, shaking her head decisively. To give her credit, she didn't hold back with her opinions as far as he could tell. That was fine. He hated it when people didn't say what they were thinking, and if they were going to be partners, talking out the case was essential. She added, "Let's *not* forget the corpse. It's quite a leap from thievery to murder."

"I don't disagree. Reubens didn't have a cause of death for the one in the Tobias house, but the jump victim is cut and dried. Manner of death . . . yeah, not so sure. Nut job or just weak? I can't decide, can you?"

"No, but let's not put it that way to his widow."

"Do you think I would?"

She didn't look sure, which wasn't flattering. Maybe they were getting to know one another. He could be too blunt; no secret there. But not all the time, and never really on purpose, and everyone had their moments. "Thanks," he said sarcastically.

"I didn't even answer."

"Didn't have to. Let's try to catch Michelle Tobias

first, and I'm not accepting any bullshit from her father about her being too upset to talk to us."

"She doesn't have to, so that might not be your choice. You know that as well as I do."

He pulled onto Lincoln and gunned the Mustang, switching lanes, speeding a little. "Just watch me. It would be helpful to gain at least a little insight. I did manage to pry Dr. Canton's address out of him and hopefully she's not high on happy pills this time of the morning."

"It would be helpful," MacIntosh muttered, looking out the window. "But talk about a rough couple of days. I feel sorry for her."

"I feel sorry for her too, but only if she wasn't part of why her husband decided to take a swan dive off a tall building. For all we know, she's a bitch."

She gave him a disillusioned glance. "She seemed nice to me."

"But then again, some women can pull that off, trust me. Lots of false advertising out there."

The address was in Cedarburg, just northwest of the city, the house itself not showy, but obviously expensive, and there was a nice BMW in the driveway. Someone had planted pots of impatiens in a variety of colors, set all along the brick walkway, which was flanked by two ornate Victorian streetlight imitations. When they rang the bell, a small dog started barking until a stern voice spoke and the sound ceased almost immediately.

The man who answered the door was middle-aged, slightly paunchy, his hair light and thinning. He looked at them with no friendliness, obviously disapproving over his lack of a tie, but Jason didn't give a shit about that. It was going to be freakin' ninety-eight degrees and he wasn't choking to death with a tie around his neck.

"Yes?"

"Dr. Canton? I'm Detective MacIntosh and this is Detective Santiago of the Milwaukee Police Department. We apologize for the intrusion but we would like to speak with your daughter if at all possible." Ellie extended her badge.

"I'll talk to you on her behalf. Come in."

Well, shit. Not what they wanted but better than nothing, and they had driven out, so why not. Jason followed Ellie inside, a quick glance showing beige walls, an uninspired rug on the floor of the foyer, the pictures on the walls scenes of gardens with pastel tones. They were invited to sit on a brown couch that was new, but still dull in his opinion, and Michelle Tobias' father chose a dark green chair, which was probably expensive but still as bland as the rest of the house.

Then, before either one of them could speak, he said flatly, "My son-in-law is dead, and I'm not going to lie to you, I'm glad, but I do thank you for returning the dog, Detective Santiago. It means a lot to my daughter."

What?

Ellie had to admit she hadn't had very many interviews begin with such a stark, unforgiving statement about the victim. Even Santiago, whose face always wore a slightly sardonic smirk, looked surprised, his dark blond brows shooting up. They exchanged a glance, brief, but the first spontaneous silent communication between them, and then her partner leaned forward and said, "You are welcome for the dog, but is *do no harm* out the window, or in this case over the side of a parking garage, Doctor?"

Nice, Santiago.

He'd returned the dog? She had to admit it threw her

off and she'd have to think about it later, because any goodwill from Michelle's father was negated by her partner's last statement.

She quickly said, "Glad, sir? Care to explain why?"

"He wasn't my patient and I didn't make him jump either, so that reprimand doesn't apply. I have an unimpeachable alibi, and so does my daughter."

But, she noted, the older man was too reserved, his hands on his knees, his control contrived. He had eyes of an almost indeterminate color, probably blue, but there was a hint of red in the white around the irises and she wondered at once if he'd had a long night or was a drinker.

Could be both.

"Glad was the wrong word," he added immediately, but there still was not a lot of apology in his tone. "Not sorry is a better way to put it. Excuse my lack of eloquence since it has been a fairly shocking past twenty-four hours, as you can imagine."

Ellie nodded. "Okay, we're listening. Your son-in-law is no great loss as far as you are concerned. Does that sum it up? And you were where when you got the news of his death?"

"I'd picked up my daughter and taken her directly to see her therapist after I heard about the fire. We had a second emergency appointment even though it was a holiday. I have the doctor's number." He took the card from his pocket and extended it. "His office can confirm the appointment. The fire and the body in the house . . . I knew Matthew wouldn't handle it well."

"It seems to me you should have taken your son-in-law to *his* therapist," Santiago drawled. "He's the one that ended up dead. However, I'm fascinated. Why did your daughter need to be rushed off because *he* wouldn't handle it well? He beat the shit out of her on a regular basis or something like that? We have no record of any domestic violence calls."

Profanity in an interview. Great.

Just her luck she'd be assigned to someone with the worst interviewing technique on the planet. Metzger claimed he could interview a witness and make them weep out their story without lifting a finger, but so far, Santiago seemed just abrasive. She quickly intervened, "Was he abusive when he was upset, sir?"

"Not in a physical way, but let's just say I was worried something exactly like what happened would be his response to the stress of losing the house." Dr. Canton reached up to rub his cheek, seemed to think better of that telltale sign of nervousness, and casually dropped his hand back to his knee. "He's never been stable. I tried to tell my daughter but she wouldn't listen. Take his back injury. He milked that for all it was worth."

"Is that why you didn't help them with the house?"

This time she literally turned and stared at Santiago. Dr. Canton seemed just as taken aback by the frank question.

Jason Santiago, casual in an open-necked shirt, his blue eyes direct, just shrugged lightly. "They bought it on contract from a man who seems to have some interesting financial practices and we haven't really dived in yet very deep on that either." He glanced around. "You've got money. It seems to me you could have lent a hand."

The older man took a moment and his jaw tightened. "My daughter is a grown woman. I couldn't stop her from marrying Matthew and I am not obligated to pick up their bills. If he couldn't come up with a down payment and a credit score high enough to please a bank that really was not my concern."

"Gotcha." Her partner just looked bland. "You love your daughter a lot, but not enough to give *him* your money. I can see that. You are trying to protect her now. So do it and tell us who else hated his guts. In your opinion, did he jump off that roof, or was he encouraged in some way, either mentally or physically, to do it?"

"I don't know that anyone hated him." Dr. Canton backpedaled a little, and if Ellie didn't appreciate Santiago's style, at least he had the guy rattled. She could give him that.

"*You* did. Or it sure seemed that way from what you told us a few moments ago."

"I never said hate."

"You aren't sorry he's dead. I've felt guilty for squashing a spider. At the least admit to strong dislike."

"I'm not admitting to anything. He wasn't particularly responsible, that's all."

"Kind of sounds to me like you thought he was a loser. As far as we can tell, you might be the only one with a motive, but give us time, maybe we'll come up with someone else. But, of course, maybe we won't." Santiago took in a breath of evident annoyance.

"What are you pushing toward?"

"What are you pushing against?" Her partner looked ingenuously puzzled. "If we are working toward the same thing, maybe we can make some progress. Just tell us plainly why you didn't like him and no irresponsibility bullshit."

"It's not—"

"That's enough." Ellie stepped in. Now—*now*—she got it.

The day she was hired, the chief had sat her down in his office, much more plush that the plain room in the Lincoln County Sheriff's Department that her former boss had called his own, and given her the assignment to work with Jason Santiago.

"He's hell and gone too aggressive," Chief Metzger had told her frankly, his eyes not exactly amused. A burly man in his late forties, he wore impeccable suits, was fairly well liked as far as she could tell, but he didn't pull punches. "After I interviewed you I had a feeling you could balance him. I hope I'm right. People are going to trust you and he is going to ask all the probing questions. Don't get me wrong, Detective, not because he's smarter, or quicker, or at least I doubt he is, but because when he thinks it, he asks it. It just comes right out of his mouth. Nothing big as far as real complaints yet, but I don't want anything big, understand?"

An easy response to that hadn't been on the tip of her tongue so she'd said nothing.

Metzger had gone on in a pragmatic tone. "I haven't decided yet if his method works, but I can tell you this, he pisses off almost everyone he comes into contact with, and yet he has a very high arrest record. He knows who is guilty, but he needs to realize that isn't enough. He isn't in essence the cliché term of a loose cannon—nothing like that. We've had a few in this department, but he doesn't fit. He just refuses to even try tact, but he isn't out there making serious mistakes very often either. Just now and then he crosses a certain line. I am not sure if I am describing it well, but he has great instincts even if his style could use a little polish. However, he's already been reprimanded, he does not play well with others, and I am not going to lie to you, cooperation is not his strongest virtue."

It really hadn't sounded like her dream job. Big city meant more cases, and she liked the idea of that . . . The one she'd finished in northern Wisconsin had been a fluke, no doubt about it, that was never going to happen again, or if it did, it was unlikely it would be during her tenure at the sheriff's department in a county that had less than twenty-three thousand residents.

"I want to hire you," he'd gone on with calm intonation, "because I think you are a very good detective. A little more experience and you could be a great detective."

"Thank you, sir."

"So is Santiago. He might even be great as well if he can be pushed in the right direction, but see, I am not completely convinced that is possible." Metzger had sat back, his smile not indulgent; it was far too enigmatic for that, but there was at least a contemplative edge she caught.

"Might?"

"I see the modifier caught your attention. Yes, might. If I were more convinced I'd not even worry about this. You mind I'm putting you in this position?"

She didn't even get a chance to answer.

"It could be my fault. I haven't been able to find a good match for him so far. He's ex-military and I have a weakness for that. I *think* he'll tone it down for you. He may listen even when he doesn't want to do so, but most important I also believe that if he doesn't, you'll tell me. That's what makes it feel right for me."

She couldn't help but ask. "And if he doesn't?"

"I did just say I want you to tell me. You heard that part, correct? Partners have each other's backs. That is part of the code, an intrinsic nuance of successful police work. But if he really is a problem, I need to know it."

"I heard it." She wasn't sure if it was amusement or dismay she was experiencing, but she'd definitely *heard* it.

"I'll fire his ass. He's close." He leaned brawny arms

on the desk. "I'm not going to kid you on that one. I'm not projecting my job on you, but I can't go on the street with him either. This is an opportunity, which you already know, but this is how it is, Detective MacIntosh. He's decently well liked, but no one wants to work with him. His last partner said it was like trying to train a grown dog who already liked to piss in the house. Your thoughts?"

"I'm not fond of unruly animals, sir."

He looked her in the eye and nodded. "Duly noted. But if you help me save this one, I'll remember it, you have my word."

Well, son of a bitch . . .

So she'd sat there in the uncomfortable chair in front of his desk and folded her hands and taken the job. She'd said, "Absolutely, sir."

At this moment, she thought she understood exactly what Metzger meant.

But Jason Santiago had taken time to look for the dog. Why he hadn't just said so was annoying, but maybe underneath that smartass exterior there were a few redeeming qualities.

Drawing herself back into the situation, she smiled in a conciliatory fashion. "What Detective Santiago means is we need a short list of people who might have disliked your son-in-law and it needs to start right here in your household. Can we speak with your daughter now?"

"No."

Chapter 8

Sitting in a bar on south Kinnickinnic Avenue, I started to play a game. Bayview used to be strictly blue collar; it was a small steel factory town back in past times, but was now trendy and eclectic.

I watched a young couple at another table and imagined what they looked like naked, like a soft porn movie in my head. Not doing it necessarily, but naked. The woman had long dark hair and big breasts clearly being shown off by her tight knit sleeveless shirt.

"Another beer? Same kind?"

I glanced up at the waitress, nodded once, smiling, and went back to it.

The young man was probably more attractive than his companion. In my opinion he was dating the tits, not the girl.

He had muscular arms and a slightly square face, short brown hair that he obviously styled with gel, and a hint of scruffy beard that he probably thought was pretty chic because it was so popular right now, but in my opinion he would have looked better without it.

As the waitress delivered my second drink, I thought about following them home. I could do so pretty easily, I'm good at it. Often enough it was part of the entertainment, the challenge . . .

I just might. It was tempting. Maybe that's why I enjoy the game so much.

Ellie usually just read the reports, which were often boring, and she couldn't detect the finer points anyway. What she really needed was a one-on-one with the medical examiner if that was possible, so she'd called down and been told the autopsy was almost over.

"Do you see this?"

It would have been better if Dr. Reubens hadn't gestured with his knife right along the breastbone in a graceful arc that was almost artistic. A part of her winced.

She saw nothing but a flayed body that had been stitched back together. The crisscross on the chest never failed to shake her, but she'd wanted to sit in on this one in person as he made his summary.

"Yeah, what is it?"

Dr. Reubens, who was by far the youngest ME she'd ever encountered, elaborated. "Point of impact. He literally did a swan dive. Hit the pavement chest first, which is an interesting choice. Most of them jump feet first."

"Except maybe he was aiming to go headfirst and really seal the deal," she mused out loud. "Ever try a dive into a pool and not get the angle right?"

"I think we've all experienced that, Detective, but in this case, he was no doubt killed instantly. It snapped his spine." Dr. Reubens shuffled through a few papers and coughed. The room smelled strongly of disinfectant and something else she couldn't quite identify and really didn't want to analyze, but then again, it was the morgue.

"No sign of anything that indicates suspicious death?"

He met her gaze, frank and steady. "Sorry. I can't help there."

"I take it you are going to rule this a suicide then."

He stripped off his gloves. "What I think is that he wasn't harmed in a manner that left visible evidence of criminal intent. He died of a variety of the effects of his fall—crushed lungs, severed spinal cord—all of which were potentially lethal. I could go into all of it, but I can't see the point unless you'd like to hear it."

Unequivocally, she wouldn't. Ellie said, "You think the toxicology screen is going to come back clean."

"I can never speculate." He had a decent smile when he chose to flash it. "Detective, I know you are new to this department but I am going to venture a guess they've already told you I'm picky about that sort of thing. It isn't personal when I don't offer an opinion before all the test results are in. It is more than professionalism was drummed into me by my predecessor and I learn lessons well. Eight years of medical school, a three-year residency, and a fellowship will do that for you. I refuse to *guess*."

"But there are signs usually if someone is a drug user. He had a bad back from what I understand."

"Narcotics for the pain? It's possible. It would impair him to a certain degree. That is an unfortunate side effect of the schedule II medications we prescribe and one of the reasons people so often abuse them."

"I just wondered."

He walked around the steel table, his gaze on his cold, unmoving patient. "If it has been going on for a while, yes, there certainly can be signs of drug abuse. I can tell by the changes in some organs, like the liver for instance. Mr. Tobias might have had a mild problem with alcohol, but there is such thing as nonalcohol fatty liver disease, which can't be discounted. When pathology sends me back the blood screen, we will know if he was intoxicated when he fell, was pushed, or jumped off that building."

"I'm more interested in trying to establish a clearer idea of his behavior and habits, bad or good," Ellie explained. "His father-in-law is not a fan but he really walked around why he disliked him so much. Santiago and I wondered if there was some reason, and drugs came to mind. He also refused to help them financially, which as he pointed out, he isn't obligated to do, but he's a physician pulling down six figures a year and yet they had to buy a house on contract. There's a reason he didn't offer to give them a bit of a boost."

"Not all physicians are rich, trust me." Dr. Reubens gave a rueful laugh. "You should try my school loan payments on my salary, but I do see your point. I'll be in touch as soon as possible. Two bodies in the same case in such a short period of time indicates urgency is in order. I understand that."

That was certainly true. And especially for her. "This is my first crack at a case that doesn't have an obvious suspect," she said frankly. "I wouldn't mind a decent showing on this one. All help is appreciated."

"I understand you caught the Northwoods Killer, Detective. As a matter of fact, I think I heard you administered justice yourself." His gaze was appraising, which was something she'd run into more than once. The nickname too had surfaced after the case was over, and she didn't particularly like it, but the media had managed to sensationalize the fact that a female cop had killed a serial killer who had preyed on women.

"I shot him," she said matter-of-factly, the memory of that cold, grim evening probably something that would never fade. "Let's keep in mind he had two hostages and he'd shot me first. I wasn't acting as judge and jury, just defending myself and two more potential victims."

Dr. Reubens lifted his hands in a swift gesture of apology. "No judgment here. I'm sure you saved the judicial system a great deal of trouble and the taxpayers a lot of money."

She had been over what happened about a thousand times and never could dig up a single pang of regret. It didn't happen yet again as she left the room after thanking him for his help and wondering if she would ever shake off the notoriety. The stairwell—she spent way too much time at a desk so she took the stairs if she could—still held that faint unpleasant morgue odor, and she left the building through the glassed foyer. It was like being blasted in the face with a full-on hair dryer when she stepped outside, and it didn't bode well that towering white thunderclouds were building anvil shapes in the distance, white on blue, monoliths like pagan symbols, the gods of the Wisconsin summer. The sidewalk stank like urine as it baked, but it was still better than the morgue.

Maybe a good storm would break the oppressive heat.

For whatever reason, she shivered despite the temperature outside.

Jason had braced himself for the conversation, but that was a piece-of-shit proposition. It really, in the long run, didn't matter to him, but the outcome was a symbol of his failure in his personal life.

"Is this this about my substandard footwear last night?"

"Oh, please."

Kate tossed her shirt onto the floor, but unfortunately it wasn't one she'd just taken off. A natural slob, she just missed the box she was packing. Then she turned, her dark hair swinging, and said, "This is going to hurt to hear, but I'm bored."

Ouch. *Great*, now he was boring.

It did sting. Not that it mattered, but still, she *was* moving out.

"How so? Bad sex?"

She slanted him a derisive glance. "No. Why do you think I even stayed as long as I did?"

"That's a relief." He pointedly looked at his crotch. "Hear that buddy? Ain't your fault."

"Don't try to be funny. Seriously, Jase, you might want to think about a few things."

He might want to think about a lot of things. But there were just some things that unfortunately he didn't want to think about at all.

"Like?" He sat back on the faux leather couch, trying to look as if he cared, but she *was* a graduate psych student and not fooled one bit.

She exhaled and pushed a lock of dark, short hair off her forehead. "Like at least pretending to have a desire for more than this." Her hand indicated his apartment. "It's all right, maybe for a college student, and I understand that police detectives don't make a load of money, but this place is . . . *immature*."

He'd thought about taking down the mirrors with liquor ads on them, but he worked a lot so he hadn't gotten around to it, and honestly, he liked them. "Thought you might help me with that when you moved in, so take some responsibility. Besides, no one moves out because of the furniture."

"It's what it represents."

Okay, now they were getting down to it.

"Go on, soon-to-be Dr. Macomb." He took a hit of his beer. Hey, he was entitled. His girlfriend was breaking up with him if the boxes were any indication. "Give me a soon-to-be-professional opinion at no charge. How much of this is about Brian . . . Wilfong, is it? Why do I think you've been comparing more than notes in class?"

She had better aim into the box she was packing with a pair of panties he preferred off her more than on her anyway. She was almost exactly his height, which he usually didn't like for some reason that could no doubt be turned into something that made him ill-adjusted, but the generous tits were real and she liked having them touched. A lot, actually. That aside, she was smart, and when it came down to it, he liked smart women.

"You see," she said in a tone that reminded him of his long-gone mother, "your real problem is that you're not good in situations that involve stress. You might think about working on that since your job involves stress one hundred percent of the time, which doesn't give you a lot of time off. Don't accuse me. Think about yourself."

"Now I'm confused. I'm always thinking of myself. Isn't that your very point?"

She slammed the box closed and ran tape over the lid. "You can be such an asshole."

"Asshole? I object to that particular label," he countered. He might actually miss her, but not the long debates over human motivations and how environment could shape a person or the opposing argument that it was genetics. She wasn't the only one who got bored on occasion. "I prefer graciously challenged."

"I'm afraid you're stuck with asshole." She removed a few more garments, shoved a drawer shut, and didn't look at him.

Yes, Brian all the way. He hadn't seen it coming, but in the rearview mirror it was crystal clear.

Jason asked, "What did I do? This can't be about the party."

"Oh, you are right about that."

"Then . . . what?"

"You don't know?"

"That's possible." He drained the beer, put his feet on the coffee table, and shrugged, not half as nonchalant as he pretended. Then his tone went lower. "Katie, look—"

"I don't want to go, but I have to." She dropped to her knees on the wooden floor and efficiently sealed up another box. "We have a singularly symbiotic relationship in which we feed off our mutual flaws. If you want it in higher educational speak, I like fucked-up men, but you are way *too* edgy for me. You like intelligent women because you might be the most competitive person I've ever encountered, but you can't play nice if you feel threatened on that level. I don't know who will work for you, but it isn't me. Your new partner has pushed you. She's good, she's competent, and Metzger is really on board with her working with the department and you hate that."

Hate was kind of strong.

Goddamnit. He wished he could disagree completely.

"I don't wet the bed," he offered, because really, he

wasn't sure how he felt about her leaving. "Can you give me a free consultation before you go? What are the odds I'll start doing that?"

"Carry this out to my car." She inclined her head toward a box. "And then I will be out of your hair and you will, I predict, be relieved."

He got to his feet. Annoyed, relieved, which was he? "A scientific opinion?"

"No," she said with a thin smile. "Just intuition. I've always been more into this relationship than you." She tossed her bag back over her shoulder. "If you want to laugh, the funny thing is I knew it from the very beginning. I would like to stay a lot more than *you* want me to stay. "

Not that funny really, he thought as a few minutes later she put her car in gear and pulled away from the curb. He wasn't amused, but then again he wasn't a damned psychologist either. Turning, he went back into the apartment complex, walked up the one flight of stairs to his unit, and entered into a combination of welcome solitude and the bereft feeling of missing pictures on the desk in the corner and the empty sound of the clock ticking in the kitchen.

He stared at the clock moodily. She hadn't taken it, which said something. He'd only bought it because she liked chickens and the ridiculous thing had a rooster on the face, pecking at something on the ground, maybe kernels of corn, he'd never paid attention, but he did notice it stayed, and she'd left.

He was left with the goddamned cock clock.

His mother had left too. It meant nothing really, but it stung a bit. If he was like Kate, with her overemphasis on everything that might make a psychological impact, he would read more into it, but the truth was . . . at the end of the day, she'd left him.

Simple. Fine. She left. He'd dealt with it before, and he could deal with it now.

The apartment had a small balcony that faced a pool only used maybe three months a year, four if it was a good summer, square and fairly big but unimaginative, blue and with some scattered chairs and umbrellas. He couldn't remember getting into it even once, but it was crowded today with the heat. He wandered outside and dropped into one of the two lawn chairs and decided a little people watching might make him feel better.

And for whatever reason, he didn't so much think about Kate's departure as he did the case. She might be more intuitive than he thought. Besides, he really couldn't do much about her moving out but he could hopefully solve this murder. No use wasting his time on regrets.

So . . . body one was an unidentified female in a torched house.

Body two, the owner—kind of—of said house splattered on a sidewalk downtown. No way it wasn't related, and no way so far to connect them. Antagonistic father-in-law, meek wife who barely spoke a word . . . and just plain nothing else.

It was possible, he decided while watching two kids who couldn't be more than six fling a ball at each other and splash in the pool, that Matthew Tobias had secrets. People who killed themselves had secrets, whether they were deep and dark, or just slightly private. If they didn't, they wouldn't be left alone for five minutes.

Fucking someone else?

He just didn't buy it. The guy wasn't the type in his opinion, but then again he really didn't think he'd have the balls to off himself by jumping off an eleven-story parking garage either. For sure when he'd interviewed him Tobias had been nervous, but then again, his house had just been burned down with an unknown person in it smoldering along with the carpet and the cheap furniture.

Helton, the real owner, middle-aged, with a tobacco cough, wasn't helpful. He was in Florida for a wedding apparently during the fire, and when they showed up on his doorstep, he was still unpacking. Airline tickets don't lie considering heightened security, and the man swore he had no idea who the victim might be or why anyone would have chosen the Tobias house.

The more Jason thought about it, Tobias committed suicide in his opinion. Offed himself by jumping, and it muddied the waters, but it was not pertinent to the real intent of the homicide they were investigating. A casualty, but not a contributor.

Dismiss it.

Fine.

The sky had taken on a hazy hue due to the humidity, the clouds holding together like the gluey air got to them too, and he was sweating through his T-shirt. The kids in the pool shrieked with joy as they splashed each other. . . .

As he tipped his beer back, he wondered if he'd ever had that kind of innocence, and came to the conclusion that "probably not" was the answer.

Chapter 9

The building looked roughly the same; brick with gen-
teel ironwork over the windows that was supposed to
be decorative but really represented that the level of crime
in the neighborhood required some sort of security. Two
kids on skateboards went by and looked at me curiously
and I realized I was driving too slow and sped up a
little.

I used to live there. I'm not ashamed of it, or proud of
it, or really anything else in between.

I just used to live there, in that building.

There was a woman, walking alone and wearing a
baggy pink-striped dress, holding a purse, her pace slow,
her face tired, shoulders drooping . . .

She reminded me of someone . . . and the monster in
the swamp stirred in my brain, sluggish but rippling the
surface of the stagnant, steaming water.

Maybe that was a sign.

JULY 6

Ellie was sleeping, deep and dreamless as far as she could tell, and the sound of the alarm jolted her out of a comfortable place.

No, she registered later, not the alarm, but an actual ring on her cell . . . and who the hell, she wondered as she squinted at the clock, would call her at four in the morning? Next to her Bryce stirred and rose up on one elbow, groping for the light.

"MacIntosh." Her voice was throaty with sleep.

"It's happened again."

She blinked, not quite awake still, but Santiago's tone had an interesting quality; he sounded just the same at this hour as he did midafternoon. A little brusque, sure of himself, nonapologetic.

She sat up and brushed the hair out of her face. "Okay, I'm listening. What happened?"

"Metzger called me. There was a fire in an apartment building that was reported around one this morning and has the exact same methodology. There's a charred body inside. Fire department goes in, think they are containing a situation, destroy pretty much all the evidence and then realize they've got a corpse on the table in the middle of the room."

She was already out of bed, feet on the floor, searching for her discarded clothes. "Address?"

"I'll pick you up."

Well, this was slightly embarrassing, though she wasn't sure why. "I'll meet you there."

"Why do I have the feeling you don't have a pen on you, or anything else for that matter," Santiago said sardonically. "Same place as last time? This will be faster. I'm already on my way."

Unfortunately, he had a point.

"Fine, I'll be out front in five minutes."

"Sounds about right."

She pushed a button and Bryce said in a voice still slightly thick with sleep, "I take it that isn't good news. I'll make you a cup of coffee."

"Most of my phone calls from the department aren't good news and coffee would be great." She found her underwear and headed for the bathroom. Teeth brushed, hair swept into a ponytail, sleeveless blouse—she didn't have anything else there—and shorts with tennis shoes and she was ready, slipping her gun into her shoulder holster, reminding herself that if she was going to spend the night so often, maybe she should bring some more clothes over if Bryce didn't mind.

He *wouldn't* mind.

She knew it, and couldn't decide how she felt about it.

The Mustang was a little loud for the hour and the peaceful street. True to his word, Santiago pulled in about the same time she came out the front door. She opened the door and slid in, balancing her cup as she fumbled with the seat belt. He never bothered with greetings, so neither did she. "Where did this happen?"

"Bayview again."

"That's interesting. Maybe we've got a pattern."

"We might. Hold onto that cup, this is a sweet ride, but not necessarily a smooth one."

He was right, the precarious matter of holding her cup upright and his speed making it difficult to talk anyway. He hadn't done much better in the clothing department, wearing shorts and a Hawaiian-style shirt, and if he'd combed his hair, it hadn't worked out all that well. It was still pitch dark, though she could swear that the temperature was in the seventies with matching humidity even at this hour of the morning.

The scene was a disaster.

Fire *was* considered a disaster, she was informed as she stooped to duck under the police tape, a very messy business, and the timeline needed to save the other apartments in the building made for an expedient entry and enthusiastic response from the efficient Milwaukee Fire Department.

Damn.

Once they were inside the building, they were stopped. "We can't let you in yet, ma'am." A firefighter, streaked with soot and water still dripping from his slicker, stood in the hallway, flanked by several uniformed police officers. One of them recognized her, a curly haired young rookie, and as she reached for her badge, he said helpfully, "This is Detective MacIntosh from homicide."

"Oh. Sorry." The firefighter smiled through the grime. "People are crazy about being evacuated. They want to see how their apartments fared and a few of them are going to be unhappy, but the fire is contained and extinguished, and hey, I say if you're still alive, you did pretty well."

A healthy attitude. "Someone didn't survive, or so I understand," she said. The hallway stank of smoke and wet drywall. It was still hazy and one of the officers coughed repeatedly. Her own eyes were already watering. "That's why we're here. Safe to go in yet?"

"Structurally, yes. There still could be hot spots though. You'll need to clear it with someone higher up than me. Right now we've been told to keep everyone out."

"Then point me in the direction of your supervisor."

He did, which proved to be someone harried and uncooperative who told her they hadn't yet cleared the building and to go get a cup of coffee or something. Santiago surprisingly didn't argue.

"I'll buy," he offered. His eyes were red from either the smoke or the early hour. "I need some. Unlike you, I haven't had any. There's an all-night place around the corner."

There was, but it was jammed with anxious people rousted from their apartments, so they settled for a fast food restaurant instead, taking their cups back to the scene, standing outside, watching as equipment was hauled out of the building. Her partner wasn't given much to talking in the predawn hours, Ellie discovered. She was sweating already in her light shirt.

When the surly supervisor finally came out to signal them clear, a deputy medical examiner had arrived, and the crime scene unit techs were standing around, talking about the heat, the temperature outside, and the predicted high for the day.

"Midnineties. Lake will be busy today," one of the techs said to her, rubbing the back of his neck. "I was supposed to go sailing, dammit. Let's get this done."

As they walked back into the building, Santiago asked him a question about his sailboat, obviously well versed in the subject, but she didn't pay much attention. Canoes she knew about, from special handmade fiberglass river canoes like the one her father had by Badger Boats, built way up near the Hayward flowage and almost forty years old, to aluminum commercial lake canoes with a completely different shape to handle bigger water. She'd inherited that old river canoe after her father had passed away at far too young an age and her mother decided to eschew the frigid northern winter for sunny Florida. She took care of it, but it was getting harder

and harder to find someone to repair it. Before the move
to Milwaukee, she'd taken it out only on rare occasions
because she was so worried about damaging it. Still she
loved the feel of gliding through the water, and truly, it
handled like a well-trained thoroughbred racehorse,
sleek and fast . . .

Now, reentering the building contaminated by the
pungent smell of the recent fire, she wished for a cool,
crisp autumn morning and a quiet paddle on the Wisconsin River, alone, the leaves whispering in a slight
breeze, the air so clean you could inhale it like drinking
a glass of fine wine, the current flowing like silk under
the canoe.

Why the hell had she moved down here again? At the
moment, she wasn't sure.

"I don't know about you," Santiago said, pulling gloves
from his pocket, "but I'm getting fucking tired of this
particular smell. I didn't apply to the fire department for
a reason. Jesus. I couldn't do this."

He was right, it was noxious. Part of it, she knew as
they passed the tape and walked into the apartment,
was that among the various other smells like melted
plastic, sodden half-burned carpet, and whatever other
damage the fire had done, there was something else.

This time the body was on a kitchen table, or what
was left of one from the metal legs that were splayed
around the corpse, the structure itself collapsed. Unlike
the last one it was visibly a woman, but the body was
badly burned enough that facial recognition would be
impossible.

"Point of origin," the firefighter who had been man-
aging the scene said in a dour voice, pointing at the

grisly display. "Whoever you are looking for started the fire by lighting your victim on fire. There was obviously other accelerant sprinkled around because the whole place started to go up fast and it wouldn't happen that quickly without it, but I'd say the main purpose for this was to burn the body."

He spoke with enough authority that Ellie didn't doubt for a minute his opinion, but there was the now eerily familiar mess of soaked debris, which meant all the evidence was virtually obliterated. Santiago must have been thinking the same thing because he said sarcastically, "Maybe he dropped his driver's license or something."

"Feel free to look around for it, and I hope you are not criticizing the fire department." The other man stomped off and shouted something to someone in the hall, and with some reluctance, Ellie forced herself to really look at the body.

Not fun, but necessary.

It was familiar because of the unnaturally crossed arms, the same ghastly smile, the clothing either melted onto the body or burned away, but the suggestion of a human form was much more pronounced. "I'm going to defer to the ME's office, but I'd say this one didn't burn as hot," Ellie ventured, staring at the body but not touching anything. Technicians were starting to process the scene, and quite frankly, she was close enough.

"The victim isn't as crispy," Santiago agreed, crouching down to inspect the floor. "Less carpet burned, in general the place not as trashed. There are still pictures on the walls."

"Apartment." She glanced around. "No sprinkler system because this is an older building, but neighbors who not only notice the smell of smoke but have a vested interest in calling in a possible fire right away. It just was put out quicker. What's his pattern?"

Santiago rose. His blond curls looked liquid in the light now coming in through the broken windows as the sun rose. "Yeah, I agree. It didn't burn nearly as long."

"Why was this one at night?"

"I'm wondering that too. The other was in the middle of the day. Considering the placing of the victim on the table, it surprises me the progression of the crime would vary."

That was actually a pretty intuitive insight, but she shook her head. "I don't think the progression varied as much as the location. House to apartment. Why?"

"That is an interesting question. And who the hell is she? According to the frantic old guy who lives next door, he woke up to the smell of smoke. He swears he was just asleep before that and heard nothing."

It was true. His consternation and horror matched pretty much how the Tobiases had reacted. They would look into him, of course, but now that there was a pattern of sorts emerging, Ellie was trying to get a feel for who they might be looking for.

"It took a lot of nerve to carry the body up here. The hour was helpful, but someone still could have been coming in late and seen him. He had to break in; what if the occupant of the apartment woke up . . . why'd he choose this location?"

"Big balls," Santiago agreed. Glancing at the warped orange countertops, singed black now, and the debris all over the floor, he carefully stepped around what appeared to once be a plastic chair but was now just a mass on the floor, and looked around the kitchen. "The place needed updating. So did the Tobias house."

"Lots of homes and apartments do. Ever watch HGTV?" She let her gaze rove over the destruction. "Is that relevant? I can't see how. Not yet anyway. What's the connection?"

"There's the body on the table," he pointed out, scouring the room, and—if it was a little grudgingly admitted—she had to acknowledge he was completely professional on the scene, letting the CSI unit work, allowing the medical examiner on call latitude with deference. "Let's not skip over the fire. This is new to me but I am starting to think if I wanted to kill someone, I might just decide this is the way to go. No need to tidy up after yourself; big hoses and men in rubber boots will take care of it."

"Is covering up evidence the reason to do it this way?" Ellie surveyed the damage, looked again at the body, and an inward chill of apprehension went through her. "If so, we need to find out what this guy has to hide."

Chapter 10

It really isn't about control.

Quite the opposite. This sounds strange, but it is about not *having* control and a different thrill ride altogether. I know it, and I don't fight it.

I stood on the street and watched the fray; fire trucks and police cars and people standing around talking in subdued voices . . .

A mistake, of course. Visiting the scene of the crime. In this day and age, detectives recognize that it happens and look for it, so everyone would be scrutinized at some point, and I'd be up for inspection, then either dismissed or considered. I could make an excuse, but still it was a risk.

It seduced me.

I *wanted* to be there. To see the smoke still oozing from the rooftop, to imagine the damage inside, the beauty of it all. The sun was coming up, illuminating the rooftop, tinting the haze red like a veneer of blood.

* * *

Carl slid into the booth.

The two people sitting across from him looked tired. Maybe he did too. His contact in homicide had called him right after the news broke about the second murder and fire. Santiago he knew. They'd crossed paths often enough. MacIntosh was different. Honey blond hair, fairly young, with maybe a hint of smudged mascara around her eyes, though her gaze was very direct. Rachel would envy her figure, which seemed naturally trim, but then again, he liked curvy women.

Still only early morning. Everyone around was drinking coffee and eating pancakes and scrambled eggs. He asked for a decaf and a cinnamon roll and looked at his two companions in question.

"A water." MacIntosh was cool and professional. "Otherwise, I'm fine."

"Denver omelet," Santiago said in his nonchalant voice. "Bacon instead of sausage and I sure could use some good coffee. Just black."

At that point Carl decided two things. Neither of them liked sitting next to each other on the opposite side of the booth. The discomfort could be for any number of reasons, but none of those reasons were good between two partners.

The second was that he thought they both were probably good cops. He'd been on the force long enough to know the difference. Hungry but not crazy—he'd met a few crazy ones—and even at six in the morning they looked at him with straight inquiry in their eyes.

Well, he could satisfy their curiosity over his call but their personal differences were their own problem.

The bustle around them was loud enough he felt comfortable saying in an ordinary voice, "Five years ago, as far as I know, your perp probably took his first lap in the pool. Both Metzger and I remembered it and that is why I'm here. I was homicide then, and it was my case."

"Five years?" Ellie MacIntosh looked incredulous. Her eyes were a unique hazel, the green brilliant behind the gold flecks. She folded her arms on the table. "Okay, we appreciate this. Tell us why you think the cases are connected."

That was easy enough. "The table and the arson."

"Well, shit the bed Fred," Santiago muttered, his shoulders settled against the vinyl padding of the booth. "This is interesting. He send you?"

"Metzger? Not specifically. But he encouraged me to pass it along. We talked about it when you had the first victim. It struck a chord with both of us even though it was a little different. Male victim, his own house, but the table . . . Now I'm thinking maybe you have the same problem I had five years ago. Three tables and three burned bodies? Can that be a coincidence?"

"Okay." Jason Santiago looked at him without particular resentment but he wasn't friendly either. "What do you have to tell us about that first case? As long as you keep in mind this is our investigation, I am willing to listen to whatever you have to say."

Well, they weren't exactly strangers so he knew that much about his colleague. Santiago was no punches pulled, not ever.

Fine.

"Tell us." MacIntosh was a little intense herself, her gaze direct. "There was a table?"

He nodded. "It's a cold case now. Five years cold. Still, the body on the table and the burned house? I am not sure how to put this exactly; both of you are police officers so maybe you'll understand I just had the feeling he wasn't done back then. This job is driven a lot by instinct and hunches. My hunch then was that whoever committed that crime hadn't done all he wanted to do. It seems to me that one was dead on."

"Ah, fuck me." Santiago ran his fingers through his already disheveled hair.

"No thanks." Carl grinned briefly, but it faded. "Look, this is all yours, but I'd like a hand in just because he used to be mine. Just keep me informed, okay? If this is the same perp, he once belonged to me and I never caught him. Here's the file with all my notes. I hope it helps."

His cinnamon roll arrived just as he pushed the paperwork with his fingertips toward MacIntosh.

Bryce had made coffee. He'd made eggs too, scrambled lightly, like Ellie usually preferred, and toasted a couple of bagels. It was convenient he worked at home, and often as not, by his own admission he forgot to eat breakfast anyway, so this was probably good for both of them.

He scooped eggs out of the pan. "Most important meal of the day."

It was midmorning and she had been gone for hours. When he slid the plate of food in front of her, Ellie said, "I'm starving, but . . ."

"Bad, huh?"

"Bad," she confirmed, remembering the apartment. She was still a little queasy. It wasn't at all easy to dismiss.

"If it goes cold, we can warm it up or I can make more." He took a forkful and said nothing else. The eggs were light and fluffy, and the coffee was fresh, so no doubt it all tasted good, but he hadn't had her morning. She always talked about cases eventually, but it needed to sink into her skin, her soul, her psyche.

She took a sip of coffee and then looked at the wall.

She knew there were unattractive shadows under her eyes. A light jacket that no one could possibly wear in this heat hung over the back of her chair, but it hardly matched the rest of her clothing. She could have showered back at her condo, but somehow it had seemed natural to go back to his house.

The night before had been somehow . . . different when they'd made love. There had been an urgency when Bryce had undressed her, his hands busy, his hungry mouth on hers in a kiss that was not like his usual almost gentle style, and he'd definitely been less than selfish in making sure she'd enjoyed every minute, which wasn't new exactly—in bed they'd been good together from that very first time—but something had changed and she not only wasn't sure just what that might be, but at a loss as to how to ask the question.

For the life if her, she couldn't figure out to how to *phrase* the question. She wasn't even sure she *wanted* to ask. *So, the new position, what is that all about . . .*

No, that didn't work. Fantastic sex. Why even question that?

"I need to go back as soon as they've cleared the scene."

"That doesn't surprise me, I guess." He took another bite, leaning his elbows on the antique round table he'd bought one afternoon at a garage sale he'd dragged her to—her dad had been like that, always off looking through antique shops and going to estate auctions. Bryce had been convinced at the time it was walnut—she remembered his enthusiasm—and he was right as it turned out, for once he'd paid to have it refinished, it was a true beauty with ornate legs and an inlaid top that had been almost invisible under the scratches and water damage. The kitchen windows were set in an octagonal design and boasted a view of a very private backyard with mature trees and terraced flower beds full of perennials planted by the previous owner. It was a nice place to sit.

The minute she'd hit the door she'd gone straight to the shower and dropped her clothes in the laundry room, so at the moment she wore one of his old T-shirts.

She took a bite of eggs and answered the question. "We need to start interviewing witnesses. It was impossible until the tenants were allowed to go back into the building and considering the time of night when they were evacuated, some of them went to stay with friends or family." The eggs were delicious and she took another forkful with more enthusiasm. "This is the exact same scenario as the last one, which was only two days ago. Maybe the ME's office will be able to help us, but so far we really just don't have much. It isn't their fault, but let's face it, you were right when you pointed it out, the fire department obliterates the evidence."

"Clever."

Ellie picked up her bagel, stared at it as if she didn't know what it was, and set it down again. "I know. Or I mean, I know *that,* I just don't know what it is. What *this* is."

Bryce put his spoon in his coffee and stirred. "This is exactly your kind of case, you know."

Her gaze flashed up to look at him. Her hands cradled her coffee cup. Was it really only ten o'clock? "Meaning . . . what?"

His grin was crooked. "I wish I didn't know firsthand, but I can say with some measure of authority that you won't stop until you catch him. The case last year . . . I can't say I enjoyed being the prime suspect in a serial murder investigation, but I was reassured somewhat at the time that you were smart enough to figure out I didn't do it and I didn't even really know you then."

That served to lighten the mood actually. Her mouth twitched into a rare smile. "Somewhat?"

He shrugged, telling her he hadn't been entirely positive he wasn't going to be nailed as Wisconsin's next notorious killer, even if he wasn't guilty of it, despite how good at her job she might be. "It was touch and go there for a while, admit it. But I admit my faith in you was about all the hope I had. Everyone else was ready to hang me. So, why is this going down so fast?"

That was the question of the hour, wasn't it?

"I don't know." She ate slowly in small bites. "It has to mean something. We have video of the crowd. It's standard now. After we get through with the initial questioning, half the department is going to watch it. Who knows, we might turn something up."

"Two bodies and one suicide. I'd say the *entire* department should watch it. Three dead in three days?"

She set down her fork. Miracle of miracle, after what she'd seen just a few hours ago, her plate was empty.

Ellie rose, dusting off her hands. When had she devoured that last bit of her bagel? She wasn't sure, but she was positive it was good for her. "That might not be a bad call, but these aren't our only homicides and I'm new. I don't get to make those kinds of decisions."

"Yet?"

It hung there. She saw it didn't surprise him at all that she was at least considering one day moving up in law enforcement. She was still young, only thirty-two, but she'd been a detective for a while and the case up north wouldn't hurt later in her career if she was in line for a promotion.

But for now . . . this case . . .

"What are you guys calling him, or is that sanctified information?"

"What do you mean?" She looked at him.

He laughed. "Come on, Ellie. I'm going to bet the department already has a name for whoever you are investigating at this time. What? Fireman?"

"This isn't a television show."

"No, it isn't, unfortunately. I really wish people weren't out there dying."

She considered him for a moment and then shook her head. "Fireman isn't bad actually, but might offend some other civil servants that I have seen quite a lot of recently and who risk *their* lives for other people, not take lives. One of the other detectives referred to our resident match-happy friend as The Burner. It stuck."

"The Burner."

The kitchen was her favorite part of his house, upgraded to tile and concrete and stainless steel, the windows letting in a lot of natural light.

On a morning like this one, she needed the sun streaming in, making square patterns on the floor, touching her shoulders . . . outside it was hot, but inside she was cold.

She also had needed to not be alone and Bryce was a logical choice, the one to turn to.

Was he what she needed right now, or was he what she wanted for a lifetime?

But at the moment, in the sunny kitchen, she thought it was probably *yes*.

Was probably good enough?

"Santiago?" Bryce lifted his brows in slight inquiry, prompting her.

He really looked incredible in the morning, which was vaguely irritating. When she was rumpled and hadn't showered she looked like crap, and here he was, careless gray T-shirt with a Marquette insignia on the front,

wrinkled shorts, and tousled hair, and he could do a fea-
ture on the front of a magazine.

"Santiago, what?"

Bryce set aside his cup. "I'm going to take an educated guess and assume he was the one who christened
the perpetrator in your latest case."

"You'd be wrong. Why would you think that?"

"Short and flippant. Sounds like him."

"It was Carl Grasso. He had the case first if this
proves to follow the same lines, and he was actually the
one who christened our killer."

"Grasso? For whatever reason his name sounds familiar."

"He killed two men in a self-defense shooting about
the same time The Burner decided to pop up. *If* it is the
perpetrator."

"I see." Dark eyes held hers. He agreed slowly, "Yeah,
that does ring a bell. The police department kind of kept
it low key but I remember it vaguely because Suzanne
was with the prosecutor's office back then."

She was never crazy about the mention of Bryce's ex-
wife.

"They moved Grasso to another section and saved
face for homicide." She changed the subject. Bryce didn't
like her partner, she didn't really either, so why discuss
him? Besides, her job seemed to take up the majority of
their conversations and she felt guilty about that now
and then. "How is the book coming?"

"Not bad," he responded noncommittally.

He was writing a novel—he did have a Ph.D. in literature after all—and while she couldn't describe him as
secretive about it, he wasn't very open on the subject and
she was *interested*. "How are things in West Virginia?"

"For the main characters? Fairly bleak, I'm afraid."

His tone was self-deprecating. "I'm still not sure why I decided to embark on a journey quite this dark, but then again, I'm not cut out to write a genre novel."

He'd really only given her a vague comment that the book was a literary work set in the Appalachian mountains.

"What about your personal experience?" she observed dryly. The case up north lingered, in both their minds at a guess, but Bryce didn't talk about it often.

He'd not only found a murdered woman's body, but seen a point-blank shooting where the person on the receiving end died. Both those incidents were fairly hands-on when it came to researching a crime novel, though she doubted he looked at either one that way.

It was a little tough to figure out how to get their way around what had happened. Oddly enough, while it should make them comrades in arms, it sat there like a stone wall at times, separating them despite the attraction, the proverbial elephant in the room. The case was solved. It should be over.

It wasn't. Not quite. Obviously not for her when it came to her occupation or her colleagues wouldn't bring it up. She doubted it was out of Bryce's mind either, especially since it was how they had met.

"Just think about it," she said, only half joking. "I could be a source of research."

His dark eyes were steady. "No."

"Good to hear."

"God, Ellie, you already knew that." His body shifted in the chair.

True.

Fine, time to switch into another gear. They obviously had some trouble with this topic of conversation. "So, what's the premise? At least tell me that."

"Do you really want to know?"

That stopped her. "If I didn't, would I ask?" she finally said, taking a drink of coffee as she took her plate to the sink.

"So far, no."

She turned around. "I've gotten the impression you don't want to talk about it."

"A work in progress is a little hard to define."

There were things she didn't know about him. Well, she could qualify that by saying that even though the Lincoln County Sheriff's Department had crawled all over him with a microscope last fall, and she knew almost everything on paper possible about Dr. Bryce Grantham, there were parts of him that she didn't quite *understand*. It could be entirely her problem. She liked facts, straightforward and irrefutable, and he was a complicated entity rather than a linear individual.

But, truth be told, she liked that about him. The intellectual bent and the complexity. Simple apparently didn't appeal to her, and eventually, points connected.

In her experience, most everything did. She rinsed her plate and felt immensely better, though after that crime scene, eating hadn't been her first priority. Had she been asked outright, she would have declined food, but he'd taken one look at her and just fixed breakfast. For that alone, he deserved a little attention to his life. All too often her job got in the way of deep discussions on more than one level.

"Do your best. I'm really interested." She picked up a towel and dried her hands. "Wow me, Dr. Grantham."

He laughed. It cracked the tension, and besides, she really liked it when he was spontaneous, which wasn't often. Brainy men might be sexy, but they weren't easy to deal with all the time.

"That's a tall order. I don't think you are wowed very easily, Detective MacIntosh."

"It wouldn't hurt to try. You are pretty secretive. What is this book about?"

"I can't decide if I should tell you."

The combative light in his eyes was intriguing. Usually Bryce was laid back, calm, a contrast to the men she dealt with on a day-to-day basis. She said slowly, "I suppose if you are exploiting the Northwoods Killer case, I—"

"Do you really think I want to relive that? I think I just made it clear I don't." He meant it too; she could see it in the twist of his mouth and the decisive shake of his head. "Please, Ellie, give me more credit. I'm not going back there. Not ever. This isn't a crime novel really. It isn't about what happened, it is about how the people involved handle it."

He was adamant enough that she believed him.

"Then?"

"To sum it up loosely, it's about a dysfunctional family—by the way, show me a functional one—that dabbles in some less-than-legal activities that fairly often have them at odds with each other. But when the youngest son is killed under mysterious circumstances, they reassess their dubious lifestyles and priorities and pull together. Toss in some revenge to the mix, and that's a thumbnail synopsis."

"Sounds good," she said, and meant it. "I like it."

"Enough about the book. Hopefully one day you'll get to pick it up and read it. Maybe this crime scene will be more productive and the ME can help out a little more."

Back to her job, her problems . . .

She sure as hell hoped he was right. For the sake of the two charred corpses they had on their hands. "I really *am* kind of counting on some forensic evidence on this one. Santiago is convinced Matthew Tobias is just a sideline casualty. A straightforward suicide predicated on the loss of his house when he was already unstable. We did confirm he'd been recently fired again, just like his sister told us, but he had an interview the day his house burned. I don't know what to think, but I'm inclined to dismiss his case as unfortunate, and not a homicide, though when you think about it, whoever burned that body in the Tobias house is indirectly responsible for his death."

"How could anyone ever predict that?"

"They couldn't," she agreed, the warm sunshine coming in the window incongruous to their conversation.

She added with quiet introspection, "But in reality, it is two murders for the price of one. When we catch him, I'm going to do everything I can to see that involuntary manslaughter is tossed in with the rest of the charges. So far, I don't even know anyone was murdered. All we can really prove is abuse of a corpse, which is an offense, but hardly serious enough for what I think is happening."

At least it was Bryce who had redirected the conversation back to the current topic. "And what do *you* think is happening, Detective MacIntosh?"

Good question. "Oh, he's killing them. I don't know why yet. I don't even know how, but he's killing them, and he's burning the bodies, and I can tell you unequivocally I am going to catch him."

Chapter 11

In some circles I move easily, and in others, the past might show like a badge on my sleeve. It isn't that I'm not aware of it; I can be a good imposter when it is a necessity.

Actually, when I look at it that way, I suppose I am an imposter most of the time and that is the point of it all. I want to be real.

To myself, of course, I am genuine. I always know what I'm doing even if I don't understand it completely, and I am always aware of the possible consequences. It isn't a difficult equation; mistakes will happen on both sides, it is just a matter of degrees and finesse. Every single time I think about the people who rise in the morning to go to their lackluster jobs, only to return to their generic homes and watch inane television shows as they eat food that will clog their arteries and give them a blessedly early death, I am glad I am me.

Whatever it is I am, monster or man.

Unfortunately, I have thought for a long time I am both. They aren't mutually exclusive.

I weighed the knife in my hand just out of habit, looked at the white-faced woman lying so still before me, and, smiling, became the monster.

There was one thing about being an ex-homicide detective, Carl thought as he negotiated traffic along the lake: It was a bit of a relief to be off the chain. Sure, he still had to adhere to protocol—he was still an officer of the law—but no one was paying attention to what he did with this investigation. They were all watching MacIntosh and Santiago.

So he was free to poke around, break a few rules, and generally not worry about the finer details that might just get a man in trouble. He'd even taken a few days of leave, which he definitely had coming. Metzger had signed off on it without a word according to his supervisor.

His car seamlessly changed lanes, the expensive vehicle an affectation he supposed, but he could afford it so why not?

Except it might stand out in the neighborhood he was headed to, but he had no doubt the community would make him as a cop right away anyway, so the car was probably not a mistake. He had insurance, and he carried a Glock .45 issued to him by the state of Wisconsin. If anyone tried anything, it could be resolved one way or another.

Still, the rows of seedy restaurants and pawnshops baking in the afternoon sun weren't exactly appealing, and if he didn't have a specific appointment, he would never venture over here.

There were contacts you never lost. Ex-perps mostly, not murderers but small-time criminals who lived on the fringe, and quite frankly, he'd overlooked a lot of punishable crime for information during his career. It wasn't as if he was unique; a lot of police officers did it, and in the end, it saved the tax-paying public money. Prosecuting anyone was costly, and if all they were doing was running a bit of illegal gambling on the side, or something else small, what really was the point? Yes, he agreed the law was the law, but there were varying degrees and he'd always felt that way. Picking up a kid for smoking a joint was hell and gone from burning someone's house down with a body in it.

But the kid with the joint sometimes had great information.

He parked in front of a place that only said Liquor on the sign, turned off the car and pocketed the keys, and then stepped outside. If he weren't wearing shoes, he was fairly sure the pavement would have seared off the soles of his feet. Inside the place was dark, the windows taped over, and one lone television played a baseball game above the bar when he opened the door.

"Carlo." John Malcolm looked nervous, wiping his nose with the back of his hand, glancing around the place. Only two other tables were occupied and no one seemed interested. "I got your note. Haven't seen you in a while."

"You haven't been dealing for a while." Carl slid into a seat. There was a haze of cigarette smoke in the air and the music was just a little too loud for noon.

Thin, narrow shouldered, and probably anemic, John shook his head, his unwashed hair brushing his neck because it was too long. His shirt was unbuttoned halfway down his scrawny chest. His appearance varied with his state of affluence. Today things must have been at low ebb in the cash department. "Hey, I don't deal. I use. You know that."

The kid was smart, that was what rankled him. He could do better, he could do *things*. Go places. Not just sit and cook over a low burner. What a waste of a normally functional human brain that was more capable than most.

Carl regarded him over a cracked table that had seen better days during the Eisenhower administration. "I know a lot of things, and then again, unfortunately there are some things I don't know."

"Son of a bitch," John muttered, shifting in his chair, his eyes scanning the room again as if the clientele had changed in the past minute, which it hadn't. "Do your best to not get me into trouble, okay?"

"Have I ever?"

"Not yet." A grimace. "I'm here. But talking to you is, well, whatever . . . You have a reputation. What do you need?"

He had a reputation. All right, he'd admit that. The killings were not something he could ever shake.

"You've heard about the two burnings, right?"

"Okay," John said slowly, staring at him hard. "I watch the news, so yes, but I didn't think you were homicide anymore."

"My career isn't really your concern." Carl folded his hands on the scarred table, trying to ignore the blast of rap from the speakers. He'd never been a fan of that kind of music. "Anyone have any ideas?"

"What makes you think—"

"If they are talking about it on the news, they are talking about it on the street. You are on the street all the time and you have a special skill set most stoners don't, so talk to me."

John had a small scab on his chin and he scratched it off, avoiding Carl's gaze. "Maybe," he muttered. "But keep in mind, the sort of man you're after isn't inclined to a lot of conversation with close friends."

"And how do you know that?"

"Jesus, Grasso, for the same reasons you do. Some men move in packs, and some are loners."

"We have us a loner?"

His companion nodded. "Yes, this one is part of the latter group, and I am going to tell you one thing, I'm not scared of him."

Glasses clinked in the background as a preteen boy bussed the next table. How the hell the place didn't get busted for that, he had no idea, but if the kid needed a job and wasn't serving alcohol, he wasn't going to say anything.

Carl had to admit the defiant look in his informant's eyes was interesting. "Really? Go ahead. Tell me why you won't be the next charred body."

John looked away, his eyes distant. "I suppose, since you've been shaking me down for a while, you know I was a psychology major at one time. Is that why you're asking? You said you wanted to meet for information but might also pick my brain a little."

It was impossible to keep a slight smile from surfacing. Carl grinned, fingered his glass, took a long drink of iced tea, and set it aside. To his relief the music had shut off. "Come on, John. You actually have a degree in psychology from DePauw University in Indiana, which is a fairly prestigious school, and if you had the balls or inclination to kick your bad habit, I suspect you could get back on track and straighten it all out. You aren't a total write-off yet, or a real scumbag. I should know, I've met a lot of them. So yes, that's why I'm asking. Tell me what you think."

There was a silence between them. A big one. Actually, since the first time he'd arrested this young man over a year ago, Carl had wanted to express what he'd just said, so he could cross it off his to-do list now.

John blinked and looked out the window at the steaming midday street. "I'm not sure I can answer. Or do that other thing either."

The other thing? "Kick it? I highly recommend it. Most of us do shit all the time we aren't convinced we can do. Ever considered it? Just chuck the drugs. It's dragging you down. Join NA. Do something."

He wasn't supposed to get involved . . . that was off the table according to policy, but goddamn, sometimes you couldn't help it.

"I've thought about it, but like I said, not sure I can do it. I tried once, but it's been awhile. I wanted to open my own practice one day, you know? Clinicians make a decent living. Private practice, set your own hours, have an office . . . I started my Ph.D., but . . . well, it didn't work out."

"Just skip med school. A prescription pad might be a death knell."

He nodded in agreement. "I'd have to stay away from that. If I could write my own scrips . . . that wouldn't be good."

The kid was nervous, but not scared . . . didn't know anything worthwhile at a guess, but might be able to give a little direction.

Carl flipped the edge of his napkin negligently. As if he didn't care, when against all odds, he actually did. "Try graduate school again."

"Maybe, but aren't you here to talk about The Burner?"

"I am, but do me a favor and think about school. How the hell did you hear that nickname?"

"News again."

That would be Rachel. Carl said an inward curse. She still had friends at her former station and he had no illusions that she might pass along information. The professor was her new persona, but the reporter was still in there.

Good. She owed him now.

"Graduate school. Fuck . . . the application process, you have no idea . . . fuck." John hung his head in his hands. "Reference letters? Where am I going to get those?"

"I have some friends and I think you could get back in if you tried. Get clean and call me." Carl settled his elbows more comfortably on the table. It was a little sticky, but what the hell, he could always rinse off later. "If you were free of the drugs, you'd do fine. Everything in this life depends on how much you want it. But okay, that's up to you, and let's go back to my original question. Anyone talking about the murders besides the pricks on the news?"

"You are asking if anyone immediately guessed who it could be. No. It isn't gang, and it isn't a regular pyro, or if it is, I don't know about it or him."

He signaled for a second beer for his informant even though he wasn't drinking. Carl would give John a few bucks too, just for showing up. Not too much, because he knew where it would go, straight up his nose or into a vein, but he'd give him enough to get a decent meal. "All right, let's move along to the second part of this. Tell me what you can."

"About who is doing this?" John readjusted, his perception altering, his focus going clearer. Even his face changed, giving a hint of that young psych student. "I'll do my best."

"Why is he burning them?"

"My first impression might not be your favorite, but if you want it," John said, nervous, fingering his beer. "It's kind of weird but . . ."

"Weird is fine, I'll take weird. Just give me whatever you know."

"When I heard about it, the first thing I thought was maybe the killer was a cop."

"If squat is what you want, then you have it." Jason tossed aside the report onto Ellie's desk in disgust. "Merry Christmas. Send me a pretty card later when the season is in full swing. One of a pine tree with ornaments will work just fine. I've never put one up."

"It's a little hot for Christmas . . . and never?" She glanced up, just the barest hint of a smile of her face. "No tree ever?"

She looked very nice in some sort of frothy pink shirt that gathered under her breasts and a pair of white shorts. It was still the weekend so they were technically not on duty, and for whatever reason he was tempted to answer her question.

Maybe it was some passive-aggressive impulse because Kate would resent the hell out of him opening up even in a small way to someone else. He hadn't done it for her, and he wasn't sure why.

"No. No tree."

MacIntosh just looked at him.

Why in the hell had he ever said that about the tree? He had no idea so he brushed over it. "It's a little hard to think about snowmen and holly jolly whatever when someone is out there lighting people on fire." He pointed to the file. "That's the doc's opinion along with his notes. Other than the fact that the victim was older, we don't have anything more than we had before. Dental records? Forget it. She had false teeth."

"Oh, that's great." Ellie ran her hand through her fair hair and blew out a short breath. "Cause of death?"

"The body was too burned for him to really be sure, but he thought it might have been asphyxiation."

"Smoke in the lungs?" She was glancing through the report already but he had read it twice himself and knew what was—and wasn't—in there.

"No. Like our first one, she was dead before she was set on fire."

She nodded, her brow creased, scanning another piece of paper before she set it aside. "I finally got the person who rents the apartment. He called back about five minutes or so ago. His name is Kilmarten and he says he has no idea who it could be. He's incredibly ticked, by the way, about losing all of his video games and his television. The dead body didn't compare."

"That's helpful."

Jason dropped into the chair by her desk and rubbed his cheek. "Our guy, The Burner . . . maybe he belongs to some sort of pagan religion and believes in purification by fire or some such extreme bullshit that *my* pagan soul does not embrace."

"Could be, I suppose. That's as plausible as anything else. Three dead in three days. That's extreme to me."

"I don't know if we can count Matthew Tobias. He jumped. We only have two murdered as far as I am concerned."

"*Maybe* he jumped," she corrected. "I wish the tox screen would come back on that."

"Yeah, well, our pathology department is a little overworked."

"I'm feeling a little overworked myself."

He, on the other hand, had nothing else really to do. The investigation at least gave him something to focus his energy on rather than sit and feel sorry for himself because Kate had decided to move on to greener pastures.

Brian Wilfong. Fine. He wished her joy of that supercilious little prick. He hated pretention.

Still, he was all alone. His pasture was dull gray, dry as dust, and not likely to get any rain soon.

"It's a long weekend," he said neutrally. "This isn't northern Wisconsin, America's vacationland."

Ellie looked affronted. "Don't make the mistake of thinking that the sheriff's department doesn't have plenty to do up there. Yes, the detectives aren't strictly assigned one type of case, but they are busy."

There was a slight snort in his laugh. "What? Investigating how one would-be hunter who had scotch with his coffee shot another one because he was too stupid to realize deer don't wear camo jackets?"

That was insulting, he knew it, and yet it came out of his mouth anyway. Maybe Kate was right, he *was* an asshole.

"I know you aren't thrilled MPD hired me," she said evenly, looking at him, her hazel eyes direct and unflinching. "I know you are even less thrilled to be assigned to be working with me. But they *did* hire me, you are my partner, and we have an important case to solve. You don't have to like me, I'm fine with that. But you do have to work with me. I'm aware you think I got this job because of one case, but I was a detective before the Northwoods Killer started abducting young women, so don't think I lack experience in this line of police work."

This was kind of a long overdue conversation. Maybe

he had a bit of an attitude . . . okay, hey he did, but he was entitled to a few questions, he thought. He propped his elbows on her desk and there might have been a hint of belligerence there. "How many homicides, MacIntosh?"

"Does it matter?"

"Maybe."

"How many serials have *you* worked?"

"Before this? None."

"You see?" She folded her hands and squared off with him, eye to eye. "You are going to have to just accept the answer that I've worked homicide cases before and know what I'm doing. You and I aren't running a contest."

"That's because you'd lose. I'm not sure I trust your experience."

"I'm not sure I trust you, period. There, do we both feel better?" She picked up a sheaf of papers from the desk and straightened them. "Going back to our investigation, maybe tomorrow, when people get back into town, and when the apartment building has all the tenants in their units again, we will find out someone saw something. I want to know how in the hell a person can get in without anyone noticing them either carrying a body, or if the person was still alive at the time, with a companion. I know it was the middle of the night, but people work different shifts. The risk was huge."

Fine. She was right, actually. The case was the important thing. "Has to be a male perp," he said, which had been his opinion all along. "The ME says they are dead before the fire is set and that the first one was decomposing before he decided to build his little bonfire. If he's right, they have to be carried in. You think the second one is different from the first? I don't."

"A woman could kill someone and stuff them in a

suitcase before rigor sets in, and then just wheel them through the door." She sat back, her face thoughtful. "Maybe we should ask about that. No one thinks about someone with a suitcase. The last time I flew my bag was overweight and cost me a fortune because of the penalty, but I had no problem rolling it through the airport and was surprised when they told me how much it weighed. I couldn't have carried it, at least not any distance, but wheeling it around was a cinch. We can't entirely rule out a woman."

"That's not bad," he conceded. "Possible. We'll ask about suitcases."

"The fire department broke down the door. We still have no idea how he got in."

"I do think we know how he got out. The window was open, probably to facilitate the fire, but also as a means of exit."

"Two stories?" she objected.

"Well, we know the corpse didn't set itself on fire and there was no one else inside and the door was locked until they kicked it in. If it was tampered with first, it will be hard to tell. Look, I don't know about you, but if I have air-conditioning, in this weather, my window is not open. He went out that way somehow."

It took a moment, but then she nodded. "I think you're right."

"Then how the shit *did* he get in?" Jason thought about fire and empty apartments and open windows with a considerable drop to the ground that might involve broken bones, and muttered, "I think we're looking for a fucking Houdini."

Chapter 12

I really don't have an agenda.

Agenda. Such a stupid phrase, coined by those who follow trends, and I suppose the world should be glad I don't inspire trends. It was entirely personal, so the speculation on the news just irritated me.

It might be more aptly said I wanted it over. You know, like once something is set in motion it is just easier to let the flame lick up the fuse and ignite the blast. Like sex, the climax is what it is all about anyway, right?

Son of a bitch. How I wished it was over and done.

Maybe it would be better to let it go. I knew it would be easier to handle it that way, actually. Walk away. Nothing forced me do this. But, honestly, I was really looking forward to the inferno.

As far as I can tell, that's been my problem my entire life. If I could walk away I would never have started this in the first place.

Ellie didn't usually play hunches. She had them occasionally, but Bryce was right. Police work required a perfect

balance between instinct and fact: It did not allow sup-
position and yet relied on it. The law was the law. Figuring the rest of it out was up to human beings, and they
were fallible, which was tricky when they were pitted
against each other.

And she did have a hunch. If you could even call it
that. She had a lingering feeling that Michelle Tobias
was a dead end . . . but maybe a hypothesis and a clue
could be in there somewhere.

Nothing more.

Yet she still had driven over to Cedarburg again.

The door opened slowly and she didn't miss it as
Dr. Canton regarded her presence without even a pre-
tense of enthusiasm.

Fine. If he wasn't happy to have her there it didn't
hurt her feelings.

"Dr. Canton."

"Detective." A tense muscle bulged in his jaw. The
open door drafted out the scent of cheeseburgers and
chocolate cake.

Just the same, she hadn't gotten the sense of a warm
family home. "Is your daughter still here?"

"I think we've been through this, and this is a bad
time. We just finished dinner."

"No offense, sir, but finished means I'm not interrupting. And a better time would be . . . when?"

"Not now. She's been humiliated enough."

"Her husband died and someone was incinerated in
her house," Ellie pointed out. "How is that humiliation?
I understand it is extremely upsetting, but humiliating?"

To him, she thought as they stared at each other. It humiliated *him* that his son-in-law had committed such a
public suicide—it had been in the papers—but she didn't
give a rat's ass about his perception of the situation.

She thought he was a jerk and obstructing justice, but she'd tell him that later if he didn't allow her to see Michelle. "I've got a couple more questions . . . I told her that might happen when we last talked."

He didn't stand back but blocked the doorway, and all of a sudden she actually wished she'd talked to Santiago about this. That was a revelation all by itself. Had Jason Santiago been there, she had no doubt they'd be inside the house at this very moment. This was different than the first time. The bulldozer tactics weren't pretty, but they worked. No finesse, all muscle and attitude.

But, he wasn't there. *Lesson learned, maybe?*

Tonight, though, it didn't matter. Well, it mattered, it was just not a topic for discussion. Ellie said succinctly, "I have two questions. She answers them and I am on my way. It will take minutes . . . maybe even seconds."

"What questions?"

"As they are for her, sir, I'd rather direct them to Michelle."

"She's asleep."

Ellie glanced at her watch. "It's seven-thirty."

"Maybe you can concede, Detective, that it has been a trying past few days."

At that point, she shrugged. It always amazed her how even people who weren't criminals distrusted law enforcement. "I concede quite a few things, Dr. Canton. I concede that someone was burned in her house. I concede that right afterward her husband either killed himself or was murdered. I concede she is probably tired, because, you know what? I'm tired too. I concede all of that. Can I see her?"

He was going to stand there, the troll under the bridge, she saw, until maybe something in her expression changed his mind. He finally nodded, but he said on a cautionary note, "She's fragile. I just hope you take that into consideration."

Note to self: fragile.

Already on the radar.

"You do realize what I am here for is to help, correct?"

That set him back a little anyway. It took a second, but he grudgingly nodded.

She said persuasively, "Then give me my five minutes with Michelle, and I am going to say ahead of time, we need to be alone."

He didn't like it. She'd known he wouldn't. "Why?"

"So she feels free to be honest with me about Matthew." Ellie slightly lifted her shoulders. "Look, sir, let's both admit that because she knows you didn't like her husband, she is not likely to admit he had questionable habits or friends. Do you think she is going to tell me her husband was a poor choice in front of you? I would think she doesn't agree with you since she married him, but if she does, I'd like to hear why and she's not going to tell me with you in the room."

That was frank and to the point. From their previous conversation she had a sense of Michelle Tobias and as it settled and became part of the investigation, she understood that an aggressive male made the woman nervous, probably because her controlling father was in her face all the time.

No wonder she'd chosen Matthew, who had seemed not precisely weak, but at least unassuming. The symbolism of the choice hadn't escaped her. Maybe Santiago not being here was wise after all.

"Okay." Michelle's father grudgingly opened the door. "I suppose this is inevitable. I have no desire to be charged with obstructing justice."

Ah, someone had been talking to a lawyer. "Thank you," she murmured, entering the foyer.

Why *had* Matthew killed himself?

It needed to be answered, in Ellie's opinion, before the investigation could go forward. The bodies were obviously not giving up the needed information and while she didn't understand why the murders had occurred, she was much more confounded by the suicide.

There *had* to be a connection.

What was it?

She was shown to a deck that reflected heat and was overshadowed by a large oak in one corner. It looked out over clipped grass and a distant fence, rough-hewn on purpose, and on the slab below there was a hot tub and a stack of towels on a wooden bench.

Michelle came outside to join her with obvious reluctance, her eyes dry but bloodshot, her clothes not rumpled but not neat either, as if someone might have suggested the yellow sundress with the thin navy stripes, but had forgotten to mention shoes. It was hot enough it didn't matter, but it did say something about the witness.

If she even was one. Ellie wasn't convinced of that, not yet, which was why she was making a second sweep.

"Hi. I'm Detective MacIntosh . . . we met the day of the fire, remember?"

"God, was that only two days ago? I swear I feel like I'm in a tunnel." Michelle brushed back her hair and dropped into a chair on the deck. "Sit, if you want."

What Ellie would actually prefer is a cool glass of wine and a poolside chaise to prop her feet on, but there were those pesky murder victims out there . . .

Incinerated and left like a grim calling card.

"I am deeply sorry for your loss." She really was. It

complicated the hell out of the case and her restless need to understand it was what had brought her back. "Tell me something I would never know about your husband."

Michelle Tobias blinked. She did look fuzzy around the edges, like she'd been given a sedative, which Ellie would guess was the case. "What?"

Ellie gazed at the trim yard to give her a moment, and then looked at her directly. "Something we can't get from phone records and interviews with the staff at his former workplaces . . . Tell me a fact that is right off the wall. An idiosyncrasy, a quirk, a detail I would never guess. That is actually why I am here. Something was wrong. I want to know what it was. Did your dad give him his prescriptions?"

"No!" After a second, Michelle, set a trembling hand on the table and repeated. "No."

"Was that part of the problem between them?"

"There wasn't—"

"Come on, Michelle, there was. Just be honest."

"Where's the other detective? Santana?"

It was a desperate question, at a guess, to put off thinking about the answer. Did anyone actually *want* to talk to Santiago?

"Santiago," she corrected gently. "Can you give my question a little thought? I'll wait."

"Okay."

Michelle pursed her mouth and looked as if she was pondering, but Ellie thought maybe whatever she was taking had her too groggy to be able to really come up with a decent answer. The hum of the locusts was loud in the background, the air stagnant. Even a hot breeze would have been welcome. A trickle of sweat ran down her neck.

"Okay, fine. I don't know if this counts, but Matt

hated my dad." Michelle's eyes were glassy and she looked away. "They never liked each other. My father wrote him a few prescriptions in the beginning, right after he hurt himself, but then he cut him off."

"I've gotten the impression from your father that he thought he was hooked on pain meds. What else? Surely you have an opinion on why he decided to jump off that roof."

"He was clinically depressed at one time, but it was better." Michelle stirred a little, restlessly moving her legs. "Or at least that's what the doctor told him he thought was wrong back when it started. Depression. He couldn't sleep, hated going to work, didn't eat."

"I'm not an expert, but that does sound like depression to me." Ellie weighed her next question. "Do you think it was bad enough to make him do what he did?"

Michelle nodded, her throat rippling as she swallowed. "I think losing the house might have been a little too much. The back injury . . . I think he really *was* addicted to pain meds off and on. We argued about it. I practically got down on my knees to beg him to stop."

A sob followed that confession.

That fit. Awkwardly, only though . . . Ellie wasn't sure she bought it. "I realize you didn't own the house and Mr. Helton is going to collect the insurance, but that really isn't the end of the world, is it? More like renting, and at one time or another most people have done that. I'm doing it right now. It isn't perfect, but you both were alive and well. Why the suicide?"

She lifted her head. Mascara had run to the corner of her eyes, giving her the look of a stage actress. "He loved Harry. That could have been it."

"Harry?"

"Our dog."

"As I understand it Detective Santiago brought the dog back."

"He did . . . I was grateful."

Ellie was still not quite sure why, after his mocking derision, her partner had spent the better part of his evening looking for a stray dog, but he had, and he'd gone up at least a small notch in her estimation.

Michelle went on. "Everything has been so *awful*. By then he'd already left."

"Matthew? To go where?"

"I don't know," she said on a sob. "He didn't tell me. He didn't say anything except that he didn't want to stay with my parents."

"I'm sorry." She meant it. "What else can you tell me? Do you know anyone in Bayview? Have you ever been to this address?" Ellie produced the card on which she'd jotted the apartment number and street. "Does it mean anything to you?"

Michelle looked at it but there was no guarantee anything registered. "No."

"Do you know anyone named Kilmarten?"

"No." She shook her head and she leaned back, her eyes drifting shut. "God, I'm tired. I'm just *so* tired."

"Michelle, if your husband wasn't getting his prescriptions or drugs from your father, where was he getting them?

"I don't know," she said, like a limp doll in the chair. "I really don't. He has an old friend that is a doctor now. Maybe from him."

"His name?"

Michelle looked dazed, as she had through the whole conversation. "I don't remember right now . . . maybe I can call you."

That was helpful. Well, perhaps. Ellie knew she was

jaded, but she doubted it would ever happen. Just in case, she left another card and gratefully turned on the air-conditioning in her car full blast as she drove away.

Ellie's desire to go out for dinner, even to Lulu's, was utterly gone. Instead she thought she'd stop and pick up a couple of steaks. She wasn't at all in the mood for lights and people; she just wanted a quiet dinner and a nice glass of wine at home.

Home.

She still wasn't sure, even as she took the turn for the expensive meat market downtown where Bryce preferred to shop, that her psyche was wired to program in his house as home. A part of her was practical enough to realize she spent very little time at her rented condo and by no means did she consider it to be a permanent arrangement. Another part of her rebelled against taking such a drastic life step.

And actually, he hadn't asked her to move in either.

It did not help her small inner war that about five steps into the small store, the first person she saw was his ex-wife.

Well . . . *damn.*

They'd only met once before but there was no mistaking that perfect swing of dark hair, the elegant profile . . . and of course Suzanne Colgan-Grantham shopped in this particular location, she did everything from the top shelf, and besides, the loft she and Bryce used to share was not very far away.

Still, the encounter was unfortunate. If Ellie could have turned and run, she would have, but it was already too late. She'd picked up a basket and was about five feet away.

"Detective MacIntosh."

Actually she was a little startled that the recognition

was so swift considering they hadn't seen each other since late last fall. She said warily, "Hello."

Bryce's ex-wife wore a flattering red silk sleeveless tunic that came down to her hips, and a pair of white capri pants. Her toenail polish matched her blouse and her skin was as perfect as Ellie remembered. On the other hand, *she'd* been up since about four in the morning and was pretty sure she looked as tired as she felt.

"I'd heard you'd moved south." Suzanne's smile was about as sincere as a cat apologizing for devouring a mouse. Almond-shaped eyes accented by perfectly applied cosmetics regarded her with steady appraisal. "I assume Milwaukee is a bit more exciting than a county job."

Of all the fucking people to run into . . .

The Santiago-like sentiment of that thought almost made her laugh. Almost.

She nodded. "Ms. Colgan-Grantham. Nice to see you again."

"Bryce said you've been promoted to MPD homicide. Congratulations. We were bound to cross paths sometime, but I assumed it would be at the courthouse."

Oh, and that was something to look forward to. His ex-wife was an attorney; a pretty high-powered defense attorney at that, and she was probably right, they would eventually have to deal with each other. Ellie hooked the basket over her arm. "I suppose we might run into each other."

When on this side of hell had Bryce talked to his ex? Their parting of ways had been far from amicable.

Maybe over their steaks, they might need to have that conversation. He certainly hadn't mentioned it.

"It sounds like you all are probably more than a little busy right now."

She was doing her best to forget the case for a few hours, not rehash it in the gourmet bread aisle. "Unfortunately, we are. It has actually been a rather long day. I hope you have an enjoyable evening."

Ellie couldn't bring herself to say it had been nice to see her. The insincerity of it stuck in her throat. Instead it had been uncomfortable and awkward and just about the last thing she needed. As Ellie turned to walk away, Suzanne said pleasantly, "Tell Bryce it was good to see him the other night."

The other night?

Maybe if she hadn't been so tired she could have guarded her reaction better, but evidently her surprise showed. Suzanne just gave a satisfied smile and walked away.

Yes, they were going to have to talk about this. Definitely.

But not tonight.

Chapter 13

If creation is an art form, surely destruction is even more so.

Combine the two and it can be . . . beautiful.

The house was filthy, broken crates in a haphazard pile, a rolled-up piece of ratty carpet against the stained wall, two chairs with the caning broken out of the bottom toppled over in the middle of what had once been the living room. It smelled of disuse, stale and empty, with maybe a hint of dead mouse.

No table.

That was fine. I'd brought one with me. Carefully I unfolded it, snapping the legs in place, not even bothering to hide the smudges my shoes made in the dust. I moved quickly, quietly, and with swift efficiency.

Maybe my soul was that lonely creature in the swamp, long since drowned, haunting the edges, covered with slime, grotesque and alone.

Where the hell we go, I'm not sure at all. If I believed in an avenging God, I would have confronted him a long time ago.

Or maybe it would be the other way around.

My sins were piling up, building like a shaky house on stilts, all that murky water flowing underneath . . .

If I didn't need to do this . . . but I did.

I grabbed the handle of the bag and tugged. It was too early for rigor, which was an advantage, for at the steps I just stopped at the top and shoved, watching the dark form tumble clumsily downward until it hit the bottom with a sickening thud.

I whispered out loud, "Welcome home."

JULY 7

Carl pressed a button and Rachel answered on the third ring.

"Tell me something, how soon can you get a story on air?"

She didn't hesitate. "Fairly soon . . . today. How big are we talking?"

"We have another murder, same MO. National channels will be picking this up."

"What is in this for you?"

"Just point out that Detective Ellie MacIntosh is on this case and maybe a hint about the murder five years ago. There's been a third murder—or a fourth if you can count my old case."

"Seriously?" Her voice held a hint of shock that he was fairly certain would echo through the entire state of Wisconsin.

"Would I call otherwise?"

"I can't promise how exactly they'll present the story, but I know they'll want the tip."

"Thanks. I need to go . . . thanks."

"Call me," she said quietly.

* * *

Jason surveyed the scene. The place was a tenement at best, long since abandoned, the fire had started earlier in the day according to what they were told, turning into a conflagration as the entire decrepit building went up like a well-lit torch. Luckily, next to it was a weed-choked empty corner lot, littered with cans and bits of trash with a broken basketball hoop at the far end, and on the other side the building there previously had been torn down.

It wasn't the finest neighborhood. The only two cars parked down the shimmering street were spotted with rust and one of them was missing a front bumper.

"We're just going to start calling you to every fire in this damn city, Detectives." The fire chief, in full gear, didn't sound like he was joking. "Once it was contained one of my men spotted what looked like a possible body below through a hole on the first floor. Point of origin a basement apartment at one time. It's a mess down there and swimming with water. I don't think I need to caution you to be careful, but at least the electricity is off. You'll need to wear hats." He jerked his head toward one of the trucks. "Jimmy will give you each one."

"This is out of control." MacIntosh said it in a matter-of-fact voice a few minutes later as she slipped on the hard hat and fastened the strap, echoing his thoughts.

Jason didn't disagree. The frame was intact but the door itself was missing and the dark hole didn't look very appealing. He almost slipped on the greasy stairs, said a very bad word, and righted himself at the last moment. MacIntosh didn't even glance back, her flashlight beam skittering over the blackened walls, a mask just like his over the lower part of her face to prevent inhaling potential toxins.

The basement was old, the ceiling half collapsed, the awful smell something he was getting used to, but the table was new.

That was interesting.

This time the body was displayed as usual, but it was different, not part of the usual scenery obviously, and this was actually the first clue they might have delivered at their doorstop. He said tightly, "He brought the table."

Ellie stared at the body, not rattled by the gruesome sight, probably because, lucky them, it wasn't their first horrific scene in the past few days. Her brow knitted. "I noticed. That means this isn't a random choice. He knew what he needed wasn't going to be here."

Water dripped everywhere, just like all the other crime scenes, but this was worse. The floor, walls, ceiling, all soaked, ruined, and it probably hadn't been good to begin with from the general state of disrepair.

Jason walked around, his feet splashing water, the place way too warm considering the smell. The foul liquid was ankle deep in some places, ash and water and God only knew what else, probably dead rats . . . Jesus. He said, "He has a connection to this specific place."

"How can we know that?"

He liked that it was asked with due consideration. That it was his theory didn't mean it was tossed out the window. He'd had more than one partner and some of them wanted their ideas to be considered first and then to hog all the credit.

"Would you ever even guess this was here?" He tested a rickety step. "I wouldn't. If all he wanted was to burn another body there are a shitload of other places that would work better and be easier."

"Shitload?"

"The official departmental word for it. Try it."

She didn't. "Like where?"

He grimaced. "This is in the city, but it has some significance. He chose it. Took the trouble to buy a new table. That might be his big mistake. If we can track down what retailer sells that brand of table, maybe someone will remember him."

"That's a possibility and more than what we've had before now." Ellie bent down and, with her gloved fingers, touched an old rag on the floor that could've been a piece of clothing. She glanced up at him and her hazel eyes were narrowed. "What are we dealing with here and what set it off? This is like wildfire. One after the other. He's on a rampage."

And it would be their asses if they didn't stop him. He knew that already. His testicles were tightening in the crosshairs. Whether she knew it or not, the chief had stepped in for him already—shit, Internal Affairs had a hard-on for him ever since he'd strong-armed an arrest back when he was first promoted and put the kid in the hospital. There had been a few other complaints involving foul language and suspect harassment, to which, if he was allowed to reply, he might point out that the suspects were scumbags who deserved it. What was he supposed to do, send them flowers? Each day he went in, he expected to be called into the office and, given his background, he'd be one of the first to go if they decided to make changes in the department.

Look at what had happened to Carl Grasso. A former legend but busted down. Individual style was frowned upon in the homicide division. True, the guy had gone over the top—way over the top—but it wasn't anything he hadn't thought of once or twice himself.

"I know." Jason couldn't even imagine trying to glean

clues from this decrepit space, all of it saturated and destroyed. The crime scene unit was going to have a ball making sense of any of it. He took in a breath cautiously, and exhaled. Everything stank of smoke and decay, and he was getting tired of that particular odor.

"It's our job to figure out how to stop him," she replied grimly.

"Lucky us," he muttered.

"Let's both sit in on this one."

Ellie glanced up from her computer screen. The report was late, but quite frankly, how in the hell was she supposed to keep up when someone was dying practically every single day? Even a trip to the morgue was preferable to all the paperwork lining up.

"It's late," she said, glancing at the clock. "After six. Surely Dr. Reubens is going to wait until tomorrow morning." She'd been trying to catch up on reports, which was not exactly easy, and they had spent most of the day trying to find a witness or anyone else who might help them with the latest crime scene, which had been even harder.

"He just sent me a text and he's not going to wait. It said specifically 'gloves on, mask in place.' Maybe he has plans tomorrow. God knows we've all worked quite a few days straight and it seems like that isn't going to change until we get this guy." Santiago ran his fingers through his blond curls in a manner that was becoming increasingly familiar. "Three bodies in five days? Anyway, I'm heading down and I thought it might not hurt if we both heard his notes during the procedure. We need something."

The suggestion was somewhat of an olive branch and she recognized that. She still hadn't told him about her visit to Cedarburg to see Michelle Tobias without him the night before, mostly because it hadn't done anything to help with the case. Maybe it would pay off if Michelle ever called her with the name of the doctor who was giving her husband the drugs.

Ellie rose and clicked a key to shut down the screen. She'd text Bryce from the elevator to tell him she'd be late in case he'd planned something for dinner. There was no formal date. They'd left it at a vague maybe over whether or not she'd stop by. "Let's go."

As awful as it sounded, she was looking forward to how cold it would be in the morgue. The air-conditioning upstairs was not keeping up, and since the visit to the scene she felt as if she needed a long, cool shower.

In reality, the next hour did not help. Yes, the temperature was more acceptable, but autopsies weren't her favorite pastime, and Reubens, with his schoolboy face and businesslike approach, wore a headset and dictated notes as if they were not in the room. Every medical examiner was different; she had no problem with the way he did his job, but sometimes the medical terminology made it hard to understand exactly what he was saying until he submitted his summary and opinion.

Like the other burnings, at the end, she got the impression there was no clear manner of death.

"This is your guy's work again," Reubens said, his pragmatic voice loud in the silence of the room after he was done. "No inhalation toxicity. The victim was dead first, and burned after."

"Any idea of her age?" Santiago had been remarkably silent for him during the whole procedure. Not one rude comment. In fact, she was starting to think the morgue bothered him more than he cared to show.

"No uterus. That doesn't necessarily mean anything,

but it is an indication that maybe she was at least in her middle age. No one would ever recognize her visually, you don't have to be a physician to discern that, but her organs were fairly intact. I didn't find any definitive sign of a cause of death."

"Other than the crispy-as-hell body?" Santiago looked pointedly at the blackened corpse on the stainless steel table. "The fucker lit her on fire."

Reubens didn't quite smile, but it was in there somewhere, maybe a hint of humor in his blue eyes. "Yes, the 'fucker' lit her on fire, as you put it, Detective. It wasn't what killed her, though. Like the others she was already dead. This one has all her teeth, so if you can come up with a name, we can probably figure out who she is."

"But we aren't going to," Ellie said, thinking out loud. "We aren't going to come up with a name. I can feel it. He's just too damn smart. Usually *who* is what drives the investigation in a case, but this is about *why*."

"I bow to your expertise, Detective." Reubens shrugged and glanced at the clock on the white, sterile wall. "And I wish you luck, since I'm currently working overtime. I've a vacation scheduled in a week, so can you pick up the pace on this one? I've already bought my tickets, rented the place on the beach, and I have a date with paradise."

"We'll nail him to the wall," Santiago said with more confidence than *she* felt.

"I'm sorry but I'm with Detective MacIntosh." Reubens peeled off a glove and carefully deposited it in a container for contaminated matter. "Bodies are usually the topography of a crime. Some findings are like a mountain, huge and obvious. If a victim is stabbed with forty-seven wounds to the abdomen, chest, and neck, I can safely conclude that it was homicide and an interesting degree of hatred involved." He went to the sink and rinsed his hands despite the gloves. She would too. The water splashed off and he glanced back over his shoulder. "On the other side of the coin, when a perfectly healthy person dies of no apparent cause, that raises my hackles too. Most people aren't intelligent enough to pull off a successful murder—they just aren't. It isn't easy to do. I'm smart, you are both smart; there is little argument that you deal with this every day. Do you think you could get away with it?"

Good point. He was perfectly right. She wasn't sure she could. It was a delicate balance of the crime and the investigation. Hard to say what a person might get if he chose to break the law.

"Maybe."

Reubens shook his head. "It requires too much. Let's face it that intelligence isn't enough. You also need luck, and all of it good. There are just too many variables."

He was right, and that was why they usually found the culprit, but usually was not always and that galled her. Ellie said, "Burning the bodies, that's . . . crafty, clever, whatever you want to call it."

"Clever works." His smile was rueful as he wiped his hands on a towel. "It doesn't leave me with a lot to give you. Medical science has made some leaps in the past decades when forensics came into its own in a big way. I can do a lot with very little evidence, but I'm not finding anything. As long as we both understand that, we'll do fine together. Only in one of these cases can I say I think I know the cause of death, and even then, it's not certain."

"The burning of the bodies," she said tentatively, "in your opinion, is it to so compromise the evidence that an investigation is impossible?"

"As to that, I would say with conviction, yes, but as I understand it, he's killing them elsewhere. That location might still hold clues."

She noted it down, not that she hadn't already come to that conclusion all on her own. "Anything else?"

Dr. Reubens looked at her, his face somber. "I am afraid, Ellie, you are up against someone who does not like rules very much."

It was Santiago who said with sanguine humor, "That could be his mistake. He and I have a lot in common."

"That's amusing, as I was under the impression your job was to enforce the rules." Reubens had slipped off his lab coat and put it in the rolling laundry basket along with his surgical hat and mask. His brown hair was tousled and it suited him far better than the usual carefully brushed strands.

"Doesn't mean I have to like those rules," Santiago said laconically, and Ellie was fairly sure he meant it. "Thanks for staying late, Doc. Have a nice night and a good trip. I'm kinda hoping not to see you again before you leave."

"The feeling is mutual, Detective."

Chapter 14

They are out there. Looking for me, asking themselves unanswerable questions because even I don't know how to define it. Predators after the ultimate predator, their stakes almost as high as mine.

Not exactly.

There wasn't a lifetime in prison waiting for them. The state of Wisconsin does not embrace capital punishment, but still . . . they have their purpose and I have mine. I wouldn't be given much leniency and a lifetime in a prison cell is not my goal. All I really want is to banish a few ghosts . . .

That's a lie. I want . . . it. The thrill. It is hard to shake. I'd always been afraid of it, of the lure.

I have some habits they frown upon in law enforcement.

With a small twist, the lock gave.

I popped the door, waited there, listening for any sound of habitation, and when I didn't even get a hint of movement, I stepped inside.

It smelled old, like the closet of a woman past middle

age, with an odd fragrance of dated perfume that had been kept too long in the bottle . . . and maybe a hint of whatever she'd had for dinner. Something from a can, no doubt. I have my moments, but in general a good memory.

The wine bottle on the counter in the silent kitchen told me some things never changed.

She'd be asleep for it all . . .

Bryce must have been working because he didn't hear her knock and since she had a key, Ellie wasn't sure why she bothered anyway. She let herself in, the wash of cool air welcome, and when she looked down the long hallway, sure enough he was in his office. She could hear the faint sound of the television, kept low because he really didn't watch it much but sometimes he caught the news.

She walked to the door, always a little hesitant to disturb him. He worked from home but that didn't mean he wasn't working.

He was at his desk, staring at the screen on his computer, apparently deep in thought. Sure enough in the corner on a mahogany table that discreetly housed various electronic equipment, a flat-screen television flashed images. There was also an Oriental rug; a grouping of two comfortable wing chairs and a low, polished table; and several bookcases. If nothing else, from his dissolved marriage to Suzanne, he'd walked away with some lessons in good taste.

Suzanne.

Ellie was really debating how to bring up that subject. Or even if she should.

Her knee-jerk reaction was to ask him if he really had seen his ex-wife and failed to mention it, but she wasn't entirely sure she had any right to be ticked off about it.

She was the one who had made it clear she wanted to take it slow and easy.

Except she had turned her life upside down and moved to Milwaukee.

He'd be perfectly right if he pointed out that she'd never once said it was because of him, and Ellie wasn't at all sure she was ready to admit that yet anyway.

She cleared her throat. "Hello."

Bryce turned, a slight smile surfacing. "Hello."

"I knocked but then used my key. I wasn't sure you were even home."

"Working a little." He gestured at the laptop on his desk.

"The book? Am I interrupting?"

"I'm kind of at a stopping point, so no, you aren't."

She held a bag and lifted it. "I stopped and picked up some food. If you've already eaten, that's okay. The medical examiner is really trying to help us out and he stayed late to do the autopsy on this last victim. You hungry?"

"That's a strange combination. Autopsy and take-out food. But actually, yes, I am hungry. Just keep the details to yourself if you don't mind." He hit save and stood. "Lunch was how many hours ago?"

"Your favorite deli. I was close by." Ellie led the way to the kitchen. "Pastrami for you. Some coleslaw. Roast beef on a bagel for me, unless you want to split and share?"

"Turn off your phone for dinner? Just for thirty minutes."

She gazed at him curiously as she set the bag on the table. There was something a little off about his demeanor. "Sure. Yeah, I suppose so. I haven't been off duty in five days. Probably a good idea. One quiet dinner isn't too much to ask."

In the end they did share, splitting the sandwiches. He drank a cold Leinenkugel with his meal and she had a glass of wine and was just starting to unwind when he said, "I watched the news."

"You usually do." She had to admit she was a little mystified by the way he was acting.

He suggestively lifted the bottle of wine. "A little more?"

"No thanks. I'm about to fall asleep as it is. Did you know it hit 103 today? I have no clue what the heat index was, but it felt off the charts."

"It was 110." He set the Chablis down. "Heard it on the local forecast."

Ellie regarded him across the table. There was a moment of silence, and then she said in clipped tones, "All right, what is it?"

"What is what?" He didn't pull off the blank look very well. She liked that about him. People lied to her constantly, but he couldn't. Maybe that was why she didn't want to ask about Suzanne. He would tell her the truth.

"You just don't hide things very well. How we ever thought you were a killer . . . Never mind that, but, Bryce, just tell me, okay? Something has you off balance, I can see it, you were uncomfortable the entire meal and have been since I walked in." Her voice was flat and uncompromising. "Tell me."

He blew out a short breath. He disliked confrontation, which made them an interesting pair, but might just be a personal preference on his part as his ex-wife was an attorney. Maybe opposites did attract, she had no clue, but the issue at hand was he looked very much like there was something he needed to tell her that he didn't want to reveal.

Someone in the neighborhood hadn't used all their firecrackers on the Fourth. She could hear the staccato sound in the background, but it barely registered. The cicadas chirped in the trees also, a more soothing summer song.

In the end he lifted his shoulders in surrender. "You were on the news."

That stopped her dead. Whatever it was he didn't want to tell her, she didn't expect that. "On the news? Me? Why?"

What the hell are you talking about?

"They made a point of the case last fall and that you were working this one." He stood, took both their plates, and moved toward the sink. "Not a lot of detail but a video of you ducking under police tape, and a note about this maybe being a serial and you were assigned to it. I just happened to catch it."

Surely he wasn't serious. But then again, his tension ever since she walked in the door told her he was excruciatingly, absolutely serious.

She sat in the chair and watched him rinse their plates. Finally, she said, "I'll take that second glass of wine, and when you are done, can you please sit down across from me again and tell me what this broadcast said?"

Bryce glanced back over his shoulder. "I really just caught your name."

"My name?"

"And the footage. You looked good."

"Dr. Grantham, I suggest you don't equivocate." She meant it too. It was clear in her tone.

"When you call me that it brings back memories of a not-so-happy time. Let me get the wine."

She wasn't letting him get off that easy. As he retrieved the bottle and tipped the golden liquid into her glass, she said quietly, "Bryce, just tell me why there would be any reason for me to be mentioned on the news."

He met her eyes and it wasn't just the issue at hand, but her heart stopped for a moment. He didn't want to tell her. He just didn't. She could read it on his face. He said reluctantly, "The recent murders."

"So?" Her fingers toyed with the glass but she wasn't going to take a drink until he answered. "We don't know anything. What could they possibly be saying?"

Bryce settled into the opposite chair. He shook his head. "It was just a short piece about how you are on the case. Linked it back to last fall and tried to make it look deliberate on the part of the police department."

"In what way?"

"Apparently you are the current force to be reckoned with in the effort to stop serial murders in this neck of the woods, so to speak . . . or that was just my impression."

"Shit." She picked up the glass and took an inelegant gulp of wine. "What station?"

"I'm not sure. The television is probably still tuned to it. You can look if you want."

She set down the wineglass and stared at it, thinking. *Disaster?* Not really, not in terms of anything except it proved someone was feeding information to the press and she was pretty sure it wasn't Metzger.

Santiago? There was an issue of professional jealousy whether he would admit it or not. This suddenly put the pressure on her in a big way.

"No need, the station doesn't really matter." She sighed. "It's out there now. Good God, we have a job to do. I'm not opposed to the public being informed if there is a threat, and this is one . . . let's not kid ourselves, but Metzger didn't condone this, I know that. Why would anyone even care if I'm on this one . . . it isn't news, for heaven's sake."

"Ellie, you caught the killer who had abducted at least five women and brutally murdered them. I see why you don't want the attention, but it is interesting you are now working *this* case. Look at it this way, at least you were not the main suspect in the other case. I admit I was pretty happy they didn't mention me."

"I don't think I blame you there." Ellie regarded him with contemplative introspection. "Neither of us is going to find what happened easy to live down and it makes our relationship interesting. If the media really gets ahold of that, we should be prepared. I really hope no ambitious reporter ever looks at me closely enough to figure out we are seeing each other." It had worried her just a little, all along. Santiago knew, obviously. It was why she strictly did not discuss her personal life.

"I was cleared. If I remember correctly, you were the one who did that for me." His dark eyes were direct.

"Bryce, I realize everyone does not know this, but I slept with you when you were still a suspect. I was fairly sure of your innocence, but—"

"Hold on." He lounged back, his tall body not precisely relaxed, but giving that impression. "*Fairly* sure? I can't decide if that is a compliment or an insult."

She gave him a level look. "Sure enough, apparently. However, I am not too thrilled about anyone finding out that you were so involved in that case and now we are . . . here."

"Where would here be, Ellie?"

Now that was a legitimate question. She wished she

had the answer. If she wanted to ask about Suzanne, this seemed to be a good time.

But it didn't have the right feel, and she wasn't up to hearing it if the answer was something she didn't want to know.

Was he pressing her? No, actually, that was not like him, and it was one of the reasons she felt comfortable in their relationship.

There were a few other reasons she felt uncomfortable too, but probably more her problem than his, and she was not in the mood to address them right now. "Can I answer when this is all over?" she said, and did her best to stifle an unwanted yawn.

"Yeah, because I put you to sleep, or at least tonight I do. What would you do without me?" His voice held a hint of quiet laughter.

"Hey, long day."

Damn long day.

She was exhausted. Mentally. Physically. The works.

But still . . . maybe not *too* tired.

Maybe. He wouldn't push it. That was a nice given.

"A dip in the pool?" She wasn't really all that interested in swimming, but then again, she was hot and sticky, even in the air-conditioning. "Suits optional?"

His brows shot up. "I'm not going to say no to that sort of invitation."

She stood, tugging off her top and dropping it on the floor. Then she shimmied out of her shorts. "Bring me a towel, if you don't mind."

"Yeah, right, like I'd mind." He stood, watching her walk to the door in just her bra and underwear. "It might be a little cold in the water since I turned off the heat a few days ago when they came to clean it. Seemed redundant."

"It sounds perfect, then." Ellie opened the French doors and walked out. Technically one house behind his could see the backyard if they were upstairs and paying attention, but otherwise, it was pretty private and she was past caring for the most part. It was dark now, and the lights weren't on. She sat down on the edge of the pool, slipped off her panties, and unfastened her bra before sliding into the water.

Perfect. The air was humid but the water a few degrees below tepid. She dived under, surfaced, shook back her hair, and felt clean for the first time all day. There was no way to do the same thing for her mind, forever contaminated by the memory of the crime scene, but at least she could wash some of it away.

Bryce came out, took in her discarded underwear, and swiftly stripped out of his trunks before making a dive that neatly split the surface of the water. He came up next to her and his arm went around her waist, pulling her close. "You've had one hell of a day," he said, his mouth grazing her temple.

"I know," she agreed, pressing her body against his. "Make it better."

"Like this?" His mouth touched hers and she sighed into the kiss. It was good, and the cool water against her bare skin was an aphrodisiac after the meltingly hot day.

His hand smoothed her shoulder and cupped her bare breast. "Hmm. Perfect."

She couldn't agree more.

Chapter 15

Reckless is stupid. I'm not stupid, I refuse to believe that . . . Determined maybe . . . but that's softening it. What is it? Driven?

Does that work?

Yes, driven might be it. To be done with it all—there's some appeal there. I just want to finish. Cross that line, whatever it might be. Not a lot to ask, really. To tidy up the mess, sweep it away, move forward. I'd like to live a normal life. No one would ever know. I believe the creature in the swamp will slowly subside, sliding into the black muck.

Maybe. I could be fooling myself.

There was a problem with heinous monsters. They don't follow directions often.

Mine is particularly venomous. It doesn't sleep much, and those are the worst kind.

I shook out a little white tablet into my palm and stared at it. I had more work to do. I'd have to sleep later.

It slid gently back into the bottle.

JULY 8

Carl punched in the code. The gate opened, his car slid through, and he parked the BMW next to a gorgeous potted plant, delicate pink flowers of some kind spilling in a lush fall over the side. He'd never watered it in his life, but someone had. At that moment it occurred to him he might need more hands-on contact with the people who worked for him, but his phone rang. He dug it out of his pocket and answered. "Grasso."

"Hear the latest on The Burner?" The chief was way too neutral on the other end of the line.

He could honestly say he had. "You know I have."

"MacIntosh was on the news last night. Did you have anything to do with that?"

"How would I?" He shut off the alarm and twisted the lock on the front door but he wasn't nearly as calm as he sounded. Rachel had come through apparently. "What did they say?"

"Just that she was on the case. I thought of you." Metzger sounded irritated now, but then again, he usually did, so the tone was more familiar than the detachment. "What was the name of that reporter you were involved with?"

"You mean years ago? She's a professor now. No longer works television."

"I don't care. I'm just going to ask flat out. Are you feeding information to the media?"

"Why would I do that?" His tone was careful, subdued, removed. And he wasn't lying either. Rachel had come through brilliantly, but he hadn't lied. She wasn't employed by the station that had broadcast the piece.

"Come on, Carl."

Metzger never had been a fool, but what he couldn't prove . . .

"I want him caught, Joe. He's really pushing us."

"Ah, what a surprise, we *are* playing on the same team. Here's a bulletin, I want him caught too. That's why I gave you a little latitude. Look, we never had this conversation, understand?" his boss said decisively. "If you interfere with this investigation, I'll have your badge. I stuck Ellie MacIntosh with Santiago, which is no picnic in the first place. Don't try to make the pressure so intense she can't possibly do her job. I know you have sources and I know you can leak details. If you want back in, help, don't hinder. Someone recognized you in the crowd outside this latest scene, and no, it wasn't either of the detectives I just mentioned. They had their hands full. I'm pleased you contributed the cold case file. I think you could do a lot for the investigation, but stop the press leaks. Are we clear?"

"You usually have a way of getting your point across, Chief."

There was a click and he found himself standing there, phone to ear, all alone in a finished conversation.

Despite the wrist slap, he still thought the story was a good idea, and he'd known Metzger would guess it was him. Santiago wasn't personable enough to court the press and MacIntosh would never do that to herself, so, yeah, him. Before Metzger was promoted to chief, he was a damned good detective.

This would push all of them. MacIntosh to live up to the legend, Santiago to get there first, and as for him, if all he did was contribute the cold file and provide some support and it made the administration happy, fine with him.

Maybe he would take a nice trip to Mexico or the Keys when this was over. He really hated vice. He was born to solve murder cases, not bust teenage girls hooking on corners. The transfer had been a slap in about a dozen different ways, but what really hurt was not being able to do what he wanted and that meant true detective work in his opinion. Sure, vice was important, he didn't belittle that, it just wasn't his style.

It was always satisfying to solve a case, but this was a big one and he wanted in the thick of it and for now had to just skirt the edges. But fine, if that was the way it had to be, he could deal. The big house was cool after the inferno outside, the rush of air soothing, but it was also lonely, empty, unsatisfying.

Another murder? Right. The crappy apartment building, the dead lot next to it . . . yes, he'd gone by, checked out the circus, stood outside with the gawkers.

Everything was really heating up, wasn't it?

It was a very hot morning. What was new about that?

For the first time they had a glimmer. Not much, but a hint of a solution, just a small break.

That was his gift as an investigator if he had one. This . . . *feeling*. Jason asked as casually as possible. "Tell me again what you saw."

The woman looked down, looked back up, and then down again. She was stout, and wore a shapeless dress and mules on her feet instead of shoes, and they weren't all that clean. Gray hair worn short, a smoker's cough, and cracked nails. "Not much," she admitted. "Kind of a flash. I don't know cars. It just looked . . . I don't know, out of place. Like not something that we see in our neighborhood."

He leaned forward. "So . . . middle of the night, car

with lights pulls up to an abandoned building, someone carries out a large object, but you don't call the police. Do I have that right?"

She twitched the fabric of her dress and must have caught the sarcasm in his tone because she frowned. "That makes it sound bad. It's sketchy enough around there. No use pissing off the wrong people. I have a rule. If someone is being stabbed or shot in front of me, I call. Anything short of that, I don't. Try to not give me shit. I'm talking to you right now. Had to take two different buses to get here, but I came. Once I heard about the fire and that someone had been burned inside, I remembered the car."

Okay, all right, she had a point about doing her civic duty. He wasn't from the hood but he had worked scary parts of town and usually it was a lot easier to get along with your neighbors if a person kept his mouth shut. "And we appreciate it. Did you see the person who went into the building? Was it a man or a woman? Tall? Short? Skin color?"

She shook her head. "It was dark and the streetlight over there doesn't work. Can I complain to the city about that while I'm here?"

"Sure you can." He tried his most affable smile. "I'll point you in the right direction. Let's get back to the car then. Any marks or anything else you can tell me about it?"

"Black."

There might be thousands of black cars in the general metro area, probably tens of thousands. He scratched his temple with a pencil. "Nothing else you can give me?"

She snorted. "If you want the make and model visit the local car dealerships. Let me put it this way, it didn't *belong*. Black and expensive. A sedan without rust and a thousand dents. An insignia on the front we don't see too often."

"Four doors or two?"

Her forehead creased as she gave it some thought, nicotine-stained fingers worrying the material of her dress. "Four, now that you asked. The person went around and opened the back passenger side."

"And that's when he or she pulled something from the car? You said you saw them go in. Did they drag it, or carry it?"

"He. I'm pretty sure of that. And carried, I think, but the car was blocking my view, and it was one of those things, you know. I noticed it seemed strange but I wasn't paying all that much attention. I just got up to go to the bathroom and happened to glance out the window."

"Gotcha. Thanks for coming in. I'll point you to city hall if you want to complain about that light." He wrote down her name and number and politely walked with her when she rose to shuffle off, but his mind was working, sorting it out, taking the measurements, adjusting his perceptions.

An expensive car.

Or corrected, just not a junker. Old ladies who probably drank gin before breakfast were not the most reliable of witnesses.

On the other hand, she had absolutely no motivation he could think of for coming in and lying to him. That there was a black car didn't really make bells ring, but maybe that there was a sleek black car could at the end of the day help out . . .

"Your mother?" Frankton, a junior-grade detective with open aspirations, was sitting with a hip hitched up on his desk when he returned. "Stopping by to deliver cookies?"

"Aunt," Jason responded blandly, dropping into his chair. "On my mother's side. I am sure you saw the family resemblance. Can I help you?"

"How's the case going?" Frankton was thin and whippy, with a well-trimmed beard and wire-rimmed glasses.

"It's going, I guess. Looks like maybe we have an eyewitness, but she didn't give me much. I need to tell MacIntosh."

"You like working with her?"

"Doesn't matter, does it? I work with her." He shot the other officer a look. "You are asking . . . why?"

"Just curious. She's nice to look at, that has to help. Great ass."

For whatever reason that annoyed the shit out of him. Jason leaned back and drawled, "I've been told I have a pretty nice ass myself, maybe that's why we're assigned together. Is there some reason you're here, Frank?"

"Actually, yeah, there is." He tossed a piece of paper on the blotter by the computer. "Here's your tox screen on Matthew Tobias."

"Finally." Jason snatched it up and scanned it. "The guy was loaded up on antidepressants and pain meds. His sister did mention he'd had a back injury, but according to this report, his intake was pretty excessive when he jumped."

"Looks like he decided to dull the pain of man meets concrete."

"Or he was just fucked up in general."

Frankton's beeper went off and he unclipped it, muttered something about having to go, and walked away. Jason wasn't going to miss him either. He rested his elbow on the desk and thought about burned houses, bodies on tables, and an expensive car in a downtrodden neighborhood.

His cell beeped and he answered on the third ring. Before Ellie could really say anything on the other end, he interrupted, "I've got an eyewitness and we need to find out where Tobias was getting his meds."

"Has it ever occurred to you to offer at least a basic greeting?"

The censure in her voice made him crack a short laugh. "Now you sound like Kate."

"You've mentioned her before. I take it she's your girlfriend."

"Was. We recently parted ways and maybe you're right, it all could have been due to how I answer the phone." He did his best to sound like he didn't care, and maybe he didn't. It hadn't been long enough for him to decide. Just that morning he'd taken down the rooster clock and shoved it in a hall closet, which had actually given him a sense of satisfaction. "I assume, by the way, you called for a specific reason yourself."

"What about Tobias? The screen back?"

"Oh, yeah. It is sitting on my desk. Just got it."

"Bring it. And I," she said with her usual cool intonation, "have a missing person report that looks promising. I'm on KK right now. Where do you want to meet?"

She was a fast learner for someone new to town. Kinnickinnic Avenue was kind of a mouthful, so most people called it KK.

He said shortly, "How about Anodyne?"

The coffeehouse smelled fantastic, the enticing aroma drifting in the air because they actually did roast the beans on the premises. Ellie ordered a plain French roast, paid for it, and chose a table in the corner. Dropping her bag on the floor, she pulled out the sheaf of papers and clicked her pen.

Santiago took his time and she was still jotting down notes when he walked in—sauntered might be a better word—and spied her sitting there. He didn't order anything and, as he took a chair, said, "Metzger caught me in the hall and I had to fill him in. What have you got?"

"Maybe you should go first. The term 'eyewitness' plus the tox screen trumps my possible missing person."

This afternoon he wore a short-sleeved shirt with a tie and his pants actually had crisp seams, but he never managed get his hair quite under control and it waved around his face. He shook his head. "Don't get excited. I have one black four-door sedan, something carried into the building at about the right time of night, or morning I guess it was, but no physical description of a suspect. The woman lives in a building down the street and the light on the corner is out. The only thing that might help us is that she thinks the car was high end, but I think you remember that neighborhood. What she thinks of as expensive might not be the same as the average person might."

That was disappointing. Ellie stirred her coffee, wondering if she should have ordered an iced one instead. "But she really saw our guy? Man, that's frustrating. Couldn't she tell you anything? Height? Weight? A general idea?"

"No, I'm afraid not. He carried in either the body or the table while she watched. I'm going to say it wasn't a woman because bodies are not light and I've never thought it was a woman anyway. The old lady was on her way to the can and just caught a glimpse."

A valid point. Ellie was about average height for a female, in good shape, and she would not be able to carry in a dead body unless the person was a lot smaller, which wasn't the case with the two victims. Dragging would be the only option. Still, she argued, "Once you got that door open, even someone small could tumble the body down the stairs."

Santiago shook his head. "I don't buy it. You still have to get it up on that table. That requires lifting it. Dead weight is just that. Our perp is a guy."

That made her curious. "Serials tend to be, but not always. Why?"

"Female serial killers target men, males target women. It isn't an exclusive club, but pretty close. There's usually a sexual component to it all. You get to go next and then we'll talk about Tobias. So, who's missing?"

She answered readily. "There's a few, of course, in a city this large. Some teens, but that doesn't fit our victims. Two stand out to me, especially this one. I think we should take the time to interview her family." She shoved a few of her notes across the polished surface of the table. "Vera Hatcher. Lives alone, but she has a dog and I guess it was raising all hell yesterday. Middle-aged lady from a nice suburb over by the lake, not seen since Friday as far I can tell. Neighbor reported it. Loves her dog, and wouldn't just walk away. Two kids, both grown, who have no idea where she might be. I talked to her son on the phone. He lives over in Minnesota in the twins. She had a hysterectomy about ten years ago."

Her partner looked interested. "Okay. Could be our last one . . . teeth but no vagina. Dental records?"

"She still had a . . ." Ellie caught his grin, and her annoyance went up another level. "Dammit, do you have to be so—"

"Yeah, I can't help it, I guess."

"I asked about the dental records. The week isn't helping us much because it seems like half the country is on vacation. It might be tomorrow."

"We get a match—"

"Maybe we get a solid lead. I'm hopeful."

The place wasn't as crowded as usual, the heat maybe, and Santiago picked up the pack he'd carried, took out a bottle of water, and twisted off the cap. He took a long swallow, his throat working, and then set it aside. "Too fucking hot for coffee. Are you nuts?"

"You suggested we meet here."

"Yeah, I suppose I did. So what do you want to do next?"

"We have three victims. I'm not counting Matthew Tobias right now. Should I?"

"I don't know." Santiago's eyes were a steely blue. "He was pumped full of meds. I called his father-in-law, pried the name of his physician out of him—he's an asshole, by the way, the father-in-law, not the physician— and contacted the office. They haven't gotten back to me yet, but someone was prescribing him some serious shit or he was getting it off the street."

"That's interesting." She meant it and didn't mention that her visit to Michelle Tobias supported that theory. "I wondered if we were too easily dismissing the suicide. Let's not forget the cold case Grasso gave us either. It's piling up and we have a lot to work with right now in my opinion, but just not much time to do it."

"Metzger is putting together a task force."

It didn't surprise her. She said slowly, "I've worked one before. The rapid-fire sequence of the crimes calls for it, really. He wouldn't be a good chief if he didn't, and he's probably getting pressure. It's a solid call."

"It's bullshit." Santiago aggressively tugged at his tie, his eyes holding resentment. "Give us a chance. We've had no real time between crimes to investigate. I told him so. Boom. One after the other. I got a little in his face."

That was brilliant considering he wasn't on Metzger's good side anyway. She merely raised her brows. "Way to manage your career. How'd that go for you?"

He grimaced and didn't answer directly. "What I'm saying is that until we have to share, let's bust it on this one." He stopped and considered her from across the table. "I suppose you heard about the press leak."

She'd known it wouldn't go unnoticed. "I heard. Bryce saw it on the news."

"Bryce? As in Grantham? Of Northwoods Killer fame?"

Fine. She'd asked about his personal life. Her mistake. He had somewhat of a right to ask about hers now that the door was open. "You've got a good memory. That was last year."

He shrugged. "I looked up the address. Took me two seconds. Just kind of curious because I was getting the vibe you didn't want to talk about it and wondered why."

"You getting that same vibe now?"

He ignored the sarcastic comment. "Once I saw who owned the house, I made the connection. Since I picked you up there in the middle of the night, I assume you two are playing house together. Interesting way to pick up a guy, MacIntosh. Didn't you arrest him on multiple murder charges?"

This was exactly what she *didn't* want to happen. Bryce had been cleared, so it was hardly unprofessional to be involved with him, but she knew she'd catch grief from her colleagues. Cops tended to be less than merciful, and being a woman in a male-rich environment meant she was under more scrutiny anyway.

"No, he was never arrested." Deliberately she set down her cup. "And it's not really your business."

He raised his hands, palms up, theatrically. "Okay. Personal confessions aren't really my thing anyway. Let's just get this case solved."

Actually, for the first time since they had become partners, she agreed with him 100 percent.

Carl sat out by the pool with a glass of whiskey and thought about how it was all going down.

Fast.

This was his favorite part. Thinking about the crimes, how so far they had no idea how the victims died or why the fires were set. The varied locations were also part of the puzzle, but as far as he knew—and he was pulling in favors to make sure he knew if there was progress on the cases—there was no viable theory yet as to why the three different spots.

The water shimmered and the underwater lights were on, giving the illusion of a turquoise lagoon. He was lightly sweating due to the temperature and the humidity, but he was wearing only his boxers and it wasn't too bad. Although, the mosquitoes were hell this summer, even in the city, so he had several citronella torches going.

Five years between murders was a long time to wait. But suddenly there were three more victims. If this was his case, what would he be thinking about the time gap?

He took a sip and contemplated the flickering light of the closest torch. Prison? Could be. Often enough, it happened. The guilty party gets sent away for something else so his opportunity is taken from him, and when he gets out, well . . . everything goes south again.

But Carl was pretty sure everyone was getting a sense of how smart their killer was, so prison was probably not the answer to him or anyone else.

Why five years? That was an interesting question, wasn't it?

He drank his whiskey and thought about the complexities of human emotion, and how he'd been convinced that killing five years ago was about retribution. The good Reverend Cameron, the victim of the first Burner crime five years ago, would have said vengeance belonged to the Lord.

Carl really didn't agree with that and never had.

Chapter 16

That ticking clock in my brain was an entity that hung in the background, always there, reminding me of what I had not accomplished in my life. There are many things, of course, that aren't going to happen to us. Inevitable, who can do it all? A Nobel Prize, an Academy Award, founding a Fortune 500 company, hitting the home run in the World Series . . .

Being considered a serial killer.

It was like peering through a haze of smoke, always trying to see what might be out there, the hidden dangers, the other monsters on the hunt.

This time I'd dismembered the body.

Not much of a choice, really. A change of plans was in order.

So I cut her up carefully, placed the body in the bag, and thought about how it would all play out.

Fire could purify almost everything.

I parked the car and got out, the long drive familiar, different and yet unchanged, quiet, the house silent and dark.

The place looked the same for the most part, a few shingles missing, the paint not as bright, but then again it was dark out and the macabre cast to the scenery didn't help with my perception of what it looked like now, twenty some years since my last visit.

Heat lightning flashed in the distance, but I doubted the promise of rain.

Getting out of the car, I inhaled the fecund scent of midsummer plants and humidity and went around to open the trunk. I was a little smarter each time and had used plastic bags, not that I had any illusions. If they really suspected me at any time, the police would be able to retrieve forensic evidence from my car. Lots of it probably.

So the key thing was that they should never suspect.

The crickets were loud. I was thinking that as the porch light flashed on.

Fuck.

The swirl of the lights, blue and red, made the scene look like a carnival.

Greendale. South of the city, quiet, the typical American community, small and cozy, and . . . the depository for murder.

Metzger was already on the scene before them, his face tight, his eyes showing a dark gleam in the revolving illumination, and he was visibly sweating, but then again, it was still hot even after dark. He told Jason, "The sheriff is going to want to talk to you. What the hell is going on? Change of city, new place? This asshole is trying to ruin any chance I have of a decent night's sleep." He turned, hands on hips. "MacIntosh, can you please tell me you are making some sort of progress."

"Sir, we're doing our best. This is all moving pretty

fast." She looked a little white around the mouth at the direct inquiry, and really, Jason didn't blame her, though at the same time he resented like hell he wasn't the one being asked. He had seniority.

"I was hoping for a little more than that. Now we have jurisdiction issues."

Okay, Jason wasn't her biggest fan, but still Ellie didn't deserve the blame for the change in the location. Part of it was that damn piece on the news that made everyone look to her.

So he did what he did best and interrupted. Rudely. *Fine*. He did rude better than most. It was a gift. "Yeah, well lodge a complaint with whoever is hacking up innocent citizens and burning them. Doesn't make our job any easier either, Chief."

Metzger's gaze snapped over to him. "Shut up, Santiago."

"Yes, sir." The edge of insolence was probably a bad idea.

"I want a suspect within twenty-four hours."

Ellie looked off balance, her hazel eyes wide, as if she didn't know where the demand was coming from, but he'd worked with the chief longer and understood the short fuse. When he'd come into his job, more than one officer had questioned Metzger as the choice as the head of the entire precinct. The chief wasn't bad—actually he was a pretty good administrator—he just wasn't all that understanding when he was under pressure, which was a distinct disadvantage if you were head of a big force in a major metropolitan area.

Time to go to work.

"We'll get back to you." Jason caught Ellie's elbow and jostled his partner forward, out of the wash of emergency response and further into the crime scene, which happened to be a small house a few miles from the western edge of town. It was fairly wooded around the structure itself, still a sizable chunk of land by city standards, at least five acres left of the original farm, which was why no one else saw the fire right away.

Unfortunately it looked like the owner had been at home.

"We got an interrupted 911 call," the local sheriff said with a certain level of discomfort as he met them at the base of the steps and introduced himself. The look on his face indicated he didn't deal with a double homicide, especially not like this one, on a usual basis. "We look at all of those, of course. I sent out a cruiser to check. It's pretty quiet down here. The officer knocked and a man came to the door, apologizing. Said his kid was fooling around with the phone. That happens now and then, and the deputy said everything seemed fine, so he left."

If Jason had felt a flicker of guilt for how the chief treated his partner it was gone and the case was back to being priority number one. Not to mention how she'd shaken off his hand halfway down the steps. "He see a car? If the answer is yes, tell me it was black."

"You can ask him, we haven't gotten that far . . . When I realized what this was I called DCI."

The Division of Criminal Investigation supported all Wisconsin law enforcement. Especially in runaway situations like this one. Small departments especially need the extra expertise of detectives and labs with extensive resources.

The sheriff rubbed his jaw. "Then I called your chief too, in case there was a connection, and took my men out. The minute the fire department was able to get the situation under control, some of the deputies went in, but they weren't all that unhappy when I pulled them

out either. I've heard about the burnings on the news."
The sheriff, stolid and tall, with hair going white at the
temples, waved at a persistent mosquito. The woods
around them squeaked with frogs and cicadas. "And
here I was feeling sorry for you guys and it knocks on
my front door."

"We've been feeling sorry for us too," Ellie said, gaz-
ing at the blackened front of the house.

"If what you've been dealing with is half as bad—"
He stopped, and his voice caught. "I used to be a state
trooper. Worked accident scenes all the time. This is
something else."

Jason didn't at all like the way the guy was shaking
his head; it meant something particularly disturbing and
he was already having trouble sleeping since this had all
started. "Please tell me the kid that made the call isn't
dead in there. I can't take the kids."

"There's no kid. Never was. The owner of the house
was in his sixties, recently retired, and had just inherited
the house from an aunt. He spends a lot of time in the
Twin Cities at his place there according to the neighbors. He's inside, dead from several gunshot wounds
along with what appears to be a dismembered body.
The good news is the fire department put this one out
fast. One of the neighbors was driving by and saw the
smoke."

"He's inside dead . . . then who answered the door?"
Ellie had rallied, shaking off the rattled persona for a
more composed, coplike demeanor. Her voice was sharp
and cool.

"You tell me, Detective. Mr. Jarvis lived alone."

The deputy proved to be not as helpful as Ellie had hoped,
obviously off balance since he'd actually talked to the

man who had probably just butchered a body, chagrined he didn't get the sense something was wrong, and also half-scared he'd probably looked a cold-blooded killer in the eye.

The description was vague. Thirties or even forties, mild-looking, pleasant and completely calm, light brown hair, apologetic smile, features blurred a little by the screen. Clothing? The officer thought baggy shorts and a T-shirt, nothing on it he could remember . . . could have been a Badgers logo.

Oh, yeah. *That* narrowed it down in the state of Wisconsin.

The only bright side was the young man thought he could finger him if he saw him again.

But only *thought*. And Metzger wanted a suspect in twenty-four hours.

She said to Santiago, "If the fire started later, and it obviously did, and our guy was here when the deputy came along, that means he parked somewhere."

"It's dry as dust, and I suspect rescue vehicles have run over everything of value, but we can try. Let DCI take care of it." Her partner snapped on gloves.

Ellie was still processing this new development, her brain churning, in her gut trying to find a direction. They hadn't been in the house yet, but at least the fire had been contained fairly quickly. She wished the interview with the deputy had given them more, but it was something more than a vague sighting of a faraway figure and a black car, a drugged-up unemployed man who had just lost his house, and a missing persons report that might, or might not, pan out.

"I know the scene is going to be like a Fourth of July hog-shit contest from the way everyone is acting, but let's get to it, shall we?"

Ellie turned to look at Santiago, even under the circumstances a small hint of amusement surfacing. "A what?"

"Shit contest. You know, where you pick up a piece and see who can chuck it the farthest? God, MacIntosh, where did you grow up?"

She ducked under the tape, his face a flash in the revolving lights. "Not where you did, evidently," she muttered. "That's what you did for entertainment?"

"It depended on where I was."

"What does that mean?"

He didn't answer and he was right. It was personal again and she didn't want personal. Instead he said, "Metzger gets frustrated. Ignore it. All you can do is the job to the best of your ability."

It was unbelievable, but maybe she owed the smug, smartass son of a bitch.

There had been a moment back there when she wasn't sure she understood just how to respond to her boss, especially the implied failure to deliver. Coupled with the recent piece on the news Bryce had told her about, she was feeling the pinch.

This would be their fourth homicide scene and included two victims.

No wonder Metzger was tensed up.

She was a little tense too.

"I guess let's see what we've got." Her voice was irritatingly uneven. The porch was wide and not that clean, especially now after firemen and other personnel had tramped across it, muddy footprints everywhere. Not only was it wet and streaked with soot, but there were more than a few warped boards and a rickety swing suspended from a ceiling she was pretty sure she wouldn't trust *before* the fire. A dead potted plant, probably watered for the first time all summer from the hose spray to put the blaze down, sat by the door.

"Inside." The deputy who opened the old-fashioned door for them looked a little green. He was young, fresh-faced, obviously shaken. "Better you than me."

That wasn't promising.

A double murder? Ellie had hoped she would never see one again. She'd worked one actually not that long ago up north, and she'd just as soon skip a repeat performance. "One of the victims is gunshot?"

He turned to her and nodded, his smile sickly. "Two to the chest. The other body is in tiny little pieces, Detective. All on the table, just for you. I swear, in case you have any idea about me helping, if I have to go in there again, I'll maybe lose it and contaminate the scene. Almost happened the first time. I can handle a lot but . . . dear God."

That was an aberration. The table smacked of a familiar scenario, but the body in pieces?

"Something happened here," Santiago said tersely. "Holy crap, something *really* different happened here. We needed this."

Yeah, right, we need two more bodies?

"What we need is for him to take a day off and let us work the cases," she muttered.

"He doesn't shoot them, and he doesn't cut them up usually. I'd say he didn't expect the old man."

"Let's go see what our victims can tell us."

The answer to her question was particularly gruesome, and this hadn't been the most delightful case from the very beginning.

The deputy was entirely right.

It was . . . indescribable. Both bodies were in the kitchen. The table was an old wooden rectangle, sturdy enough that though it had burned, it hadn't been entirely destroyed either. The body was like charred bits on a grill, the dismembered pieces a collage, the mosaic arranged in human form. It sat near the remains of a hutch with melted glass and shattered dishes, and old, tired curtains hanging sopping wet at the broken windows, with blackened holes in the fabric that had marred tiny lilac flowers.

It was truly grotesque. She didn't blame the deputy. She was shaken too. Those grisly bits . . . *God*.

However, there wasn't time to be squeamish.

Some things never changed. The place was soaked in stinking water; the fire had destroyed a good deal of it, but not the other body.

The elderly man was different, lying on the worn rug by the back door. He was shot twice in the chest, one high and one low just above the abdomen, glazed eyes open, his expression still vaguely surprised, even in death. He wore flannel pajama pants, even in summer, and a soiled shirt, but that could have been from the fire. It looked to her like he'd been trying to go out the back of the house but was caught before he could manage it.

Santiago was right. This was the anomaly they needed.

"He *was* interrupted." She stood in the doorway, waiting for the crime scene techs to arrive, speculating. "He doesn't shoot people, he kills them some other way and burns them. What we need is to find out what happened *here*."

Santiago was not nearly as affected, or so it seemed. He surveyed the display as if he was viewing a museum exhibit, and eventually nodded. "Different. Agreed. I don't think he cared so much about the others, but he doesn't want us to identify this one. Something about that resonates with me. The old man was just home at the wrong time. Our killer thought he'd be over in Saint Paul or something. The fire didn't burn like it was supposed to, probably because of the deputy who knocked on the door. He was in a hurry, so he got sloppy."

"He must have expected it at least a little. He came prepared." Ellie went to look again at the old man, going down on her knees by the body. "He used a weapon that I suspect was a .38, but we'll have to have that confirmed by forensic evidence. Decent-sized holes, both of them. Not a big gun, not a small one. Same weapon for sure."

"Maybe a .45." Santiago took one gloved hand and shifted the shooting victim, whose vacant stare was disconcerting, so it was a relief. "Might be. I don't know if that will tell us anything. He must have picked up the casings, the fucker. We could've used those."

"Inconsiderate of him," she said dryly. "I couldn't agree more. What else do you see?"

"Other than the dismembered body over there?" He showed true emotion for just a second, a twitch of a muscle in his face, his composure cracking only for a moment. "That's not enough? Okay, besides the usual filthy contaminated crime scene no one could decipher even if there were bloodhounds and cameras and other forms of documentation, I am going to say that someone broke in here with the intention of dumping body parts on that table and burning the place down, and the owner woke up and came downstairs. Startled, our killer shot his saggy old ass, and that was the end of it. Body bits dumped, fire started."

As insensitive as that recital might be, it was also probably accurate. They both stood up, looking at each other.

Fine. Her wheels were turning too.

"He had time for the 911 call."

Santiago followed along her train of thought, indicating the doorway. "Didn't take him down with the first shot. Old man crawled to the back, grabbed the phone, pushed the buttons . . . see how close he is to the door? I'm thinking The Burner was bringing in the body from his car when he realized Jarvis wasn't where he fell. He was a little panicked, he doesn't usually shoot people, and so he finds him here"—he pointed at the lax form on the floor—"and shoots him again. Sees the phone in the old man's hand and realizes he's fucked. That's why he's prepared for the deputy, story in place, composed, and he waits to start the fire until the officer is gone."

"I can see that," she said slowly. She could, watching Santiago roam around the destruction of the kitchen, his face tense, his mind obviously turned inward.

"He's got some sort of timetable, we've been getting that picture, but the *locations* are the key. Did he live here once? I mean, think about it. He brought the body and he didn't expect the old guy. The murder was already done. This is about the *house*."

Ellie watched a piece of soggy curtain move in the breeze, which happened to be hot and stale but welcome just the same. "Okay. Okay . . . maybe that's it. We keep looking at the victims when we should be pursuing other venues." She couldn't stand to look at the table, so she walked toward the broken window. "I can buy that. He kills the victims, but he burns the houses. Give me a why."

Maybe Metzger was right. Maybe her partner was a good cop. He'd been able to get the scene a lot faster than she would, like he was living it.

He turned. "Why what?"

"Why is he doing it this way? He's taking a lot of chances."

"How the fuck would I know, but good question."

"We need that. We need a why. Not a how. That's obvious to the both of us. If you want to commit this sort of crime, you can figure out how, it's just that most people don't want to work that hard . . ."

"Damn straight. Murder is hard work."

She stared at her partner, then glanced at the thing on the burned table, and then at the dead man in front of them. She was with Metzger. Twenty-four hours might not happen, but the sooner the better.

Santiago agreed. She knew he did. They dealt with it differently, but they had the same demons. Hell, they were *assigned* the same demons.

"So is solving one. Let's get to it," she said with cool decisiveness. "Thanks to my last case, I know someone who might be able to help us."

Chapter 17

Before now there were several truths I'd denied myself. There is no such thing as usual—that's an absurd concept I don't think I ever really had, but I confess that, in the realm of reasonably normal, I thought I fit right in. I still might, but doubts were starting to gather, like quicksilver elusive shadows in the corner of my mind, by the time I was ten years old.

Fitting in and being normal; not the same.

Still, I managed fairly well. Not perfectly, of course, but enough to give the illusion of it. But all illusions can be shattered.

I'd made a mistake.

Perhaps the error of a lifetime.

Killing an old man? Really? It wasn't that I planned it, but fate often enough tossed a ball you had to dive to catch, and so it had happened. The thud to the ground, the plume of dust it raised, and the impact all counted just as much as the actual capture of the ball.

Deal with it.

I did. He'd come out of the house, holding a rifle, and

I hadn't expected him. So . . . the knee-jerk reaction wasn't perfect. He didn't die immediately either. I had to expedite it, and then the rest of it was more imperfect, which I hated.

I watched the news with a jaundiced eye, judging the reporter, the copy, the newscast in general, wondering about the stories, about the teacher in Madison who was up on charges of molestation, the latest political snafu— would they never learn, and in an election year—

And there it was. Just a pan of the building with the camera, the farmhouse not leveled as I intended, smoke still rising from the roof, the sky darkened, and people gathered around, like at a funeral, which it essentially was if you cut to the chase. It hadn't done what I wanted, but fire is like having a lover. I can never quite predict it. Oh, I know the nuances, I get the changes in temperatures and airflow, but it does not mean it will cooperate. The flame is in charge.

That's part of the fascination.

I swear it.

JULY 9

"This person," Montoya, the profiler from the FBI Ellie said she'd talked to in the Northwoods case, said to the room at large, "is exerting a powerful control over all of us, this city, and the potential victims he sees out there. It is all escalating at a rate that alarms me. He feels entitled."

The place was stifling. The power had gone out twice at the station during the day, but luckily, Jason hadn't been there either time. However, he was suffering now, after the fact. It was entirely too hot have so many people crammed into a small, airless space. There was a fan, and it was a nice touch, but still, doing little to nothing.

Jason had to admit it all sounded like stupid psycho grad school crap to him, but this was the FBI and he knew he was required to sit and listen in a polite way. Federal law enforcement had never appealed to him. Too much red tape; it was worse than at the city level and that was bad enough. Besides, he doubted he could get in, not with his past. His military record was clean, but there were a few nicks and dings on record that they would frown on. That said, it didn't stop him from waving a hand at the man standing at the front of the room.

He was never good at staying quiet. It just wasn't his strong suit. "Excuse me, but may I ask a question?"

They were in the briefing room and apparently all these murders in such a short time frame required the entire world of law enforcement to arrive. Well, maybe not the world, but there were at least twenty of them, including detectives from the Division of Criminal Investigation, some of whom Ellie told him she knew.

"Of course." The FBI profiler looked interested. "Please do."

The bastard wasn't even sweating.

Jason's initial instinct was to point out that since not one person in the room knew who the asshole was lighting people on fire, wouldn't they be more effective if they didn't sit around yapping about it and instead actually investigated? But he had the feeling that might push Metzger over the edge and he didn't want to be instantly unemployed, so he settled for saying, "What the fu— I mean, what the heck do you mean by entitled? If you are here to get me into his head, which is not a place I am sure I want to go, can you be clearer?"

The profiler, tall, with angular features, dressed in a suit that was so tailored Jason felt particularly grubby in his khakis and blue polo for the briefing even though they were both pressed and clean, cleared his throat. He said, "Certainly."

Ellie, sitting next to him, didn't even glance over in reproof, so at least he felt as if the request was pertinent. Usually, when he said something she didn't approve of, he was on the receiving end of a certain kind of look. They were starting to know each other that well.

So, then, good question.

That was progress.

"Entitlement is about a perception of deserving recompense for an effort exerted or a sense of righting a perceived wrong. He thinks: I experienced this, so I can have X." The profiler looked around the room. "The ritualistic aspect of this case or cases represents something we don't yet understand, but we will. Let's just hope it is before the next victim. I'm not quite certain why the actual process is the same and yet the locations change so radically, but I'm going to speculate that his urgency is increasing not because he's more homicidal, but because he wants to get it all over with. The places he leaves the bodies and burns down mean something, we just don't understand what yet."

"Why do you think that?" Someone else, a uniformed officer up front, asked.

Good. Jason wanted to know that too, not that he was all that certain profiling really worked. He'd figured out all of that for himself already.

"He isn't more reckless. He's *less* reckless." A picture flipped on with the singed and extremely unattractive parts of the last scene displayed for everyone on a flat screen on one wall of the room.

At least they didn't have to live it, smell it, be there for body bag exit. Jason didn't realize it, but he'd shifted in his seat and he consciously stopped himself. It had been a particularly horrific experience in his opinion.

It was Ellie who spoke up and said, "Less reckless. How do you know that?"

"Usually there is a part of them that wants the glory of being caught. That is, almost beyond exception, part of the psyche of an individual who commits multiple homicides." The agent surveyed his audience again, resting his hands on the podium. "But we are dealing with a different animal. Not this one. He doesn't want to be caught at all. The shooting was because he didn't anticipate an interruption, and the dismemberment of the other victim was done elsewhere, the body parts brought to the farmhouse and set on fire to make sure we stay as confused as we have been so far. He isn't average in any way."

"Okay, I'll buy that," Jason muttered under his breath to Ellie, "but what the fuck has he told us that can actually help?"

"Just listen."

Montoya went on, pointing at the board with the locations of the victims. "I think, unlike most cases, the motivation is the key. I believe in this one, we need to figure out why. And I rarely come to that conclusion, but after looking over the data and evidence, I completely believe *why* will lead you to *who*. Usually serial killers have compulsions we just don't get. Some of it is sexual and arousing in a certain convoluted way that is at odds with how normal people think, but this doesn't seem like it to me. He's . . . purging, if I had to guess."

The guy even had good English. Annoying. Jason never could figure out when to use who and whom.

"I told you I've talked to Montoya before," she said quietly without looking over, her gaze focused on the speaker. "I don't believe this is ever the magic wand, but I do think it can be a way to think it through. It's a tool, not an answer."

"Goddamnit, I really don't need someone to help me think it through. I've thought about it enough and come up with the astonishing conclusion that the killer is fast, quiet, and worst of all, smarter than we are."

It might have been better if he hadn't raised his voice. He could blame it on the malfunctioning air-conditioning. He was sweating more than just a little. Heads swiveled.

His partner also turned to him, her hazel eyes level and challenging. "Maybe smarter than *you*, Santiago. Speak for yourself."

At least someone nearby could hear their exchange because there was a low whistle and a chuckle. He ignored it, studying his notes, but he did temper his tone. "All I really wanted was a tip I could use or I would have skipped this. Jesus, it's hot in here."

"Keep on listening," she shot back. "With profilers it isn't really what they think they see, but more what they think *we* should see."

"What the shit does that mean?"

"Can you ever speak and not use foul language?"

"I don't fuckin' think so."

MacIntosh sent him a lethal look. "Very funny. Just listen. He's maybe going to help us, and maybe he won't. Either way, federal law enforcement is here, we need to just work with it, and if all goes well, no one else will die."

"How effing likely is that?" He raised his hands, palms forward. "Hey, effing isn't technically a swear word."

"Really more likely if we can catch him."

That was, in his opinion, a kind of big "if." As far they

knew the guy drove a black car. That narrowed it down. Not. The sheriff's deputy was a possibility as a way to nail the killer, but only if they could finger someone for him to identify.

It wasn't hopeless, but it wasn't all that great either.

The profiler was still talking. "What strikes me most was that though the scene is rushed, he was still methodical. Since he's never shot someone before it deviates from the usual plan. He stops and makes sure he has the casings; we think he used gloves to move the victim now that sometimes we can get fingerprints from skin under the right circumstances; and he still went through with what he needed to do, because he is just that cool under fire."

"Is that a pun?" Jason couldn't help it. The words just came out of his mouth.

Special Agent Montoya didn't look all that amused. With splayed hands he braced himself against the podium and said, "No, Detective. What I'm suggesting is that perhaps there is a chance we are dealing with someone who is law enforcement."

The resulting silence was impressive.

Carl extended his legs and listened, his demeanor not precisely condescending but somewhat skeptical. He felt about profiling like he felt about triple A baseball. It was close, but not really the big league team.

But, as always, he could keep an open mind. The FBI wasn't chump change, the ideas being presented were being listened to by everyone who was anyone in the department, and he needed to cash in on being offered this ticket of attendance because Metzger was throwing him a bone.

God knew he'd pushed to get it.

"Law enforcement?" One older guy, Jamison, not a uniform, a little heavy in the middle and jowls, sounded offended. "Just because he's methodical, doesn't mean he's one of us. Most serial killers don't really have nerves. That's why they can do it." He ticked off on his fingers. "No brakes, no conscience, no humanity, no scruples, no nerves. I don't think I agree."

Grasso found it interesting that MacIntosh, who might be the only person in the room who had ever been face-to-face with a serial killer—discounting the ones the profiler had probably interviewed—didn't say a word. She didn't take notes either, just sat relaxed in her chair, a bottle of water in her hand, her expression remote. It was getting to be a tiresome joke about how pretty she was, and he didn't disagree, but he wasn't in the least bit interested in the tasteless comments. He liked women—that was hardly the issue—but Metzger hired her because of the Northwoods Killer case, and here she was, assigned to this one.

It did give him a second of pause that he envied her that much, but then again, he did. He'd always wanted to work a serial, much less two of them . . . and all he could think was *lucky her.*

"You don't have to agree." The profiler panned the gathering with a long look. "And I'm not saying it is necessarily a police officer or any other type of civil servant, but I am trained to pick up nuances in the behavior of individuals who commit certain types of crimes. Obviously homicide is one of the higher levels of infraction, considering the possible penalty. We take it seriously, and so does the offender with a functional brain. There is a reason we create laws on a scale to match the crime. In my opinion, this particular criminal is very able to consider what he does from an analytical viewpoint, which does not indicate a drug-induced state, or an impulse-generated situation."

"He went out and bought a frigging table," Jason Santiago said. He added clearly, "*I* could tell you he's a planner. Might just be the four crime scenes with no real clues that tipped me off. Tell me what you think he's going to do *next,* will you?"

Montoya didn't look offended. "That, I don't know. It is possible he could be done."

"Done?" MacIntosh spoke finally, lifting her pen. "I wouldn't mind if you explained that."

The profiler just shook his head. "I think that he has a purpose to this we haven't found out yet, and it has happened before with this sort of killer. Once he's finished with it, he feels he's completed whatever journey he thought he needed to take. What you need to do is connect either the victims, or the fires, before he just quits and leaves you hanging onto an investigation that could last for months, or even years."

To a certain extent, well, duh. Carl couldn't agree more. Because there was a pattern, there was a reason . . . but they hadn't found it yet. The clock was ticking now with the task force a reality.

He signaled that he had a question. "Five years ago I worked a case that had a victim who was burned on a table. Almost the same exact methodology except he was male and all our recent targets have been female. Any idea why the killer would wait so long?"

Montoya looked at him and nodded. "Good point. I've been told that there could be a precedent, but I've also been told that there is absolutely no physical evidence to link the crimes. Part of our problem here is that because of the fires, the general contamination of the scenes, the lack of ties from the bodies to the places where they were burned, and nothing back from the medical examiner's office that is really helpful, I can't even give an educated guess. There have been serial killers in the past who have stopped for years and we still are not quite sure why. It could have a logical explanation, or it could just be a trigger. It is definitely something the task force should investigate.

The task force. Carl hadn't asked, but he'd been invited anyway. Metzger viewed the old case as relevant, and quite frankly, Carl had put his heart and soul into it, so even though it had taken this long and he wasn't back on homicide, he was at least working a homicide case.

The meeting was over and they all walked out of the conference room. He followed, deliberately trailing Santiago and MacIntosh, the tension between them palpable. They didn't exchange even a word. He waited until they gained the utilitarian hallway before he said, "Detectives, can I have a word?"

Both turned, their gazes similar at least in that they were sharply inquiring. Santiago said curtly, "About?"

That was Jason Santiago. Never all that hung up on the niceties.

Carl raised both hands in a gesture of parley. "I just wanted to say I think I might know something you don't about this case."

Up close, MacIntosh had incredible eyes, he'd give her that. That unusual not brown and not quite green, and even without much in the way of cosmetics, they were striking. "I sure as hell am listening. What is it?"

It was impossible to resist being a little theatrical and he was entitled if he was giving up this information, so he cocked a brow before he said, "Have you had a chance to read the file I gave you? The murder I just mentioned?"

Of course they hadn't had a chance to really go over it. That was several murders ago. This case was on a swift path and he might just be the gatekeeper.

"I think I might have made a connection that could help us," he said, shoving his hands into his pockets. "Buy me an ice cold beer and I'll tell you about it."

Chapter 18

A marathon is a journey. 26.2 miles to be exact, a run that tests the spirit of human endurance, the compulsion of competition, and of course, the will to survive.

It might be pure arrogance to think so, but I have all of the above. Maybe some of those characteristics in too much abundance, but I do possess them.

I am a marathon runner, not a sprinter. That I realized long ago, which is why this has all been so hard. It needs to be done swiftly and then left entirely alone.

Patience.

Stealth.

A sense of the enemy. Remorse had a place, but it depended on the situation, like just about everything else in life.

Let's not forget that by the time I was ten I'd already killed two people.

The place was a pizza joint on a busy corner, loud enough but not too boisterous, good for a conversation that wouldn't be overheard. Grasso asked for a beer and it was delivered, frothy and in a cold, frosted glass, just minutes after they were seated in the booth. The way the waitress flashed him a smile implied he was a regular. Ellie opted for iced tea, but Santiago had no trouble ordering a beer for himself—technically he really wasn't on the job. They were off the clock and working on their own time.

Seemed to be a lot of that going around lately.

She studied the man sitting across from her. He had nice enough features, was maybe a little older than she was—could be more, and his chestnut hair was starting to show tiny flecks of silver just at the temples. Otherwise, unless she counted his expensive suit that he wore as if it wasn't a million degrees outside, and his silk tie, he was decent looking but unremarkable.

Except for his eyes. They were the color of a summer storm, gray and ominous and held a clear, unmistakable intelligence.

"Tell us," she said as a couple took the opposite booth, both of them laughing, obviously not worried about murder, just wanting dinner and a drink. The young woman was plump but pretty, and her husband . . . no, boyfriend, she corrected automatically in her mind, taking in the way they looked at each other, was also a little overweight, but they were relaxed, enjoying the evening . . .

She was really hoping she'd have a night like that soon.

"I just think we're missing the trigger to your case. Ralph Cameron was a pastor at a local church." Grasso picked up his beer, took an appreciative sip, and set down the mug on a little napkin that was never going to save a table that had multiple rings on it anyway. "Upright. Sermons on Sundays, that sort of thing. Loving wife and supportive family. Gave back to the community in multiple ways."

"But someone killed him and stuck his body on a table and set it on fire five years ago."

Table. Fire. When he'd spoken up during the briefing, she'd wondered how he felt about them working his old case, but she wasn't quite yet convinced it was. All the loose ends bothered her. The case five years ago with the similar theme, Matthew Tobias and his suicide, the multiple murders in different places . . .

"I hear Metzger put you on the task force." Jason folded his arms on the table and Ellie suddenly had the feeling that maybe she was in a situation that involved two males that were circling each other like wolves outside a ring of fire.

"He did."

"Good. If you can help we want it." She wiped condensation off her glass. "We ran everything through the database but came up with nothing pertinent, or at least pertinent to us. Your case went cold. Go ahead, your turn."

He took another drink and the corner of his mouth lifted. "We *thought* we solved it. Actually, that's not quite true. We found someone who fit the profile of who might have done it, we found evidence it was possible because they had opportunity and motive, and we arrested them. It went nowhere, which was fine with me because I was never convinced for several reasons. Not then, and obviously not now or we wouldn't be having this conversation."

Santiago's elbows rested inelegantly on the table. He'd already drunk half his beer in about thirty seconds flat. "I hate that kind of crap. Tell us why you weren't convinced. Why'd you arrest her then?"

Her?

Ellie had to admit that caught her attention. Santiago had taken the file and she hadn't had time to read it yet. "A woman?"

Grasso nodded, his eyes direct. "Love triangle with Cameron's wife. Not a him, but a *her*. Get my drift? Juries often aren't sympathetic in that sort of situation and she was pretty young, barely legal. The grand jury decided not to hand down an indictment because there wasn't enough evidence and they were afraid she might get wrongly convicted. She was the best suspect we had, but that really just meant we didn't have much. The scandal was plastered across every television in Wisconsin and even the country."

Maybe—it was a glimmer—she did remember it. Ellie had been a newly promoted detective then way up in the northern part of the state, and had been pretty damn busy, but the case now sounded familiar. "She was barely old enough to be tried as an adult, right? I think I remember the arrest on the news."

"Oh, you got it. The works. Preacher's wife and a barely consensual young woman having a same-sex affair, not to mention Lisa was a troubled teen. The press was all over the murder, but the sex part was the titillation. However, since at the time I didn't believe it, now I have to say I'm more skeptical than ever with these new murders. Sure, the affair gave our suspect at the time a motive, but the method really is almost exactly the same. The table, the house goes up but the body is the point of origin . . . and it can't be Lisa Martin."

Good call. And they had more of a confirmation now that the murderer was a man thanks to the eyewitness in the form of a county deputy.

Ellie nodded, her mind busy. *Still . . .*

"Why can't it be her?" Santiago was as blunt as ever and Ellie could hear just a hint of resentment in his voice. He really did not like sharing these cases.

"She's in prison for something else entirely. Best alibi on earth. Bars, guards with guns . . . But you know, if I were you, I'd go talk to her. At the time, she was a sullen, rebellious young woman who refused a lawyer, refused to talk to us, and pretty much almost got herself tried for murder." Grasso picked up his beer and finished it, standing to set the empty glass on the table. "It's nice to have a drink with my colleagues. Thanks."

They both watched him go, elegant in his suit, his movements efficient, and Ellie waited to hear Santiago's opinion, because if there was one thing she could say for her partner, he wasn't shy about speaking his mind.

Part of his dubious charm.

"So?" She caught the eye of their waitress and gestured for another tea.

"I'm not sure." He stared at his empty beer mug, tight lines around his mouth. "What if he's fucking with us?"

"What does *that* mean?"

"Grasso is good, but you know it's no secret he wants back on homicide."

"After the past few days, he can have the job. How good? Do you trust this lead?"

"Not sure. He should have planted a gun on the second guy before he called the shootings in." Santiago shook his head in evident disgust. "But Metzger took care of him, or at least sort of. He still got demoted but he kept his job."

The clink of glasses, the televisions propped in the corners, and the hum of conversation kept her from having to comment at once, but she finally said, "Tamper

with evidence? Yeah, that's a good idea. What shootings? Everyone talks around this. What did he do?"

"Offed a couple suspects. He might have saved his ass
if he'd just planted a gun." Santiago drained his glass
and set it aside, but he didn't really answer the question.
"But who cares, that's water under a bridge you or I
have never stood on, or at least I haven't. I suppose I
can't speak for you. What do *you* think about his information?"

How, even when he was giving a compliment, did he
come off all wrong?

"Interesting," she said shortly.

"Damn straight it's interesting," he said in return, his
gaze riveted on her face. "And might be the best lead
we've had so far. Tomorrow I say we visit a women's
prison."

Carl knocked lightly. When Rachel answered the door of
the condo, he could see she'd obviously been grading
papers because they were strewn across the dining room
table.

"Did we have a date and I forgot?" she asked, and
self-consciously smoothed back her hair even though
she looked good in shorts and a sleeveless tank.

"No, I just dropped by to bring this as thanks." He
held up a bottle of wine.

It didn't take her long, but then again, it never did.
"The Burner story? Hey, I owe you in a way because my
old station manager is now offering me a consulting position. I might even take it." She stepped back. "Come in."

"I hope cabernet sauvignon is okay."

"If it's French."

He glanced at the label. "California. Shall I go?"

He didn't want to. He took in the perfect sweep of her hair and thought about the last time they had slept together. Stupid probably, but there it was. After the shootings and the internal affairs investigation, he realized that her interest in him was tied to that incident and he had second thoughts about her, about *them*.

But he'd come anyway. Carl walked past her and set the bottle down on the kitchen counter with the ease of someone who had been there before, walking around the bar to pull out the drawer where she kept the corkscrew. "Glasses in the same place?"

"Yes."

As she watched he deftly took them out of the cabinet and set them down, then opened the wine.

Mildly, she asked, "Do I need fortification for what you have to say next?"

"Probably not." His gaze was direct as he looked at her. "In the great scheme of things this means very little except to the families of the victims, and to Cameron's wife and children, but certainly MacIntosh and Santiago have some limited choices now that there is a task force. It turns out I'm going to help them out."

She understood. "Really? Congratulations."

"That's a little too early, but thanks."

When he splashed wine into a glass and offered it, she took it and seemed to consider her next comment. Finally, she just asked simply, "I thought you wanted to be a star and win Metzger's attention."

"Now I think I just need to be useful. I think he's been to the wall for me."

"I'd say. But you paid."

Oh, yeah, he'd paid. If they had tossed him in prison it would not have cost him more emotionally than his place in homicide. Carl took a stool by the granite countertop and regarded her over the rim of his glass. "If there is one flaw in law enforcement, and there is a lot more than one by the way, it is a tendency to think that more men will make a more effective solution. In this case, it works to my advantage. He put me on it."

"I believe I did a piece on that once."

She had, he remembered when she'd written it, and it hadn't thrilled anyone. Her boss had liked the idea until it had passed on to editorial review, and then he had pulled it.

"I remember." His gaze touched hers briefly. "You weren't too happy."

That was all in the past. "So you suddenly decided to help? I thought what you wanted was to solve this yourself and take all the glory."

"Glory? That's an overused phrase if I've heard one. I never quite said that anyway. There is no glory in homicide unless you are like MacIntosh and manage to get famous by a fluke. We catch them quietly and usually with boring facts. Detectives are really about as glamorous as frozen French toast. I like the new curtains, by the way." He looked out over the skyline and envied the view.

"Trust you to notice a detail like that. And thanks, I'd suggest we sit out on the balcony, but in this weather, we'd roast."

Almost immediately she regretted her choice of words. "In a figurative sense."

"I pointed them to Lisa Martin."

"Stop feeling guilty about that girl. You didn't want to arrest her." She sank down on the chair nearby in the living room and folded a leg comfortably under her. "All you did was bring her in for questioning, and the decision to arrest was not your call. That was your only lead and she didn't help her case when she admitted to the affair with Margot Cameron."

She was 100 percent right.

He moodily stared at the ruby liquid in his glass. "I don't like cases based on motive. They're usually flimsy and can be manipulated if the defendant has the wrong lawyer."

She didn't disagree. "She didn't even try to do herself any favors."

"She was a kid. Besides, all she said was that she wasn't sorry he was dead and that he was a mean bastard."

"She was eighteen and that constitutes, under the law, that she was old enough to be tried as an adult, not to mention, she—"

"Jesus, Rachel, you interviewed her. Do you honestly think she was stable enough to be tried as an adult?"

It was true. Lisa Martin wasn't mentally challenged, but she was edgy, combative, and not very inclined to defend herself in the spirit of being defiant. All things he'd told Santiago and MacIntosh. The only reason he'd not suggested he go along was he was afraid his presence would ruin the interview because of the arrest. He doubted you ever forgave someone who put you in handcuffs no matter what came afterward. MacIntosh might be able to get her to talk.

Lisa had a hard life, no doubt about it. Junkie mother. He could never find out anything about her father. Now she was serving time for check kiting and fraud, multiple offenses, but at least it wasn't murder.

In his opinion, Carl thought the U.S. legal system was one of the finest in the world, and also irrevocably flawed.

"I thought the arrest was wrong too," she said slowly. "But you know all that. We talked about it then and gnashed our teeth but couldn't do anything. Why are we talking about it again now? I thought your purpose was to get reinstated as a homicide detective."

"It still is. Let's see what MacIntosh and Santiago can find out when they talk to Lisa. They owe me now. It has to be them because all that will happen is that Lisa will remember me as the man who arrested her."

"So you're using them to get information you can't get without drawing attention to your side investigation? I get it. The supposed spirit of cooperation. Sure. You'll look like a hero if your leads point them in the right direction."

"That sounds calculated and I can't say that I sat around and thought about it that way, but all I know is that tonight there is very little I can do about it. How about dinner?"

Rachel accepted the change of subject, but her gaze was speculative. "I'm not dressed for it, but there is an Italian place around the corner that delivers. We could order in."

Maybe he'd be invited to stay the night. It had been awhile . . .

He said soberly, "I don't want to be a hero." He was a born investigator, not afraid of violence, willing to bend rules if he had to—in short exactly what the law-abiding world needed between them and the bad guys. His methods weren't always perfect, but he got the job done.

But hero? *No.*

Rachel took a sip and set down her glass. "Being a homicide detective *makes* you a hero. People who catch those who kill other people are considered heroes. Now, it gets a little gray when you get kicked off the team for breaking your own rules, but you get points for trying to get back in good graces."

"I'm not interested good graces, those of Metzger or the mayor or anyone else."

He said it with enough force he could tell she believed him.

"Then?"

"I really want to work this case."

"I get it. I do. I'd love to stand in front of that camera still. Stupid in my opinion, but most of the reporters are young. At a certain age they start nudging you into the newsroom."

Carl smiled ruefully. "Sorry. You miss reporting. I know it."

"I do," she acknowledged. "But life changes. You miss homicide, but at least it sounds like you might get a second chance. Now then, if I remember correctly you like veal parmesan, right?"

Chapter 19

The past was like a booklet that had gotten wet and come apart at the edges. A little blurred, some of the pages still bright and not stuck together, glossy in places and in others like glue I can't seem to wash off my fingers.

I needed to finish.

I sat by the window and drank a glass of good scotch. Two fingers of a single barrel, single malt, my one true indulgence, though I don't do it often.

Logic told me I was going to have to wait.

The creature was incensed at the delay, but a problem had arisen and the internal struggle was going to be turned into a war and not just a battle at this point.

And here I was so close.

That young trooper, or maybe it was a deputy, had seen me. Briefly, true, and through the old screen door, which wasn't particularly clean and was spotted with cobwebs, but he'd stood a few feet away and heard my voice and looked right at me.

Not a small problem.

The old man's death would lead to a ballistics report. I knew this the minute I pulled the trigger, so I'd had to ditch the gun. I wiped it carefully, but a single half print could be incriminating enough to raise a flag and I just couldn't afford that to happen. Unless it was being kept very quiet, there was no suspect in the hunt for The Burner.

The name I didn't care for. I don't know what I'd prefer, but something less plebian, certainly. It smacked of blue collar to me, of seedy neighborhoods, and sleeveless dirty shirts, and loud music.

Not at all my style.

The clink of the ice in the bottom of the glass told me my drink was gone. The scotch would have to be my sleeping pill tonight because mixing the two was dangerous.

And I am always careful.

JULY 10

Lisa Martin was in the infirmary, which Jason had to admit was a relief. Maybe it was territory that came with being a previous offender, but prisons made him jittery, reminded him of what people could lose at the hands of the system. If anything on this planet would keep him clean besides his own sense of right and wrong, it was the idea of being locked in a cell.

Lesson learned a long time ago. It had straightened him out.

His juvenile foray into lawlessness was more than enough to convince him he didn't need to go in that direction. If he could say anything for himself it was that he was a damn fool sometimes, but he wasn't a damn fool for long.

Ms. Martin was recovering from a particularly bad case of a skin rash he was positive he didn't want to get, her entire right leg encased in bandages. She was bored, watching television when they came into the small, curtained room, and looked up from her bed with mild curiosity.

Ellie slipped out her badge. "I'm Detective MacIntosh and this is Detective Santiago. Can we ask you a few questions? The physician and warden have given us permission to talk to you."

The young woman shrugged. "Since no one comes here voluntarily, I'm gonna take your word for it. Dr. Phil is the highlight of my day, so just don't keep me long."

She was of slender build, her nose slightly too big for her face, her dark hair copped short around gamine features. There was an air of vulnerability around the set of her mouth, but an unmistakable hardness in her eyes.

Jason recognized that look. It came from seeing far too much, far too young. For all he knew he still had it.

Ellie said in a gentle voice, "We'd like to talk about Reverend Cameron." There were curtains around the bed separating the space, but no chairs, so they had no choice but to stand.

"No kidding." Lisa stared at her in derision. "Why? I told pretty much everything I knew about that bastard in court and they let me go."

"We weren't there," Jason interjected quickly. "We'd kinda like to hear it from you firsthand. Reports leave out the emotions, you know? Tell us the truth. Was he really a bastard?"

Her gaze focused on him, and he held it, letting her

see his lack of judgment. After a second, she answered. "Total bastard. You have no idea. And I didn't kill him."

"It said in the file that—" Ellie started to say, but Jason interrupted.

"How much of a bastard?" he asked point blank, because it was sure as hell easier to deal with pragmatic than with soft and caring. Female cops routinely messed up there, in his opinion, and in this case, he recognized that resentful air because he'd seen it in the mirror a few times too many.

Lisa adjusted the sheet a little over her supine body, staring at him. "What kind of scale are we talking? One to ten?"

"That's fine with me. One to ten. Ten being the biggest prick on earth."

"One hundred. Ah, what the fuck, make it a thousand."

He recognized pure hate when he heard it.

They'd agreed before they walked through the prison doors that Ellie would do the talking because Lisa was young and female, but he knew her kind, he'd been one once, so he had no trouble talking over his partner. When she shot him a look and opened her mouth, he spoke quickly. "In a nutshell, why'd you hate his guts?"

Lisa was pale, and there was a slight tick in her cheek, the muscle jumping now and then. She looked away, back at the now-silent television. Her dark hair was lifeless, without the sheen of good health. "Tell me why you want to know. Is this about Margot? If it is, no thanks. She didn't help me. I'm not helping her."

Margot Cameron, the wife, the lover . . . the woman had almost been brought up on charges of child molestation, but Lisa had been seventeen when she'd been put into foster care in their home and the charges had been dropped because Mrs. Cameron had cooperated. By the time of the murder Lisa was of age and no one could prove the affair had started earlier. Lisa certainly, according to Grasso, hadn't cooperated at all, so no formal investigation of that aspect of the case had ever been opened.

"We haven't spoken to her," Ellie said. "She lives in Utah now, but maybe you know that. We're just investigating another murder."

Or two. Or three. Or *five*.

"Well I didn't do it. I've been here for a while." Lisa gestured wide, her arm flinging out clumsily. "Ask anyone. Why would I leave paradise?"

"Why'd you hate him?" Jason asked it again in a flat voice. She didn't want his sympathy, and at her age, he wouldn't have either. That life was behind him and he was glad, but it wasn't part of his most pleasant memories and he wasn't sure he had a lot of those anyway.

After a second where they made full eye contact again, Lisa seemed to deflate. "For about a million reasons, but mainly because he was just a hypocritical, bullying son of a bitch. He beat his wife, but in places it wouldn't show, he bragged to me once that he stole from the church all the time because he was that kind of an asshole, and he . . ."

"What?" Jason was aware Ellie had gone very still.

Lisa shrugged, her skinny shoulders lifting her gown. "He tried stuff. A touch here, a little feel-up there. Margot was afraid of him, but I really wasn't. Not all that much. Pervert. He was pretty cruel to her and the rest of the kids, but he was sneaky about it, you know? Deprived privileges and punishments . . . I'm glad someone killed him. It wasn't me, but I still don't mind at all he's dead."

Pay dirt. He could feel it in the very marrow of his bones. It was *that* sort of moment. He could read people pretty well and after that one attempt when they arrived, he did note that Ellie let him have the lead in the questioning, so maybe she felt it too.

"You didn't do it. Okay, any idea who did?"

"Hard to tell. I haven't done a poll or anything, but we'd all have tried if we thought we could get away with it."

"We all?"

"Saint Ralph Cameron's kids." She made a face. "That's what he called us. Cameron's Kids. He did foster care. Made Margot do it, actually—like *he'd* lift a finger. In the church, he was viewed as doing his Christian duty."

A lightbulb lit up. Jason took in a steadying breath. "Anyone else hate him as much as you?"

With conviction, she said, "Every single one of us."

All right. He *was* good at this.

Ellie had to admit it even if she didn't like him all that much. Jason Santiago knew how to talk to a reluctant witness, or at least one like Lisa Martin, and cut through the fine nuances of trying to pry information from someone who was distrusting and just demand it from them.

And she was learning something.

Not that she really approved of his methods, but . . .

This was a real lead. If this worked they'd have the car from the tenement fire, the face-to-face with the deputy, and then this damaged girl with her hollow eyes . . . all clues leading back to the killer.

Jason crouched by the bed. Not touching it, but on his haunches so he was nonthreatening, hands clasped in front of him, his voice surprisingly soft. "Okay. Thanks.

I think you might have just helped us a lot. Why didn't your lawyer bring up that there were a lot of other candidates besides you for Cameron's murder when you were arrested?"

Before that moment Ellie would have voted him number-one least sensitive cop in Wisconsin law enforcement.

But . . . maybe he wasn't a contender.

Lisa took a minute, but she did answer him. "My lawyer was a tired, overworked public defender. Besides, Margot denied everything and did her best to bury me, painting me like some crazy stalker or something. I know she was scared she was going to get accused of the murder. She was under suspicion just like me because she hated him. Maybe more than I did. And the whole lesbian thing . . . she was ashamed of that." Lisa's voice cracked as she finished and her eyes were unfocused as one thin hand plucked at the blanket. "I was so pissed at her I didn't help myself either. I refused to cooperate, wouldn't testify, told my lawyer to go fuck himself most of the time when he asked me questions. I've had five years to think about what I could have done differently and I think the answer is just about everything, but there is one mistake I didn't make. I know they never figured out who did it, but *I* didn't kill that douche bag Cameron."

Ellie believed her. She was used to people lying to her, it happened all the time. So she was good at reading the signs, and she'd wager Lisa Martin was telling the truth.

Santiago must have thought so too, for when he straightened, he said, "Maybe, but don't take it to the bank just yet, we can get you some credit for being a cooperative witness."

"You think so?" Lisa sounded dubious.

"I can try. Who did do it? Could it have been Margot Cameron?"

"Oh, hell no." Lisa decisively shook her head. "She doesn't have the guts. Otherwise he would have been dead long before that fire. Besides, I promise you her house meant a lot more to her than her husband. She'd never have burned it down, not even with whatever she got in insurance."

"Lisa, can you give us the names of the other children you remember during the time you were with the Camerons?" Ellie wasn't rash enough to make any such promises as possible freedom and she wanted to jab her partner in the ribs and tell him he didn't have any business doing that either, but the list would be valuable.

"I can do that." The age-old weariness was gone from her voice. "A couple of them have come to see me here. But he'd been fostering for a long time. I don't know who was there before me."

But social services would have a record.

It was a start.

"I've got to make a call and I can't use my cell in here." Santiago flashed Lisa a smile and fairly sprinted from the room.

"He's kind of cute." Lisa watched the still moving curtain. "And not an asshole, for a cop."

Ellie responded dryly, "Cute, maybe, but not an asshole? Get to know him better before you make that judgment." She looked directly at Lisa. "We can't talk about the investigation we have going, nor can I give you any assurances it will help you even if we catch the person we are looking for right now, but it might. If I can give you my word on anything, we won't forget you, okay?"

"That would be a nice first." Lisa shifted, her tone not

really as resentful as resigned. "If anything happens, can you work on getting me a new lawyer? I know I don't have any money, but I sure don't want the same one I had when I went to court this last time."

"Not my call, but I can ask."

"Will you?"

This girl had been let down countless times. Ellie could see it in the resignation in her face and her disillusioned expression. She smiled and said, "I will."

"Thanks." Short, simple, and without expectations.

Ellie tried to not wince as she left the secured area.

Santiago, on the other hand, was jubilant, especially when they climbed into the car. "I think we're getting somewhere."

Ellie was driving and she started her Toyota, went past the gates, and onto the highway, heading back toward the metro area, glancing in the side mirror as she gained the thoroughfare. "I don't disagree. We've got what . . . twelve hours left according to the chief?"

"Forget Metzger. He was just pissed at having to get out of bed."

"Easy for you to say since you aren't new on the job."

He glanced at her then, a sardonic look. "Really? At least you aren't skating the line. It's no secret you're supposed to soften my rough edges. Fuck me; all I've ever done is the job."

"Then you should be fine." She wasn't going to address this now. The case was breaking, or so she hoped. "We need information . . . court records, something to tell us who else it could have been."

"I'm on it. All those kids fed through his house." He sprawled in the seat, legs outstretched, his jubilance fading to a moody expression. "I called and asked for forensics to try and bring up records but we might have to wait for the main office tomorrow. Let's see how soon they come through. I don't know if Metzger will have his suspect in the time frame, but he'll have him soon."

"Margot Cameron. Let's talk to her."

"She'll shut us down. You heard Lisa."

"She might, but we've got to do it. I know you liked Lisa—I did too basically—but let's give Mrs. Cameron a chance to tell her side. Most sociopaths are charming. I no longer trust my instincts when it comes to people who don't feel guilt. They can't feel it, so we can't sense it in them. As simple as that."

"Is that how it was with the Northwoods Killer?"

She wasn't quite sure how to answer. "I suppose," she said slowly, thinking it out. "We'd questioned him before, but not as a suspect."

"Mrs. Cameron is in Utah. All we can do is talk to her on the phone."

"But who is more likely to remember those kids, especially if she is the one who took care of them?"

"I suppose that's a good point."

"We know one of them wouldn't mind killing him, whether she did or she didn't. Lisa didn't try to hide that."

Santiago said nothing, cars passing them, his eyes on the road even though she was driving.

"I take it back," Ellie said quietly. "It isn't simple at all."

would never make the mistake of underestimating my enemies.

Never.

It was a small war, yes, and I started it, but a war nonetheless, and however ironic it might be, we as human beings do fight for small casualties as much as we do for larger losses.

No one likes to lose.

So I reconnoitered and rethought my strategy.

Just one target left, but I had the feeling opposing forces might be closing in. That was the hum, the murmur, the reverberation.

And honestly, with everything else, I just couldn't let it happen.

I'd prepared for it, of course. I'm not stupid. I don't even believe I am psychotic, even though logic can sometimes be dictated by the creature. That I was ready for the worst didn't translate to me wanting to pursue that course if it was at all possible to avoid it.

It would all be dependent on how thorough they are when it comes to connecting the dots.

Luckily, I would be one of the first to know.

"Come in. Sit down."

Ellie followed the instructions and took a chair in front of Fergusson's desk. Santiago trailed in behind her a little more slowly and almost immediately she understood why.

Lieutenant Fergusson was probably almost sixty, beefy and well dressed, his expression benign but his eyes hard and shrewd. He exuded the aura of a hardnosed cop, and by all accounts, he was one. Being summoned to his office was rarely a sign of good things to come, and Ellie was no stranger to the hierarchy of the inner workings of the police department, especially with Metzger's ultimatum hanging over their heads. The head detective ran the way investigations were assigned and supervised the results. Metzger was probably thrilled to have him back in town, especially with all that was happening. What a week to be on vacation.

Before he could even say anything, she deflected the lecture by saying, "We have a lead."

He exhaled. "That is music to my ears. All right, Detective. I know for sure you've met Chief Metzger, and we'd all like to make him happy. Talk to me. While I was in Michigan visiting my mother-in-law, which wasn't the vacation I'd prefer for your information, apparently all hell broke loose here. I am right now unhappy on all fronts."

His office was plain, smelled like a deli infused with the odor of stale coffee, and she'd heard more than once he was a very good investigator, which was probably why he was the lead detective. He'd been gone before this all started, like just about everyone else in the state as far as she could tell, so he was just getting up to speed.

Ellie nodded. "We have a link and are pursuing it. The young woman—she was barely legal at the time—who was accused of killing Reverend Cameron in a case I am told you will remember. It's similar to the ones we are currently pursuing, and she gave us some interesting information and it undeniably matches. We just got back from questioning her."

"I remember that case. She was arrested, but we couldn't prove it and she walked. Go on."

"She says she didn't do it."

"Exactly as I recall it. And you believe her . . . because?" Fergusson's brows elevated.

"For more than one reason." Ellie squared her shoulders. "Not to be too simplistic, but how the heck could she ever have heaved him on top of that table? He was twice her size. Besides, she admitted she damaged her own defense. She was essentially a kid, so I really don't doubt that part all that much. As the crimes going on now mirror what happened five years ago, I just have to wonder if we don't have a repeat offender."

"That is hardly a lead. It sounds more like you've come to the conclusion that she is innocent, but still have no idea who it might be instead. That just sounds like trouble to me. Grasso?"

"I beg your pardon?"

"He tip you off?"

She might have denied it except she was really tired and Fergusson was asking her a direct question and he was right.

Luckily, she had Santiago. "Lieutenant," her partner said politely enough but with inferred criticism, still standing behind her chair, "if you recognized the similarities in the cases, it might have been nice of you to tip us off yourself. Just thinking."

The lieutenant did not look amused. "I didn't really make a connection until you just pointed it out. Believe it or not, I don't remember the details of every single homicide in this city, and can we focus on how I was gone? Luckily, Grasso helped you with that. I smelled him all over this."

She said calmly, "Lieutenant, we have reason to believe that the same person who might be committing the recent set of burnings could be linked to the homicide he investigated years ago involving Lisa Martin. We hardly have an unimpeachable witness, but she did provide us with a thread we can at least follow. We came back to the station to do that when we heard you wanted to see us. Now, we can hash over it here, or we can go investigate. Which is what I assume you want us to do."

"What thread?"

"Cameron had kids in foster care."

"That's been looked at, I'm sure."

"We're going to look at it again."

"Very diplomatic, MacIntosh."

It probably wasn't prudent to be confrontational with the lead detective in the division, but she could hear a clock ticking in her brain. Luckily, he nodded and dipped his head toward the door, and she was up and out before she heard Santiago make whatever idiotic remark he might offer.

"He's not bad but Metzger owns his ass," her partner said as they walked down the hall.

"Metzger owns all of us," she retorted in staccato tones. "Any idea at all *when* social services is going to get back to us?"

"I'm hoping it has already happened," Santiago said and to her surprise, actually opened the door for her.

Go figure.

Do you want to take a week up north?"

Bryce glanced over. He'd just changed lanes and they were skirting the edge of the lake, the water a little rough, but the breeze was still hot, even off the water, and the sunset was starting to spread in glorious vermillion hues over the water.

"What?"

Ellie settled her shoulders against the seat. He was hardly dressed up but looked nice in a cotton shirt and khaki shorts and though she was aware of how women looked at him, maybe that recent encounter with Suzanne had brought that realization to the surface. She didn't think of herself as insecure, but she was fairly sure there wasn't anyone on the planet that didn't have a few doubts now and then.

"We could stay at my house. It has shown a few times but nothing yet, so I still own it. It will be quiet, remote, away from the city. We can just relax. I'll just tell my real estate agent to not schedule anything during that time."

We could talk.

She wanted to mention they *should* talk. About the relationship. About what he wanted and what she wanted, and perhaps Suzanne's name should be brought up.

It bothered her he hadn't told her yet that he'd seen his ex-wife.

"We could." Bryce changed lanes, his expression not showing very much. "But you are pretty deep in this case. I assume you mean once it's over."

"Just a long weekend. You could fish. We'll take out the canoe."

My father's precious canoe. I don't offer that to everyone.

"The city getting to you?"

She looked at the skyline and wondered how to answer. After a moment of consideration, she shook her head. "No, not really. No place is perfect. I admit the congestion and bustle isn't exactly what I'm used to but that isn't it. I just wouldn't mind getting away for a bit."

"I don't disagree."

She looked back at his profile. Her tone was deliberately light. "It's a date then?"

"Fine . . . Ellie, is it just what's going on or is something else wrong?" He looked puzzled, his hands competent on the wheel, but his gaze shifting over to her.

She lied. "No."

Chapter 21

It wasn't difficult to predict the outcome. It was a dream to imagine the smooth process, uninterrupted and unhindered, but in the end, I knew I'd have to make choices.

The police department was like a slow-moving overweight animal in the zoo. It stirred, it glanced your way, and finally it got up and took notice.

I really did not want that final step in the process. That animal had large pointed teeth that could sever a limb, or even end your life.

The air was hot and smelled like rain, but the predicted storms hadn't happened yet. I slid into the passenger seat, adjusted the belts, made sure it was all secure, and then slipped out.

JULY 11

"We have a positive identification on one of our victims. I thought you should see this right away."

Jason glanced up. "Seriously?"

Dr. Reubens looked positively animated, his good-natured face alight. He set down a sheaf of papers and on the top there was a photograph. "Believe it or not, I am. Dental records. Her name was Elizabeth Blake. Fifty-eight years old. Here's her address, which I don't think is where you found the body and that puzzles me, but that, my friend, is your provenance."

A name and an address. Jason scooped it up and saw the photograph was not of a person, but an X-ray of her teeth. "That's fantastic."

Actually, it was more than a little awful, but still, *fantastic*.

"Well . . . not for her family. Didn't you say that her daughter hadn't been able to get ahold of her and reported her missing?" Reubens slipped his hands into the pockets of his lab coat. "I have to confess I don't envy you that visit."

A sobering thought, but Jason already knew MacIntosh would be better at that than he could ever dream of being, so he'd just stand around looking sympathetic and keep his mouth shut. He was great at talking to people who didn't want to talk to him, but not in that sort of setting. No one would argue he just wasn't the hand-holding type.

"No offense, but there's quite a lot about your job I don't envy either. I meant we have a solid lead and this will only help."

"Sorry I couldn't respond to the scene last night." Reubens looked slightly discomforted. "I was at least an hour north of the city having dinner with a friend. Besides, Dr. Courtney is competent. It would have taken me too long to get there and you all would have been stuck standing around. I called him in and he was free."

"No problem."

"Keep me in the loop." Reubens flashed him a rueful smile. "I guess I'm off to the morgue, where apparently a jigsaw puzzle is waiting. That isn't, by the way, the easiest kind of autopsy. Any sign the corpse was dismembered on scene? I have my deputy's notes, but quite frankly, haven't had a lot of time to read over them. I've been working on identifying Ms. Blake and there is a lot of paperwork that goes along with this many bodies coming in. I did want to deliver it personally."

"We think it was done somewhere else after using luminal to discern if there was a splatter pattern, but forensics can give you better data. As usual, the scene was disturbed by the fire and the water to put it out, but there just wasn't enough blood if you ask me. We didn't find any kind of axe or whatever it is you would use—"

"Bone saw." Reubens nodded sagely. "I haven't yet taken the measurements or started my true examination, but I can already tell you that much. Clean cuts. He had at least some idea of what he was doing when he dismembered her."

"Delightful," Jason muttered. "Your reports are always my favorites. Bone saw? That's just disgusting."

Reubens adjusted his glasses. "I aim to please, or at least to inform, however the information is used. Grasso is going to be helping?"

"Hot damn. News spreads fast around here."

"For whatever it's worth, I like him. Grasso. I don't know him well, but I like him."

Actually, so did he. Like Grasso, that is. Jason drew in a contemplative breath and exhaled. "He's pretty good. I don't mind him so much. The others muscling in on this, I'm not sure of, but I don't get a say in it. DCI is here and will be until we catch our killer. I didn't see the FBI profiler giving me a lot I could use. He made sense, but then again, I'm just not sure I couldn't have come to those conclusions all on my own."

"Montoya, isn't it? I didn't sit in, but there was no reason for me to be there. What did he say?"

Jason had been thinking about it all day—and all night, which made him pathetic, but now that he slept alone, there wasn't a lot to do in the dark except think. "Guy is a loner, but most of them are. He's not really serial, or that is what I got from it, but has an agenda he wants to satisfy, something we don't quite understand. That it might be now or never, because if we don't get him, he might be done."

"I thought that usually that wasn't the pattern." Reubens looked interested in his usual abstract scientific way. "That once they got out of control, they hunted until they were caught."

"Except the ones we never get, the ones who are too fucking weird for us to even guess their next move and who quit killing, and let's not even talk about the really smart ones who just disappear."

"Any idea of what species this one might be?"

"The latter," Jason said and he meant it, getting to his feet. "Thanks for this. MacIntosh needs to hear it, and as I understand it, we'll need to spread it around to everyone at the meeting tomorrow, but you have given us a *name*. We also have an eyewitness that can probably ID him. That's huge."

"Is it? With only a probably? I don't understand. For whatever reason, I thought someone told me they came face-to-face."

"The deputy really didn't get that great a look at him. It takes a pretty cool head to stay just far enough back when you come face-to-face with a police officer during

he commission of both murder and arson. Our suspect
as a cool head."

"Like you said, the murder was probably already
done."

He thought so as well. "Much easier to transport
parts than an entire body."

"Good luck, Detective. Let me know if I can help in
any way."

"Oh, trust me, you'll hear from me."

On a note of levity, Reubens said as he walked away,
"If only I did trust you."

Outside a rumble of thunder lent a stage prop background to the conversation. Unfortunately Ellie wasn't
t her desk. Jason pressed a button on his phone and she
picked up on the second ring. He said, "Where the hell
re you? We have an ID."

"I'm in records . . . No shit? On what?"

"I must be rubbing off on you, and yes. Dr. R came
through. Victim."

There was a short pause, and then answered in a neu-
ral voice, "You aren't rubbing off on me, it's the case.
Tell me what he said."

"You said shit."

"Don't feel you can take credit for it. It is not the first
time the word has crossed my lips. It just doesn't happen every five seconds. Come on, what?"

"Fourth victim. He figured out who she was from the
missing person report you caught as a red flag. Not the
one we talked about, but the other one. We need to go
look into this and question the family, friends, neighbors, you got it."

"Reubens is sure?'

"Of course. This particular medical examiner doesn't

often approach with maybes. You know that, MacIn
tosh. He's sure."

There was a short silence, then she said quietly, "
know he doesn't . . . but a family visit? Oh God. I hat
those."

Went without saying. The most hard-core officer o
the force hated them.

He played an unfair card. "I could do it alone, but—

"Don't." Her voice was crisp and certain. "Pleas
don't. I'll be right there to discuss the details."

The sudden termination of the call didn't surpris
him.

Elizabeth Blake's daughter lived in a very conservative olde
neighborhood, and when they pulled up, DCI was al
ready there in an unmarked car, waiting at the curb. Th
lead of the forensics unit was a familiar face. Ellie ha
met him before. He stepped out with an apologetic cough
"Detective. Fancy seeing you here. I think we met las
up north."

"Hi, Jessup. It's been a few months."

The DCI tech nodded. "Can you get us keys? We nee
to process her house as quickly as possible but we'
wait while you talk to her family. Sorry we got here firs
but we really just arrived a few minutes ago."

That was fast. No doubt the task force at work. Sh
still wasn't entirely sure how to feel about it, but in th
end, God knew they could use the help.

It was a quiet street with huge mature trees, slightly
tilted sidewalks, and someone was mowing his lawr
despite the stifling heat. "I'll get you keys if they hav
them, and permission." She glanced at the house an
squared her shoulders. "This isn't my favorite part o
the job."

Jessup said soberly, "Can't blame you there."

Santiago led the way, both of them climbing the steps to the front porch, and before they could knock, the door was opened by a young woman with a tear-stained face, her mouth trembling. She had long dark hair and wore a maternity top, which made it all worse somehow, though how it could *get* worse was a mystery considering what they had to tell her. "You're the police, right?"

Ellie palmed out her badge. "Yes."

"What's happened to her? Oh God . . ."

"Can we go in so you can sit down?"

The young woman nodded, her hand over her mouth, not quite stifling the sobs.

There were some things a person just didn't have to say out loud. Ellie followed her in, taking her elbow and leading her to a small plaid couch flanked by two end tables with cheerful artificial flowers in pink vases. The floor was littered with toys, and a chubby little boy of about three glanced up curiously, but then went back to playing with a set of small cows and pigs and a miniature barn.

"Mrs. Halston, is there someone you can call?" Ellie asked it softly, fairly sure a child that young wouldn't understand the conversation but surely would not miss out on his mother's distress. "A friend? Your husband?"

"Could you just tell me?" she whispered, nodding, her voice barely audible. "I'll call my aunt, my mother's sister . . . she's so worried too."

"Then maybe someone else," Ellie said quietly. "I don't want to have to tell you this, but your mother has been identified positively as one of the victims in a recent series of homicides that you have probably heard about on the news. I think someone less involved might be better.

Is there a friend who can help you out? I hate to do this now, but we really need to ask you some questions."

Tears spilled over, wetting her cheeks. "I knew something was wrong . . . I knew it. We talk every single day but she hasn't been home, won't answer her phone . . ." The young woman got up and groped her way past the coffee table. "I can't . . . talk right now . . . just give me a minute . . ."

Alarmed, Ellie got to her feet.

"Just need to throw up . . . can you watch him for a second . . . please?" She ran from the room.

"Hey, buddy." Santiago crouched down next to the child, wagged a small cow at him, and opened the door to the barn. A cow mooed in response, and the little boy laughed.

Death and laughter. She might never get used to this job. Cross-legged, her partner played with the little boy with a certain energy that spoke to her that he wasn't indifferent to the situation either.

Fifteen minutes later the husband was home, his arm around his very pale wife. Someone had arrived to take the little boy away, diaper bag and all; a nervous-looking young woman who grabbed up the child, stammered her name, and departed with all due speed. The delay chafed under the circumstances, but Ellie wasn't sure that it was possible to interrupt someone vomiting in the bathroom because her mother had been killed by a serial killer and demand she reschedule the process.

"Tell us what happened." The husband, whose name was John, wore a blue-collar factory shirt with a logo on the pocket, and his curly reddish hair was a riotous mess from the humidity. He was slightly untidy, on the pudgy side, and seemed truly upset. "Is my mother-in-law really dead? We knew something was wrong, but of course, we hoped . . . well, we hoped, that's all."

"She is," Santiago said frankly, obviously more comfortable talking to a male than to a half-hysterical pregnant woman. "And if you've been paying attention to the news, she isn't the first one. We are trying to link the crimes. Did she know any of these people?" He handed over a slip of paper with the names of Reverend Cameron, Robert Jarvis, Helton, the landlord, and they'd specifically added Lisa Martin.

"I don't know who she knew . . . Babe?"

Connie Halston stared at it, but Ellie thought it was possible she didn't really see the names. She scrubbed away tears from her cheek. "I can't really think . . . I don't know."

Ellie had taken a chair opposite the couch and she nodded in reassurance. "That's okay. We just want you to think about it. This case is moving very quickly. Does she have a connection to any of those addresses? Ever live there? Go to school close by? Anything you can come up with might be helpful, even if you can't see how it could possibly matter. And we need a key to your mother's house and permission to search it. There's a crime scene team out front from the Department of Criminal Investigation."

Connie Halston seemed to wilt, her dark head resting on her husband's shoulder. "I don't care. Go ahead. I think I need to go lie down."

John Halston stood, pulling his wife to her feet. "I think you should too." He shot them a look over his shoulder. "I'm sorry. This can't be good for the baby. I'll be right back."

They waited, both of them, and Ellie was aware of the team outside waiting as well. He probably wasn't gone long, but it felt like forever, and when he returned, he handed Santiago a key. "We have a spare in case she locks herself out. Jesus, this can't be happening. What do I have to do to give you permission?"

"We can get a warrant, but that will take time and I don't really think we have it. Anyone else live with your mother-in-law?"

"No. I'm sure you already know this but her house is just a few blocks from here. That's why we chose this neighborhood." He stood there, rumpled and sweating, his face drawn. "I'll sign something if you want . . . or get Connie to sign it. Do you think I should call her doctor?"

This was part of the process Ellie always felt uncomfortable with. Being an authority figure wasn't necessarily a good thing when people looked to you for help and you couldn't give it. "I'm sorry, but I can't advise you one way or the other as a police officer on a nonemergency medical matter, but I will say as a person, if I were you and was worried, I would call her obstetrician."

"Thanks." He blinked and looked away. "I will. You know, this is crazy. My mother-in-law wasn't perfect, no one is, but she was a decent woman. We got along, and Connie and her mother were really close. Connie's dad died when she was little, and Elizabeth really did her best to support them both. This isn't fair. Why would anyone kill her?"

When it came to murder, it really wasn't ever fair. Fate was one thing, deliberate harm another.

"She worked two jobs, and at one time even took in foster kids, to make ends meet." He was no longer trying to keep his emotions in check, his hand shaking as he lifted one to wipe his brow.

It was as if the world stopped and pivoted. Santiago found his voice first. "She what? What the hell did you just say?"

Chapter 22

It was the best of times, it was the worst of times . . .

I'm pretty sure Dickens wasn't talking about murder.

Adversity was universal, though, for all walks of life, including people who occasionally kill other people. I have never really thought of myself as a murderer. It doesn't feel that way for me. I am not sure how to explain it, but murder doesn't quite fit.

At some point they might figure it out, but it hadn't happened yet.

I honestly didn't like this part. If it wasn't necessary . . . but it was. That was the point of it: It was necessary.

But the swamp creature disagrees to the extent that the water is clouded, and the issues aren't cut and dried, and at the end of the day, justice lies in the hands of those who no longer wish to cradle it, dripping and wet and slimy, in the palms of their hands.

I'm not a judge. I'm not a jury either. I don't even like the idea.

Always I have been an observer. I like it that way.

But Cameron had been punishment.

I hated the man, and five years after I killed him, I still hated him. Loathed him, detested he'd ever existed on this planet . . . so I had no regrets. I had made certain he knew exactly who it was also when he went not so quietly into that dark night . . .

And though he hadn't deserved the honor, I'd burned him in effigy.

Metzger was a perfect politician in most ways. Commanding without being too much of an ass, and street savvy, though he never even bothered to act as if he didn't believe he knew what everyone else was thinking.

Usually, he was right.

But not always.

The chief smiled slightly as he came up to his desk. He had a way of doing that, where his mouth hardly changed shape from the usual down curve, but somehow was different. Metzger said, "You owe me, Grasso. I have DCI helping. I have two pretty good detectives and now I am saddled with a sheriff's department thanks to this last one. There are already too many cooks in the kitchen. Promise me I need you on this and talk to me." He raised his hand before Carl could speak. "No, I take that back. *Prove* to me I need you on this one."

Once they'd been friends.

"Fair enough." He sent the chief a level look. "All I wanted was a second chance."

"I can't promise you another crack at homicide. In case you haven't picked up on this, and I do wonder about it sometimes, there are some politics involved in my job."

"I get that." Carl looked him in the eye.

"Do you?" Metzger looked right back, but then again, he was a direct sort of man.

He did, actually. "What are you asking me that you think someone else won't tell you?"

"Is this The Burner? Our original perp at work . . . are you still convinced?" Metzger sighed. "That case five years ago . . . MacIntosh and Santiago might eventually have gotten onto it, but your tip really helped. That's why I put you on the task force. They both are trying hard to prove themselves and catch him, and that is what I want, but we *need* something. I worry you're holding something back that might help this case."

He squared off with his boss, feeling his jaw tighten. "I gave them Lisa Martin."

"You swore at the time she didn't kill Cameron."

"She didn't. I stand by that. Might not be the same person, but I still think it is."

"Then let's catch who did it. The entire city is on edge by now, and I'm not sure it shouldn't be. Quite frankly, I don't want to hear about some old lady being burned to death on a coffee table in Sheboygan tomorrow night. He's moving around, and he's doing all of this with some sort of timetable we don't understand. I'd really like you to help."

"If you remember, I didn't ever want to arrest Lisa Martin."

"If only you hadn't wanted to shoot those two men." Metzger straightened, his expression about as enigmatic as ever. "Prove yourself invaluable so I can once again sell you as a good cop, will you please? I actually don't doubt the investigators on this, but I'm giving you a chance. And for the record, that is about as frank a discussion as we are ever going to have on this topic."

Carl thought the day they'd moved him to vice the

discussion had been pretty frank, brutally so, but why say so when he was being offered the golden key. "Yes, sir. I appreciate the chance."

"We always did understand each other." Metzger nodded and walked off, stopping here and there at someone's desk, sometimes smiling, sometimes serious as hell, ever the chameleon to fit the moment.

He wasn't interested in ever having to play that game. Carl had always thought if he was ever offered the job as chief he would decline, not that anyone would ever think of it with his track record, though at one time he'd contemplated it as a possibility for his future.

But he'd decided even before the shootings that administration wasn't what he wanted.

Not that homicide was all that more prestigious, but it always felt like he'd been custom made for it. He liked to hunt killers and he was good at it.

Otherwise, would he ever have been able to catch up with the two scumbags who beat up an innocent young woman and left her lacerated and bleeding on the floor of a convenience store?

The answer was no, but honestly, though he admired the judicial system of the United States of America, he'd known in his heart the punishment would never fit the crime. Aggravated assault at best. And one of them—the one she'd told him did the most damage when she'd described him from her hospital bed, tubes attached everywhere—didn't have any convictions on his record. A good lawyer would have bargained it down to almost nothing.

No way he could let that go.

No way.

He would do it again.

But that was the past.

At least the impulse to take a different tack in The Burner case had worked. He would have been more than willing to run an investigation on the side, but it was just too big.

Who knew this particular case would snowball so quickly?

He sent Rachel a quick text: *Burner task force is busy and Metzger is pushing me.*

She sent back a one-word response: *Score.*

Might still need your help.

Just ask.

It wasn't as if he was particularly sensitive, but Jason did have trouble when a woman was crying. What was even more weird in his mind was that if a *man* started crying, he was just as done right then and there. It was probably worse, why that was he could not quite figure out. In his book, men did not cry. He hadn't in years, not since he realized his mother wasn't coming back, and that was a damn long time ago.

So when the elderly man next to his desk sobbed, he dragged over a box of tissues and wondered—not for the first time—where MacIntosh might be. This was particularly uncomfortable because he actually wanted to ask some really pertinent questions and usually he just would, but it felt wrong at the moment.

He tried. Well, in his defense, he usually did, but he just came off hard-nosed most of the time. Jason tapped the piece of paper on his desk. "Thank you for this, sir."

"My daughter was a good person."

There was sincerity in that statement or else the wet eyes and runny nose were just for show. He nodded. "That is really what everyone is telling us."

"But he killed her and he *burned* her."

That point was hard to argue. "He did." Jason briefly inclined his head.

"Why?"

The million-dollar question that at this point had about a five-cent answer. "We don't know. We are looking into it."

"That's not that reassuring, if you don't mind me pointing it out. How many victims do you have already?"

"We can only follow the leads we have and do the best we can."

That was probably too damn blunt, but it was true.

His visitor blew his nose. "A long time ago . . . I was a minister. I believed in the goodness of people. I prayed for the wicked just the same as I prayed for the righteous."

If any subject made him itch to leave a room, it was religion. A grieving old man and religion together . . . "Look, Reverend, I sympathize, but—"

"Do you have any children, Detective?"

"No."

Where the hell is Ellie?

"You should. They are the greatest blessing on this earth."

Well crap, the man started to weep again. Not once, even when his mother had walked out the door and never looked back, had he seen his old man cry. In fact, if his recollection was accurate, he'd been told more than once that men did not shed tears for any reason. Even when he broke his collarbone when playing football at the park with a few of his friends when he was about twelve, he had just gritted his teeth, walked home with his one arm cradled in the other, and it had taken two days before his father thought the bruising indicated a grudging trip to the doctor.

"I'm not insensitive to your loss, sir, but maybe you should be with your granddaughter, helping her out. She needs someone to talk to I'm sure as much as you do."

The older man wiped his face and nodded. "You are a very insightful man, Detective Santiago."

"He isn't actually." A female voice interrupted the conversation. "He just pretends to be and he doesn't do that often enough."

He hadn't noticed Ellie had walked up because she stood a little bit back and his desk wasn't exactly in an executive office but more like a crowded space near the coffee machine where people passed by, some hurried, some casual, in the general bustle of the precinct. "This is Detective MacIntosh," he said, getting to his feet. "This is Elizabeth Blake's father."

"I'm so sorry." She held out her hand and her expression was somber as the older man took it. "I know this isn't much comfort for you, but she is the first of our victims we've identified and we really hope it will lead us in the right direction. This will save someone's life. Detective Santiago is right, how's your granddaughter?"

"She's . . . fine. Not emotionally, but if you mean physically, she's fine and the baby is not affected."

"I was worried about her."

Well put, of course. He was starting to see why Metzger had stuck them with each other. It didn't hurt that she looked about seventeen in white pants that cut off just above the ankle and a light blue shirt that showed off toned, slender arms and a light summer tan. The shining blond hair didn't hurt either, or the clear empathy in her eyes.

She did that really well. Actually, Jason believed it worked because it *wasn't* an act. He cared too, but it was different. He wanted vengeance for the victim. She wanted justice for the family. It sounded the same, but it really wasn't. He was concerned about the dead apparently, and she worried about the living.

Maybe the chief had more insight than Jason gave him credit for because Blake's father deflated like a balloon. He even went so far as to raise MacIntosh's hand to his lips in a gallant old-fashioned gesture, and then let her go. "Thank you. Elizabeth would like that. She really would."

"We are all human beings, even police detectives." Ellie's voice held an edge, but she smiled. "I'm a little late I know and it looks like you are getting ready to leave, but would you care to just fill me in? This is what we need to know. Did any of your daughter's foster children ever set off warning bells she told you about? I realize they are all challenging no doubt in some way, but did she complain of anyone specifically that you remember, and did their infractions include arson?"

Good question. Jason sat back down, coming to the conclusion that tears threw off males but females were apparently able to think clearly through the event, and waited for the answer with a great deal of curiosity.

"I don't know . . . surely there are records."

"Yes." MacIntosh sat down and so did the old man. The copy machine in the background whirred and it was an annoyance, but it also provided a sense of anonymity. Ellie leaned forward. "There are records of calls made and reports filed, but there's this funny thing that happens. Can I explain it?"

He nodded, and produced a handkerchief from his suit to wipe his eyes briefly. "Go ahead. I want to help. I wrote down everything I remembered."

Ellie hooked a section of her hair behind her right ear in a smooth feminine movement. "There are things you need to report to social services, but maybe you don't. Sir, let's keep in mind most of the people who take the path of accepting children that are not their own into their homes are kindhearted to begin with, and I think very often, because they are also responsible for these children, some things are not reported."

"Elizabeth wouldn't ever not report something."

"What if it would get one of her kids in trouble?"

That made him clench his handkerchief in his hand and shift in the chair. His reddened eyes briefly closed and then flicked open. "That would bother her," he said slowly. "I believe I understand what you are saying, Detective. Unless it was completely necessary, she wouldn't report bad behavior."

"She never complained about a pyromaniac?"

"She wasn't a foster care provider for long. Three or four years maybe? You probably know better than I do. Like I said, surely there are records and it was a long time ago. Over a decade at least. Maybe longer . . . yes, I'm sure it was longer ago than that. Probably fifteen years. Time goes by so quickly."

"I think I just established there might not be a record if someone was a problem, sir."

He wiped his eyes again and then seemed to ponder before he said slowly, "You know, there was a boy, I think. She talked about him setting fires. I think she finally had him sent away but I don't know if she reported the incidents or not."

Now that sounded like one hell of a clue and they needed it.

Like a tourniquet above a gaping, gushing wound.

"You don't happen to remember his name, do you?" There was a new edge to Ellie's tone.

The very first thing was to find a connection between Cameron and the late Ms. Blake.

Jason had a positive feeling about this . . . if a person could have a good feeling about multiple homicides. He let MacIntosh continue to talk to the old man and picked up his phone.

Chapter 23

Decisions needed to be made occasionally. Actually, often. What to wear. What to eat. Where to go if traffic was thick. How to manage a difficult situation. Trivial and significant. It never let up.

Who to kill and how to kill them.

I had no idea how most people might go about it, but this really wasn't about the kill for me, it was about resolution. I am as important as anyone else on this planet, and like food or water, which everyone rushes to give to the needy, I needed this. Not a difficult concept to understand.

To a certain extent I get that it is a simplistic explanation, but it is one.

I'm as entitled as anyone, aren't I?

I have a whole new appreciation for the art form of profiling. All I wanted was to be done with it. If it was necessary, then getting it over with was like ripping off a bandage and I was eager to heal this wound.

They had evidence. An eyewitness, a link back to me that was solid, and I wasn't sure if what I was about to *do was the correct decision, but like a train with momentum, I didn't want to stop now and try to start the engine again.*

What if it stalled and then I was never free?

So it might sound reckless, but I would go forward and hope for the best. This was the trickiest choice, of course.

But then again, I'd saved the best for last.

"Tell me about Grasso." Ellie was tired, her coffee was cold, and she just wasn't in the mood for more waltzing around the subject.

It did not help when Chief Metzger looked bland. "MacIntosh, you know the story."

Her hands went flat on his cluttered desk and she wouldn't have done it if she wasn't frustrated. "Actually, I don't. I know the whispers and the suppositions, but you know, I have no idea what the real story is, and I am going to tell you right now that while no one around here, even my partner, is about to admit it, they think he leaked the story of me being on this case. I do not mean to be disrespectful, sir, but could you at least do me the courtesy of telling me what exactly happened?"

The chief stared at her for a second and then said, "All right. Fine. Sit down, Detective."

She did, taking a chair in front of his desk. Metzger had a presence when he chose to exercise that muscle.

His office was stylish, and the chair she chose was upholstered in some sort of soft material and actually comfortable. He laughed quietly before he shook his head. "MacIntosh, please take my word that when I hired you, I never thought we'd have another serial here. The odds are against it in about a thousand ways, and that first burning case . . . how would I know it would turn into what it did? Give me that at least."

"I am trying," she said evenly, "to give you exactly what you want. The killer."

"No one wants that more than me."

This could be her job. Ellie took in a breath. "I wonder, sir. Any possibility it could be Grasso?"

That stopped him cold in the act of reaching for the glass on his desk. "What?"

She had not one shred of physical evidence. *Nothing.* Of course not. The killer was too smart. "He wants back on homicide and he knows how to work it. Even the FBI says it could be a law enforcement officer. He has a cold case and so he exactly mimics what happened before and draws himself in."

It was at least a little gratifying that Metzger took a minute to think about it. "Not a bad theory, but not Carl."

"With all due respect, premeditated murder is not new to him."

"Not one person who knows him will believe it."

"That might just be the beauty of it. *Sir.*"

"Detective, you add that last form of address as if you have worked with Santiago for the past few weeks. It has never done him any favors, by the way."

It was getting late, it was sultry outside, and she was tired of attempting to second-guess everyone else. "I'm trying to make sense of it. It is so neatly done that I can't dismiss Agent Montoya's theory, and I'm sorry, but Grasso comes to mind. How did he manage to stay on the force?"

"Because there was no proof that the shootings didn't happen exactly as he recounted it. No witnesses and no other evidence. One of the suspects had discharged his weapon and quite frankly, the only reason there was even an inquiry was that the second man was unarmed.

Considering you yourself have shot a suspect and killed him in the course of doing your duty, Detective, I am sure you understand that once an exchange of gunfire begins keeping a cool head is very difficult.

"Carl kept his job because he successfully apprehended two men who had beaten a young woman working at a convenience store almost to death with a metal shelf, putting her in intensive care for weeks and leaving her disfigured for life. He was reassigned to vice because he killed an unarmed man. Was it vigilante justice? I don't know. He stuck by his story throughout the investigation by internal affairs, and if they were finally satisfied, then I am as well. Does that clear it up for you?"

Evenly, she said, "That part of it, yes, it does. However, because you wanted a suspect, I'd like to put it on the record that Carl Grasso is right now at the top of my list. He is law enforcement, he knew the old murder/arson case inside and out and that has won him a foot inside the door, so to speak, sir, since he's on the task force. He even drives an expensive black car."

Metzger rubbed his chin and then he exhaled audibly. "Look, Ellie, before you toss this suspicion out there, I had better see some sort of evidence. I mean this; don't say a word until you come to me first. Even with the shootings Carl Grasso has a reputation as an excellent police officer, and being accused of something like this damages your reputation even if it proves to not be true."

He had a very valid point. No one knew that more than she did. Look at Bryce, falsely accused with his name splattered across the media, and people still connected him with those murders.

She rose and nodded, leaving Metzger's office with the feeling she'd been swimming underwater for a little

oo long, not quite woozy but getting there, tired but
still charged up.

And speak of the devil. When she rounded the corner,
she saw someone sitting in the chair by her desk, which
was more than a bit of a surprise because Bryce had
never come by the station before, his avoidance natural
because of the very conversation she'd just had with the
chief.

"Hi." He stood the minute he saw her, his smile brief.
"I come bearing gifts. Your text said you'd be late for dinner and not to bother. I thought I might bring it to you."

The man had his faults, but . . . she was starving actually and whatever was in the bag on her desk smelled
delicious.

"I didn't expect you."

He sank back down as she sat. "That would take
away the surprise, wouldn't it? I brought Thai."

"You hate police stations."

"I do. No argument there." He reached for the bag
and opened it. "But for you . . . there's beef and chicken.
Preference?"

"I'll take anything. I'm pretty sure they brought in
some sawdust sandwiches late morning, but I didn't move
fast enough. Men do know how to take care of themselves in the food department. It is definitely first come,
first serve. I was left with a small container of potato
salad, which I gratefully consumed during the briefing."

"It's what you get for being a badass cop."

"I'm not a badass—"

"I meant a very hardworking member of Wisconsin
law enforcement. Now, is there something new?"

He gave her beef, spooning it onto a paper plate, and
it was fabulous, fragrant with garlic and lemongrass
and a hint of heat.

She devoured it with what was probably embarrassing speed. "I had a short meeting with Chief Metzger. There's a task force. Some DCI and Carl Grasso are on it."

"I see. How do you feel about that?"

"He investigated a case a few years ago that was really similar," she explained. "Long story short, the cases aren't exactly the same and we can't figure out why. Bottom line is we are trying to break this quickly."

"Why wait years and then commit five murders in just a few days?"

"That is an interesting question we have actually asked among ourselves."

Bryce regarded her across the desk, fork in hand, his dinner half eaten. "The sarcasm is undeserved. I was just thinking out loud. Does Detective MacIntosh have a theory?"

She loved this about him. He was smart, and he had a rare quality that most people were missing, and that was he actually *listened*. Talking to Bryce allowed *her* to think out loud in some ways, and he was patient about it.

"A small one." She pushed her plate aside and propped her arms on the table, chin on palms. "I really can't take credit for it either, but I am wondering if we are going to find out that maybe both Cameron and Blake had the same foster kid. That's the only link. The timing is exactly right. If Elizabeth Blake had a child in her care who was setting fires and Cameron had him as well, suddenly we have a suspect."

"The others?"

"I don't know . . . the victims really are all older. Maybe they also took in kids at one time. We are waiting on the information to come back because we don't know who they are. The offices are closed and the files will have to be dug out anyway. We are talking fifteen years ago or so at least. It's flimsy anyway, but it is better than nothing. This is predicated on the assumption that Lisa Martin is a part of this and Cameron's murder is linked to the others."

Bryce shook his head, his dark eyes somber. "What would make someone go back and kill people who were kind to them?"

She always had a problem with that one too. And people who killed perfect strangers . . . and hell, people who killed other people in general . . .

And then there was Grasso. But she couldn't say anything.

"I wouldn't," she said moodily. "You wouldn't, but who the hell knows these days. Besides, according to Lisa, Cameron was far from kind."

"She could be stringing you along."

"She could be." Ellie paused. "But you know, I don't think so."

Bryce stood and took her empty plate. "Maybe she's hoping you'll somehow help to get her out of prison if she gives you valuable information. Surely that counts as good behavior."

"I'm not going to argue that one, but keep in mind we went to see *her*, she didn't contact us, and her story hasn't changed. Not to mention that she certainly didn't kill any of these women and burn the bodies. You can't have a better alibi than being locked up in penitentiary at the time of the crime."

And tonight someone else might die because they had no idea who might be next. It was frustrating to think that the information might be out there, but they couldn't get to it until tomorrow because office hours played a part in it all. The archived files they needed were going to take time, and she was worried as hell they didn' have the minutes even now ticking by.

As if he could read her mind, Bryce murmured, "Wha if he isn't done? I know the profiler said it might be over but what if it isn't?"

"If we had the slightest clue who to protect, we would." She had to fight to not sound defensive. "Othe than Cameron, Blake, and the old man who was proba bly just an accidental casualty, we don't have identitie on any of the other victims. It is hard to say for sure, bu it doesn't appear any of them were killed where they were burned, so . . . we're stumped, frankly. The table he brought to the scene himself was sold by a major re tailer with hundreds of outlets. We have someone trying to trace back recent purchases, but unless he used a credi card, and I am going to say he is too smart for that, i won't really help us probably. Forensics doesn't think the table was really all that new. Traces of food stains o something . . . he probably just brought it from home."

"That's interesting." His dark eyes reflected inne contemplation. "I wonder what the table symbolizes. don't think it takes an expert to figure out the table is intrinsic in all of this. An altar? Cameron was a minister right? So was Blake's father. Does that mean anything?"

"Could be." Ellie took an idle sip of water from the bottle on her desk. "I'm less of a psychologist than you but that's occurred to me too. At least you have the desire to create characters and get into their heads. I really don' want to know what other people are thinking. Scare me half to death most of the time. I want to catch them if they do bad things. Understand them? Not so much."

It was true.

"Let's change the subject," she suggested, the case

weighing on her—heavily—and she needed some distance. "What did *you* do today?"

It was actually a pretty innocent question. She just didn't want to talk about the case at the moment. She was stymied, they all were, and for about five minutes at least she just wanted to sit and talk about something else.

He considered his bottle of iced tea like he'd never seen one before but then lifted his gaze. "This is really strange, but Suzanne stopped by."

Okay, she wanted to talk about something besides the investigation, but not *this*.

She merely said, "Really?"

His smile was ironic. "Really. When I saw who it was, I admit I was . . . well, I don't know what I was. Cautious, maybe. She does nothing without an aggressive purpose. I was wary enough when she called me out of the blue last week, but she claimed she had stumbled across some pictures she thought I might want, so I agreed to stop by the loft to pick them up."

Ellie took in a breath. This was not a particularly good time for her personal world and her professional world to both take an unexpected turn, but at least he wasn't keeping it from her and *he'd* been the one to bring it up. "The pictures I understand, but today? What did she want?"

"She didn't tell you?" He set his elbows on the desk and looked her in the eyes. "I understand you ran into each other recently."

Well, hell. Of course Suzanne would play that card. It made it look like she was the one who had practiced duplicity. "In my defense, I really haven't had the time yet to talk to you about it."

He sat back, seemingly relaxed in his chair, but he wasn't. She recognized that singular body language that meant he was tense. "I wish you'd told me."

"I wish I'd had the opportunity, but someone is out there murdering people."

Then he said it. Starkly. Without any preamble. "She wants a baby."

Ellie could suddenly hear the ticking of the clock on the wall, the hum of the air conditioner, even, somehow, her own heart beating. She finally managed, "Excuse me?"

She'd sensed something off in the way Suzanne had acted, but then again, she didn't know the woman very well.

"I know, strange, right?" He looked away, toward the window on the other side of the room. "We were married for five years and I was the one pushing for kids and now . . . *now,* she's on board with it."

It took some effort to modulate her tone but she said calmly enough, "You are divorced."

"We certainly are."

"Do you regret it?"

"No."

That was at least a relief. No equivocation there. Ellie relaxed a fraction but her shoulders still ached and probably would until this case was over. "Then what the hell?"

Oh, good grief, now she sounded like Santiago. Again.

"She's suddenly developed a maternal instinct, I guess. She's thirty-five, she told me, and she started to think about it. Realized she was getting older and she isn't anxious to get married again."

"So she thought of *you*?"

"Please don't ask me to explain what she might be thinking. No one is more surprised than I am."

In retrospect, the recent encounter and Suzanne's attitude seemed to make sense. And she wondered if the air-conditioning wasn't working because she was suddenly clammy and hot. "Oh, I see, with you as the father? Bryce, she's a manipulative bitch."

Hopefully her voice hadn't risen to the point where someone else heard it.

"Do you think after our acrimonious divorce I'm going to agree?"

For some reason, his reasonable tone irritated her. "I don't know. Why did you even talk to her about it? Let me guess, she'd like you to donate sperm the old-fashioned way? I really can't believe this. What did you say?"

"Ellie," he said with a quiet emphasis and a small curve of his lips. "What, in your capacity as a detective who makes a living analyzing other people and their possible motivations and actions, do you think I would say?"

It stopped her.

This felt a little bit like a defining moment, and she was not sure she was in the mood to deal with it.

Not now, for God's sake.

On the other hand, this was his life. Maybe *their* life.

She stared at her hands splayed on the blotter and contemplated the answer without apology. Then she said, "I think you would tell her to know you better than to think you'd father a child with someone that you did not have a serious relationship with any longer, and that your desire for children was based on a family ideal, not just a desire to procreate."

Bryce rarely spoke before he thought it over, and she couldn't decide if she liked that habit, or if it intimidated her in some way. After a moment, he didn't precisely smile, but it was there in his eyes. "Thank you. Maybe we aren't that wonderful about expressing our feelings, but it is possible we do understand each other more than we think we do."

He just could have a point.

Still, she was angry. Not with him, but *for* him, and for herself too. "She just wanted the dad from MIT. Good genes and good looks. How calculating."

He laughed then, open amusement in his eyes. "Am I allowed to be flattered?"

"By what? The invitation or my comment?"

"I don't actually care much what Suzanne thinks. She forfeited that a long time ago."

True enough. But still there was something in his expression . . .

He said carefully, "But I *do* care what you think. This is something we've never discussed."

"What?" She was hedging, and he knew it from his demeanor, so she immediately interjected. "Children? I get it, sorry. I suppose I just don't know."

In the midst of life, we are in death . . .

The quote just floated into her mind, unbidden, but death was much more her provenance. He didn't want to have a baby with Suzanne and she was relieved on an enlightening level, but they weren't to that point where this was actually a viable discussion, were they?

Or maybe they were.

God, she knew he was serious. Was she? Yes, she was, but she didn't know—

Her phone rang and she snatched it up off the table, grateful for the interruption. "MacIntosh."

She listened for a minute or so, and then said, "I'll be right there. Give me about five seconds."

Chapter 24

The house was dark, quiet, the street wide as I remember it, the driveway cracked in that one certain spot that if you hit it just right with your skateboard it would stop dead and spill you on your face.

I have a scar to this day right above my eyebrow on the right side. I remember it clearly. Hitting the pavement, the pain, the blood . . .

It gave me pause.

I never paused.

They were looking for me, of course. They would be. I expected no less.

A certain voice whispered in my head that they should be looking for the creature, but I wasn't sure he and I were the same. We'd been together a long time, but that didn't mean we were blood brothers, joined irrevocably. I was, in fact, trying to be rid of him. To let him sink into the mire of the past and drown, the murky water filling his gasping lungs until he could no longer fight it and drift to the filthy bottom, landing there and rotting away in lonely obscurity.

What I admired was closure. Everything sewn up nea
and tidy, the past addressed, the future certainly not as
sured—no one could say that ever, but the plan execute
with precision.

Resolved? No.

The minute you think that, then a nightmare coul
walk in through your front door.

It might even be me.

She was exactly what they needed.

Jason felt the first real flicker of excitement that maybe
just maybe, this case was under control.

Well, that might be going too far.

"It is terribly hot out there." His visitor dabbed at he
face with a handkerchief. "Actually, it's really only be
cause of the weather I've been watching the news." Mrs
Hamilton was probably in her late sixties, composed
attractive even despite the age lines, her gray hair neatl
done in what he termed a housewife style, the bob brush
ing her lower jaw, her expression earnest. She wor
pants that ended at midcalf and a brown blouse, an
she carried a briefcase, which she pulled onto her la
and unzipped. Out of it she took a sheaf of papers. "
can't promise I am correct about this, but I made a fev
notes for you."

"Our job is to find out if you are correct or not. Don
worry about that, ma'am."

She nodded as if he'd said the right thing and se
down her offering. "I realize a court order is probabl
required for this information, but I'm retired now, s
what can they do if they find out? Fire me? Too late fo
that. It won't be admissible in court, but it might poin
you in the right direction. I'd appreciate it if my nam

didn't get mentioned, but if you must, then I suppose you must. I'm just an average citizen now with a tip that might or might not prove valuable."

"We always try to keep sources as confidential as possible." That was about the most he could promise until he understood exactly what she was offering.

"And I just walked through the doors of the police station to meet with you. I understand, but I get a sense of urgency from the news reports that really influenced me to do this."

"We appreciate it," he affirmed. He set the papers aside on a stack that seemed to grow ever taller and he couldn't quite get through, no matter how hard he tried. "I'll read these, and my partner will be here as soon as she can, but if you wouldn't mind going over what we spoke about on the phone, I would really appreciate it."

She inclined her head briefly, obviously not unfamiliar with the police. "I wouldn't have called if I wasn't willing to discuss it. Not the most pleasant topic ever, but if I can help, I will."

"The kid's name is Randy McNeely?" There was someone right now running him down with every method of intelligence they had at their fingertips, but Jason wanted to know he had it all exactly right.

"He's hardly a kid now. He must be in his thirties, but yes." She pointed at the top sheet she'd given him. "This is a record of when he was first placed, at least as handled by me in this city. Prior to that he lived with his grandmother until she died of a heart attack. He found her dead one afternoon after school and at that point, he was truly orphaned. That's when he was passed over to me."

Fine. Yeah, that sucked, but it didn't send most people

off to burn bodies in a series of places that at this time had no connection. If McNeely was it, he needed to *understand*.

"What happened to his parents?" He'd sift through all the paperwork later, but for now, a witness who seemed legitimate was like gold and she'd bothered to come in and was willing to talk. "What made you think of him?"

Lucy Hamilton looked at him in resigned acknowledgment that he understood to mean she didn't really want to be there. "His parents had a farm about fifty miles from here. They died in a house fire. His mother had climbed up on the kitchen table, trying to get out the window, but the smoke was too much and she didn't make it. Randy was already known for causing small problems . . . field fires, insignificant things . . . it could have been an accident; no one was sure, but there was speculation. He was just a child and the local fire department didn't think the fire was set, but most of them were just volunteers, so it could be they missed it. No signs of arson were reported. Could just be a coincidence."

"But you don't think so."

"I don't know."

Motherfucker, where is MacIntosh—

"I'm sorry." Ellie interrupted his train of thought at just the right moment as she hurried over and yanked a chair from another desk. It was already fairly late, and although the station was never deserted, it was emptier now than during the bustle of the day. She sat down and extended her hand. "I'm Detective MacIntosh. I am not sure you realize how much we appreciate you coming in."

"We have a connection between the fires and the table," Jason told her grimly. He briefly explained and Ellie listened with her fine brows drawn slightly together.

"Do these notes list all the addresses and names of where he was placed?"

"Addresses, no." Ms. Hamilton shook her head. "Good heavens, I couldn't possibly remember. I had a lot of children to supervise while I was his caseworker. Keep in mind I first encountered him many years ago. By the time he was sixteen he was out of my hands and that was over fifteen years ago."

"It's interesting that you remembered about his mother."

"Not really." The former social worker tilted her head to the side and her eyes were bleak and distant suddenly, as if she were casting back. She said slowly, "Randy was memorable. Extremely bright academically, not prone to get into trouble, but very much a loner, and he had some interests that alarmed several of his foster parents to the point where they requested he be moved. Very quickly he figured that out, and though I've no doubt he held on to his little hobbies, he knew how to conceal them much better. Like I said, he was a clever child."

"One of his hobbies being setting fires?" Ellie's voice was sharp with interest and a hint of the excitement Jason was feeling as well.

"Yes."

"I'm afraid to ask what the others were."

"I can only go by what one of his unsuccessful placements told me, but he apparently was caught attending the funeral of someone he didn't know. At the time he was still fairly young and the funeral director noticed he seemed to be there alone and called the school, which was nearby. He was truant and the description fit, so they called his caregivers. His explanation was that the picture of the lady in the paper reminded him of his grandmother."

"That's not exactly a hobby." It wasn't a secret that Jason had a bit of a rough past himself, and skipping school had once been one of his favorite pastimes.

"Well, not if you only do it once, Detective." Her smile held no humor, and behind her spectacles, her eyes were grave. "He was caught again, a couple of months later, this time the deceased being a male, and as this was a different funeral home, the director didn't know about the first incident and admitted he'd seen him in the mortuary before and thought it was odd. Needless to say, the people fostering him then refused to keep him. They had children of their own and it bothered them enough to request a transfer."

"That's a little creepy, but he wouldn't be the first kid with a fascination with seeing a dead body." Jason restlessly crossed his ankles and then uncrossed them as he pondered what she was telling them.

It was Ellie who pointed out, "Yeah, creepy maybe once, but not multiple times . . . that's strange. Couple it with his parents dying in a fire and especially that his mother was found on the kitchen table and he's definitely worth looking at." She turned back to Mrs. Hamilton. "Any advice on how we can find him?"

"I'm afraid not, Detective MacIntosh. If you had any idea how many children have come through my office, not to mention the time passed, it is just impossible to keep track of them all. Last I knew he was with a family in Greendale. But once again, that was probably fifteen years ago."

Well, shit, that sounded familiar. Ellie met Jason's eyes. "Greendale? Interesting."

He said, "I agree."

"It might be, but I can't say. When you are involved in social work, you do get a sense of which of the children are just surly and rebellious so they cause trouble, and which ones might be actually dangerous. It seems that you don't ever forget them entirely."

"Maybe you should have been a detective."

"I think I was much better at my calling than I would be at yours." Ms. Hamilton stood, holding her purse primly in front of her. "I can't decide if I hope I am right or wrong. And there is actually one more thing that might or might not be related."

"We are all ears."

"When Randy was in high school, a girl in his class disappeared. She never has been found to my knowledge. At the time, when I realized . . ." She stopped and then shrugged her thin shoulders. "I don't know what I thought, but I think you can probably guess. I wasn't the only one either. One of his teachers called me and asked if I thought it was possible Randy had anything to do with her being missing. There had been some sort of incident in class. I remember how much it bothered me then and it still does or I would not be here."

"Was he questioned by the police?"

She shook her head. "I don't think so. He was actually a charming boy in many ways, so I somehow felt guilty that his name even occurred to me."

And yet it did.

"By any chance do you ever remember him being placed with a family named Cameron?"

"I don't know." Mrs. Hamilton frowned. "Perhaps. Was he a minister?"

Jason felt a small thrill shoot through him. *Bingo.*

Ellie stood and had her phone out of her pocket, her

features set into determined lines. "I assume Detective Santiago has your number if we think of anything else, but before you go . . . do you have a friend or a relative you could spend the night with this evening?"

The street was lamp lit by mercury lights that went on automatically after dark. It smelled of hot asphalt, and every house in the neighborhood had windows open or air-conditioning units humming. Heat lightning flared out over the lake, but for the past week, any distant flash had been a false promise, so she ignored it.

Ellie said as they sped along, "You need a less conspicuous car."

"What do you prefer? Should we send a patrol car? That would make him nervous. This way, McNeely, if it is him, if he really might hit his old social worker, will just think I am a guy taking a cruise with a pretty blonde. Besides, I was just working late. I didn't expect a stakeout."

She ignored the compliment. Santiago was rarely diplomatic, so she had to wonder just what he was up to. "Doing what?"

"The Cameron case."

"We should have asked Hamilton if she was Lisa Martin's social worker—"

"She wasn't." He took a corner too fast but then slowed down. "I was reading it again when Hamilton called me. It's not in Grasso's case file."

"Grasso, yes, let's talk about him. Did he ever make the foster child connection?"

"There was no other murder he knew of at the time. And he's meeting us there, so you can ask him what connections he made."

Fair enough. They wouldn't have any more evidence

either without the helpful Mrs. Hamilton. Grasso already had said he didn't think it was necessarily Lisa Martin in the Cameron murder.

"To not have another homicide this evening, the tooth fairy could be part of the stakeout. I'll take all the help we can get," she muttered. "Not that I doubt he's good, but I don't know him and therefore I don't trust him."

Santiago drove in a careless macho way with one wrist propped on the steering wheel and it would have made her crazy, but she actually thought it wasn't an affectation. "I'm fairly sure he feels the same way about you. And look at it this way: All three of us have something to prove here."

"How so?" Lightning flashed again over the black ripples of the water, but at least the streets were fairly quiet now that it was dark.

"You're new, the hotshot. Maybe you can kick ass in a county of twenty-some thousand people, but how will you do as a detective in a city of over a million? As for me, I've been around awhile, made some mistakes, and obviously Metzger is testing me. Grasso wants back on homicide. If we break this one, everyone wins."

"We've no idea if this lead means anything."

"Sheer luck. The media can be useful now and again, though they usually just annoy the shit out of me."

He was right, that was true, but the exposure could be helpful at times. She settled back as they turned a corner. The Mustang actually had comfortable seats for a sports car, and an old one at that. "I feel like we need to connect the dots somehow. Every case is that way, but we should be able to get ahold on this one better. We have an eyewitness, a description of his car, a profile, and we might even know his name now. That's one hell of a lot of opportunity to make progress."

"He's moving fast on purpose," her partner observed in a contemplative drawl. "He's pushing it, knowing we've got all these reports to file and lab results to wait on. The medical examiner's office is backed up, and Reubens is a stickler for not giving an opinion off the cuff. So we wait. This guy isn't just a step ahead; he's a mile ahead of us. He understands how to destroy evidence by letting the fire department handle that for him, and unless you are on our side of the equation, it's actually pretty brilliant."

It was. Unfortunately.

Grasso? It still could be him, but she wasn't about to disregard Metzger's advice for several reasons. There was a flat-out chance she was wrong, for one, and Santiago was way too outspoken.

But she sensed it was unraveling, and all they needed was a stray bit of yarn to tug on to pull it apart. They might already have it if they could get their hands on the right information. "What do you think about Montoya's suggestion he could be law enforcement?"

"I think that would really piss me off and that nothing scares me more. It could be just someone associated with the police, someone who can get information on the side because they are good friends with an officer with a big mouth." He added, "Or live with one maybe."

She caught the inference.

Ellie turned her head and stared at him. "I hope to hell you are not talking about Bryce. Not only was he cleared when we caught the Northwoods Killer, but the crimes are entirely different. I already told you, he wasn't even ever arrested."

"Yeah, but you shot the suspect before all the crimes could be directly linked to him. Wasn't the first one different? I remember reading that."

"You're joking, right?" Ellie muttered, but to her dismay, a small flicker of suspicion caught flame, and then she quickly put it out. Bryce was intelligent enough to change the MO, but she *knew* him. Of course, it seemed like the wives and girlfriends were always the most shocked, and yes, the first disappearance in that former case could have been unrelated to the rest. Besides, they'd never recovered that first body . . .

Still, no way. It made her feel guilty she'd considered it even for a second.

Would she always be a cop? Probably. Always be this way? Maybe. But first she was a woman and the insinuation really ticked her off. "Look, Detective Santiago," she said with heavy sarcastic emphasis, "Bryce was only a suspect because of being in the wrong place at the wrong time. And for your information, he helped us immeasurably in solving the case, not to mention saved the life of the last intended victim. Besides, he was never in foster care. I've met his parents many times."

"We haven't established yet if that slant is relevant or not."

And she had no idea what to say in rebuttal because that was absolutely true. Instead she said coldly in an echo of Metzger's admonition, "If there is so much as a mention of his name in connection with the cases we are working now, you'd better be able to produce irrefutable proof to go along with it. This isn't a witch hunt, it's an investigation. He's been through it once before and I can tell you unequivocally that not only did he not enjoy the experience, but I'll go straight to Metzger and lodge a complaint."

"Oh Jesus, MacIntosh, relax. I was just jerking you around." He laughed.

She muttered, "Jerk being the operative word in that sentence."

Grasso had arranged to meet them in the parking lot of a small convenience store several blocks from Lucy Hamilton's house for the impromptu stakeout. When they pulled in, he was out of his sleek, dark car, leaning on the fender and drinking a fountain soda, wearing jeans and a polo shirt, both worn but probably expensive, his hair damp at the temples.

Would the woman be safe with him as surveillance? Probably, because he would have mud all over his face if anything happened to her. She would be safer than if he wasn't assigned. Ellie was sure enough of that to allow him the detail because he would be called out on it if something went wrong. She was sure he was smart enough to know when he could touch someone and when it would be the worst idea on the face of the earth.

Ellie waved like he was someone she knew but didn't expect to see, and turned to Santiago. "Go on into the store and get us both something with caffeine. I'll walk over like we are old friends who just ran into each other, and fill Grasso in as fast as possible. Then we can figure out how we want to handle watching the house."

"Yes, boss," he said with his usual flippant intonation and slid out of the car.

Chapter 25

When I realized where she was going, my heart had frozen somewhere in my chest. Locked in ice, the moment blending into a long, oblique ellipse in time where the world ceased to move around me and everything went very still.

She went into the police station.

Why?

That evoked images of two detectives I know very well are both clever and diligent, catching wind of a possible suspect.

They wouldn't know it was me, of course, unless they started digging, which they would, so it was still possible they would find it—find me. I am a student of research, a taker of information, and I understood how important it is to study.

To plan.

Catch the creature. Capture it. Put it away. I'd been trying for years and hadn't quite succeeded, but ironically, they wanted what I wanted.

We had different methods, of course. I preferred mine.

It could become arcane at any moment, dated, obsolete. But all along I knew that being able to think on your feet was the key to success. That was how I made it through high school despite a slip here and there, and on to college. I was the monster, but it wasn't entirely me either.

At the moment, I needed to make some very intense decisions.

Life-altering.

Death-altering.

I had to wonder, if asked, which most people would consider was the most important. Admittedly little intellectual puzzles interest me.

I wonder what my quarry would say, if I asked her.

Maybe I would.

But not tonight.

JULY 12

By 10 A.M. the next day there were no results.

Carl was hardly new to the process.

They hadn't made any friends by taking the initiative on Lucy Hamilton, and though they had called and eventually informed everyone else on the team what might happen, nothing did.

A good and a bad thing.

The bad part was he spent part of his night in his car, hunkered down in the seat, no light, and no entertainment besides his cell phone, which he barely switched on. A guy from DCI relieved him at dawn, good-natured and bringing coffee, which was probably the last thing he needed since he was going home to sleep for a few hours before the briefing at eleven.

The good part was he was on the job. Just being on the task force would look good.

Even if they never caught The Burner, Metzger was easing him back in the direction he wanted to go.

He went home, managed to grab an hour or two of sleep before he jumped into the shower and headed back to the precinct.

The conference room always smelled like stale coffee and sweat, some of it his. He'd been called in there when internal affairs had investigated the shootings and he wasn't ashamed to admit he had been nervous. He had never admitted he was wrong, but yes, he'd been on edge. Not the most pleasant memory. The collar of his white shirt had felt like a noose around his neck.

Still, he voted it worth it.

"No approach to the house," he said succinctly as his contribution to the conversation. "And no activity in the neighborhood."

"No fire," MacIntosh added. "Which might mean he made us, but it also might have saved Mrs. Hamilton's life."

"Social services is overloaded in the first place, it was a holiday weekend when this started and a lot of employees took this as a good vacation week, and what you want is from a long time ago." Metzger sounded as frustrated as they were and his ruddy face was tired. "Look, we were able to dig up a high school photo of McNeely thanks to a cooperative secretary and a diligent librarian. I had an officer drive it down to Greendale to the deputy who saw him point blank and the guy couldn't say anything conclusive."

"You still look the same as you did in high school, Chief?" Santiago asked, this time not being a smartass in Carl's opinion, but making a point. Metzger had started losing his hair sometime in his thirties probably, and when he'd first met him he'd been a big guy but fit, all muscle, but now he'd gone to fat a little, probably from sitting behind a desk so much.

Carl smothered a laugh and drank some more bad coffee.

Santiago went on, "I've never thought this eyewitness thing was gold. I know, I know, he saw the guy." He spread his hands. "But hell, through a screen and he wasn't really paying attention the minute he thought he was just talking to a frustrated father. That deputy had only answered about five calls just on his own before that one. No aspersions cast on anyone, but I doubt that is a high-volume department down there. He wasn't expecting to come face-to-face with a murderer and the general description he gave us could fit a lot of people. Hell, it could be me."

"Aspersions? Have you been taking vocabulary classes? Anyway, I think," Metzger said, holding his coffee cup so tightly his knuckles might have turned white, "we could currently be the highest volume department here in Milwaukee for homicides in a single week in the history of this state. Somebody better talk to me."

MacIntosh, in a pencil slim black skirt and a short-sleeved white blouse with just a hint of lace at the neckline, somehow managed to look cool, even though the air-conditioning really wasn't keeping up. She said slowly, as if she was thinking it out, "We've speculated about his link to law enforcement. Maybe he knew somehow we were watching her house."

"Hells bells, Detective, you didn't even tell *me*."

She refused apparently to even look apologetic. "We

have no idea now, and had no idea then, if any of the information Mrs. Hamilton delivered was relevant, sir."

"I don't mind if you take chances in your investigations, Detective, but keep me up to speed if—and heaven forbid—we ever have another one like it. That stands, understand?"

"Yes, sir."

He turned and Carl knew he'd be the recipient of that cold, analytical gaze and he was absolutely right and ready for it. "Look, I put you on this for a purpose, Grasso. I want speed, and I want answers."

"And you will have them, but last night he'd didn't cooperate," he said in what he thought was a reasonable tone. "I'm with both Santiago and MacIntosh. If I had to call it, Hamilton might have been next. How could we risk it?"

At least Metzger was reasonable despite the heat— and not just outside. On his terms, but that wasn't new. "You *couldn't* risk it. I'm not saying that . . . this is complicated, and truthfully, I hate complicated." He got up heavily from the table and leveled a look at all three of them individually. "Here's the simple part. Solve the case and Santiago won't get fired, MacIntosh will prove I hired a fairly unknown officer to handle this and vindicate that decision, not to mention your past with the department, Carl. I need all three of you to come through."

That was honest and brutal. Carl was hardly the lead detective, so he got the point. "No one wants to get him more than us."

"Then *get* him. Please, talk about it, and go ahead and talk about me, once I'm gone." The room was dead quiet. "I don't care if you like me or you don't . . . that's hardly new to law enforcement. All I'm asking for is an arrest. Not so much, considering you *are* detectives. I'd really like to have the assurance I chose wisely when I assigned a case of this magnitude."

"You'll have that arrest." Carl picked up his coffee cup. "I'll walk through broken glass to see it happen and, I suspect, so will they."

"Broken glass is nothing for you." Metzger swept up the reports with a beefy hand, ready to leave the room. "I couldn't care less about your dainty bleeding feet. Do something to impress me."

They all stood. "Yes, sir."

Impress the boss.

Easier said than done.

Jason could feel The Burner out there vibrating, waiting, on the edge of the abyss.

This was what he was good at. He knew the signs. Fuck yes, he should. He'd been there a time or two himself and those signs meant a thousand smoke rings rising. Visible but not necessarily readable.

Interpretation was everything.

He was missing a vital clue.

What the hell was it?

The law enforcement angle? He wasn't a believer, but that meant nothing. Could be, and like he'd told MacIntosh, it might just be someone who was privy to the information, which actually was a long list. Besides the detectives, there were clerks and the previous investigators, not to mention administration. There always were leaks because people were involved and some really could not keep their mouths shut.

"Shit," he muttered, sitting back in his chair. Around

him people were eating, chatting, laughing; the bar was noisy at lunch, which oddly enough always helped him think.

He didn't really believe Ellie's boyfriend, Dr. Grantham, was a real suspect, but at this point, he didn't trust anyone, which wasn't new in his life.

Kate could vouch for that, and would try and analyze it in the bargain. Too bad she'd walked out just as he was getting interesting.

Grantham was on his list though. He'd been suspect number one when the Lincoln County disappearances were going on and lo and behold, he comes back to Milwaukee and seven months later they have another serial on their hands. The guy was smart too, with a Ph.D. from Marquette and an undergrad degree from MIT. Self-employed, which gave him a great deal of autonomy, and he had access to Ellie MacIntosh.

"Another beer?"

Jason glanced up at the waitress. "No thanks."

"Anything else?" She picked up his empty plate and smiled at him in a way he recognized. She was pretty cute too, brunette, a little plump, but he didn't really mind that, with nice tits, and she had amazing skin, clear and pale. He wasn't much for sun-worshippers and that worked in Wisconsin, because there wasn't a hell of a lot of sun for a good deal of the year except this scorching summer.

If it wasn't for the case, he might even have flirted a little, but he was too preoccupied to be smooth, and for that matter, he wasn't good at smooth anyway. He said, "I'm fine. It was great."

No lie there, it had been a big cholesterol fest of the classic fish and chips, deep fried all the way, cod and potatoes, and he'd drenched the former in tartar sauce and the latter in ketchup. In a few years he'd have to start to eat a little better, but for now, he'd been famished and it had tasted damned good. He'd even devoured the coleslaw and it wasn't his favorite dish, but toss mayo into something, and he was on board.

"Then here you go." She handed him a slip of paper and walked away. She also had a pretty nice ass. . . .

The television hanging in the corner of the bar switched to the news and a familiar name jerked his attention upward.

The killer known as The Burner struck again the other evening in Greendale, Wisconsin, a town close to Milwaukee, bringing the death toll to five and perhaps six, if a five-year-old case can be linked to this new series of murders and arson . . .

National news. Oh, great. Metzger was probably flipping shit, and actually, Jason couldn't blame him. And who the hell was tipping the press about the Cameron murder? That hadn't been released yet on an official level, as far as he knew, because they still weren't sure about the relevance.

He glanced at the tab, put about twenty bucks too much on the counter, and left with the receipt in his pocket. The pretty waitress had written her phone number at the top and maybe later, maybe when they were done with this, he might just call her.

For now, though, he called his partner.

"See that?"

Ellie said, "You and I aren't in the same place, can you be more specific?"

"On one of the major networks there was a news story about our case and they mentioned Cameron."

She muttered something he was fairly certain he said

on a too regular basis, or so he'd been told, and even been told by her.

"He's going to go again tonight." He slid into the driver's seat, but didn't start his car. The engine was too loud for talking on the phone.

"What makes you think so?"

"I'm not much for the profiling crap, but I believe Montoya about that. There's an urgency going here, and though maybe he figured out we were watching Hamilton's last night, I still think our asshole has something to finish."

"Or he's done. We need to figure out how *he* figured it out if you're right. There's our link."

"He's not done."

"How do you know that?"

"I just do." He started the car, the engine revving up. "I'll meet you at the station."

Barely audible, her response came through. "I'm already here."

Santiago walked over to her desk and sat down in one of the chairs. She caught the vague hint of alcohol and fried food, and tried to ignore that she'd eschewed lunch completely and instead eaten a small package of pretzels. He looked a little disheveled, but for whatever reason, attractive men seemed to be able to get away with that. She said, "Hamilton has been busy. Maybe if Metzger decides we are worthless, he can hire her."

Her partner didn't look all that amused. "I'm the one he wants to fire. Busy how so?"

"Actually, he doesn't want to fire you. He's trying hard not to do just that." Ellie shoved a piece of paper across the desk. "Look at this."

He picked it up and read it, then ran his fingers along his jaw and read it a second time. "Son of a bitch. Mc-Neely was adopted at some point?"

She nodded. "After we told her last night to find another place to stay, she said she didn't have much to do but think about him, remembered the name of the caseworker who inherited him from her, found the woman on the Internet, and called her up."

"So he changed his name."

"Sure looks like it."

"Mother pussbuckets."

She laughed. "What did you just say?"

He didn't even respond to the derision in her tone. Instead he tossed the note back onto her desk and blew out a breath. "No wonder we can't find this guy. He's a ghost."

"Not entirely. Hamilton only called me five minutes ago. I've got them searching adoption records now, but she wasn't certain of the year, it'll take a little bit, but we'll find his name anyway, and hopefully, find *him*."

"Before he decides that he needs to kill someone and set another house on fire?"

Her stomach tightened. "I can't promise that and you can't promise that either. I want to arrest someone so much I'm sitting *here*, when I could be doing other things, like drinking a nice glass of white wine overlooking the pool."

"Or doing something else, like Grantham."

"You know." Ellie put her elbows on the desk, her smile not in the least an indication of amusement. "At moments like this, I really resent I was assigned to you as a partner. Keep the cracks about my personal life to yourself."

"There will be more moments just like it, sorry." Unapologetic, he gazed at the wall, his face taut. "We really need this name . . . man, we *really* need it. He's going to do something tonight."

Unfortunately, she was starting to trust his instincts. "Mrs. Hamilton is going home but Grasso is surveillance."

"We need another team. Let's let DCI cover this. I'm not sure he's after her."

"Who *is* he after then?"

"I don't know."

That was a mutual problem, she wasn't sure either, though she wasn't sure she wanted to have anything in common with Jason Santiago.

At this point, no choice.

"We could hear any minute."

"But should we really sit around and wait for that call?"

She didn't disagree. "Where would we go?"

"I kind of have a lead."

"Oh, *kind of*? My favorite. Nothing solid then?"

"I'd point out you haven't come up with anything brilliant either, but I think that would be redundant."

"Redundant? The chief is right, you have been taking vocabulary lessons. Just tell me. I'm not in the mood for show-and-tell."

She was tired, no doubt, with lines of fatigue in her face reflected in the mirror the last time she'd gone to the bathroom, and she could feel the tension in her shoulders.

Jason leveled a sardonic look at her. "Don't be a—"

"Don't say it." She replied in staccato tones that must have gotten through because he didn't actually call her a bitch. But he'd wanted to.

He settled his shoulders against the chair and elevated his brows. "Okay. So what's next?"

Ellie got up and paced across the space in front of her desk, which wasn't much, but it helped, and then she dropped back into her chair. "Look, can you indulge me here? I need to think this through and obviously Metzger expects something from me and I am not sure I can deliver."

"At least he didn't threaten to fire you."

"Pretty close."

"Almost."

There was a part of her that thought he was absolutely right. This was going to test her tenure in the department. Someone out there either knew about them sending Mrs. Hamilton into safe harbor, or watched and figured it out.

Not reassuring either way.

"We have a team on Hamilton, right?"

"Grasso."

"Good decision or bad?"

"DCI is on the ball as well. Why the fuck would it be bad? He's more experienced than either one of us, let's face it."

She wasn't going to comment, though it was tempting. "So what can we do to help facilitate this process?" Her eyes were level with his across the desk considering he was sprawled carelessly in his chair in a slouch.

He said, "I have an idea."

She looked at him, at the tendrils of damp hair curling at his temples, at the hard-edged determination in his face, and she asked, "Like what?"

"Let's take a road trip. I'll have the call we're waiting for transferred to my cell."

Chapter 26

The symbolic nature of it all didn't escape me, but for time out of mind, people have been exactly that way: busy, inquisitive, absorbed with themselves but curious about others, and the phrase "none of my business" is one of the most absurd in the history of mankind.

We all want to know what everyone else is doing. To not put too fine a point on it, we do stick our noses where they don't belong, just like other animals.

Such an advantage if you are trying to commit a crime. Someone is always willing to talk to you, to give you what you need, and unless you wear a sign that says Murderer around your neck, it is all so easy.

So very easy . . .

But it was getting harder. Did they realize that? Yes, there were degrees.

Much harder, but it just needed to be done or all of it was pointless.

The café was homey, a bit old with tile floors and retro chairs that were only retro because they might actually

be from the sixties, around small tables that didn't match
The minute Ellie walked in the door almost all the conversation stopped, but this was a very small town, and she
certainly was a stranger.

Her contact was easy to spot, sitting by himself and
chatting with a waitress who looked about fifteen and
could have been his granddaughter, and she found out
when she introduced herself and sat down, she actually
was. Mr. Raylan was in his midseventies, wearing a flannel shirt even in the heat, but still handsome in a weathered way she liked, gray-haired, his face all character
and lines.

"Sophie is in high school," he told her proudly. "She
wants to go to college and study English. Can you
imagine that?"

"I can actually," Ellie said noncommittally. "I started
out as an English major before I switched to criminal justice. You should encourage her."

"You said on the phone you were with the Milwaukee police." Mr. Raylan frowned, his silver eyebrows
drawing together. "And I've been sitting here trying to
think why you would want to meet with me. You're a
little far out of the city, Detective."

"We are investigating a case that might have ties back
here. As a matter of fact, ties to the farm you own that
used to belong to the McNeely family. I wanted to get
your permission for us to go out there and look around."

"I see."

He didn't, but he didn't have to. All he had to do was
give her the information she needed and permission to
take a walk around.

Sophie arrived at that moment with two cups of coffee and two pieces of pie. She was blond and cheerful
and said, "Here you go, Gramps. Ma'am."

"This lady is a detective, Sophie."

"Oh." Sophie looked like she wasn't sure what to say, but a new group came in and she nodded and hurried off to grab some plastic-covered menus.

"I ordered apple," Mr. Raylan said without apology. "Hope you don't mind, but I told Sophie to bring it out as soon as you arrived. It's the best here and I don't know anyone that doesn't like apple pie. Tell me you aren't one of those girls who worry about every single bite they take."

Ellie was more than happy, she was in heaven. The pretzels hadn't really done the job. There was ice cream too, in a melting, gooey glob, the scent of cinnamon seductive. "No, sir, and thank you. It looks delicious."

She picked up her fork and prompted him. "The McNeely farm?"

"Yes, I bought it years ago. After the fire." He took a large bite and chewed and swallowed before he went on. "The house was gone but the barn was still decent at the time. I'm afraid I'm not sure why you want to look at it."

"I'm interested in Randy McNeely."

"The boy?"

"The boy. Only he's a man now." The pie was delicious . . . and she was famished.

"Sure is, I'd guess. Time goes by pretty fast these days. He was nine or ten maybe when the place burned?" Mr. Raylan took a sip of coffee. "I got the property in an estate sale. It was still mortgaged and the bank just wanted to be rid of it. The house was gone, but that didn't matter to me. I just wanted the land, that's all. I farm a little, but mostly it's livestock."

"After the fire, you took care of their dairy cattle."

"Of course I did." Pale blue eyes regarded her across the uneven table. "Neighbors do that for each other."

At that point, he no longer had those neighbors, bu
she didn't point it out. This lead might easily take he
nowhere.

But the pie was absolutely worth it. Rich, sweet, and
delectably perfect. "Anything you can tell me might b
helpful. What about Randy? Didn't he go to his grand
mother?"

"Sure did." Mr. Raylan looked introspective. "Bu
Beatrice died of a heart attack and he was then shuffled
off into the hands of the government. He turned ou
good, though. He stops by now and then and I've told
him he can visit the property whenever he wants. I can'
blame him for wanting to come here and keep con
nected with the past. I might do the same, in his shoes
Did you know he's a doctor now? That's something, con
sidering his disadvantages."

The rattle of dishes and conversation around them al
faded away. Even the pie lost its glory. Ellie said care
fully, "You've seen him recently?"

Her companion looked contemplative. "Recently?
don't know. I noticed some fresh tire tracks in the lane
yesterday and I assumed it was either him or those darned
teenagers who go there to park now and again."

She set aside her fork. "Where does he live, do you
know?"

"Down your way. In the city. He's never said exactly
where."

"And he's a doctor?"

"Said he is."

Ellie could feel her heart racing. "Are you sure? Ca
you tell me his last name? We know at some point he
was adopted."

"Detective, you might even know him." The old ma
gave her a glimmering smile.

That was about the last thing she expected to hear. "Why would I know him?"

"His name is Reubens now. Dr. Reubens. I think he works for the police in some way, or that is what he told me. He was off working at some hospital somewhere else or some such thing that is required after medical school and he just moved back to Wisconsin not that long ago. Looks at dead bodies from what I understand."

Reubens. It all started to click into place, the domino effect causing her brain to race, jumbled thoughts one after the other . . . the autopsies, on his own victims? The bone saw used to cut up the victim down in Greendale, the little boy who had a fascination with fire and dead bodies . . .

She'd broken out in a sweat that had nothing to do with the heat outside. "Thank you," she said in a rush. "Thank you, Mr. Raylan. The pie is on me. You've been more than helpful."

Ellie pulled a bill out of her pocket, set it on the table, and stood. "Give Sophie a nice tip."

"You haven't even finished your pie. What did I say?"

"I'll tell you what, maybe we can make a date someday and have another piece and I'll be able to tell you all about it, but for the moment, I have to go. Can we look at your property?"

He smiled, though he looked a little bewildered. "Help yourself. And I'll take that date, Detective."

Jason had absolutely no luck talking to local law enforcement. First of all, the officer on duty was a middle-aged woman who was completely immune to his most ingratiating smile because he was pretty sure her preferences were on the other side of the fence. She might have loved Ellie. They should have switched places.

At any rate, he got nowhere asking about the Mc
Neelys' deaths because she really wasn't willing to wast
her time on it, whether or not he was with MPD.

"That was over twenty years ago. You can requisitio
the accidental death report, but not now." She looke
pointedly out the window at the growing dusk. "This i
not Milwaukee. I'm pretty much on my own and don'
have time to sift through boxes and boxes to get wha
you're looking for, Detective."

He bit back a caustic response. Well, sort of. "I apolo
gize, but I'm on a time line here and actually in the crime
solving business. When can we have it?"

She folded her hands on the desk and looked smug
"Can't say, as I am currently working night shifts and
won't be the one looking it up."

He wasn't positive what he might have said at tha
point but his cell rang and he turned around and pushe
a button.

Ellie said in an almost unrecognizable voice. "Yo
aren't going to believe this. Meet me at the car."

The road was rutted, the sounds of cicadas loud, and sh
had no doubt that even though he didn't show it, he
partner was suffering every single rut more than his clas
sic car.

She said coolly, "What are we doing? We need to g
back to Milwaukee and talk to Metzger. This is sensi
tive. We still have nothing but hearsay and conjecture."

"Let's see, Ellie: he's from here, his parents died in
house fire, we can connect the table to it, he expertl
dismembered a corpse, and the guy has a past—befor
he changed his name—of an obsession with dead bodie
and is now a medical examiner. He's killing them some

where else. He told us that himself. I'm wondering if it
isn't right here where he started."

He had a point. She'd wondered about it, but who
knew? It was all too bizarre.

Ellie looked out the window, examined the starlit
countryside, and saw the lightning bugs in the fields flash
as they drove slowly along the rutted lane. The leaves
were thick but wilted in the heat, and the wire fence
broken in many places. It smelled like dried fields of
corn and old manure. "It can't be true."

"Like fucking hell it's not. Reubens. Motherfuck. I'm
not sure I do either." His voice was rough and uneven.
"He's been here recently, right? Didn't your farmer guy
say the lane had tire tracks?"

"He did. I don't know if we should even be driving up
here. What if they could cast and match the tires?"

Santiago didn't look over. "Too dry for anything
good." His voice changed. "You always get an impression about what someone is like when you meet them,
right? I'm pretty pissed off when I think about those
reports I spent so much time reading. Who knows if
there's a shred of truth in any of them."

Good point.

The car hit a particularly rough rut and she caught
the door handle.

He had a decidedly more visceral approach to law
enforcement in general, but maybe he was right. "I listen
to my gut reaction, but I don't operate on it like you do
twenty-four/seven," she admitted, maybe a little grudgingly.

This entire evening had her jumpy. "What exactly do
you think we'll find out here? He's not going to leave
evidence."

"I don't know." Jason carefully guided the car over series of bumps and openly winced. "Shit maybe w should have brought your car. He cut up that bod somewhere. I'm sorry, but that isn't easy to do and leav no trace. My guess is right here."

"So you can now think like a serial killer?" But sh did have to wonder if he wasn't right. It was seclude deserted, and obviously there was no reason for M Raylan to come over very often since the house wa gone . . .

"You really think I'm that complicated?"

"You don't want me to answer that question."

His sidelong glance was swift and her partner gave sardonic laugh. "True enough, but I'm just trying to be lieve this. I need to feel it, you know?"

What *she* was feeling, along with a similar sense o disbelief, was that this place made a perfect setting fo murder. The headlights caught the remnants of an ol orchard, overgrown and wild, with vines through th trees, and some animal was in the underbrush by th lane, the gleam of eyes visible briefly before it vanishe There was the ghost of a fence with gnarled wire an missing posts, taken over by morning glories and poiso ivy, the evidence of human habitation slowly being swa lowed up by nature unsettling, and she was unsettle enough.

It felt . . . haunted. Maybe not in a literal sense, but b the past.

"We aren't going to be able to tell much, it's getting s dark," Ellie pointed out, suddenly uneasy. The evenin was oppressive, the breeze rustling the leaves in an eeri hint of motion. "Tell me you have a flashlight."

"Glove box."

Jason parked the car by what must have been a shed for farm implements or seed. There was the old barn, half collapsed about a hundred yards away, bleached to a weathered gray.

He got out his phone and slid a finger across the front pad. "I'm just going to fill Grasso in. If he thinks we should go ahead and tell Metzger now, we will on our way back to Milwaukee. At the moment all we're doing is following a lead. But if we investigate our own medical examiner and we're wrong, there goes my job, and it isn't going to do you any favors either. I admit the evidence is starting to come into line, but we still have nothing more than Hamilton's hunch about him as a kid."

She took out the flashlight and was grateful it flashed on at the touch of a button. "Okay, a third opinion won't hurt I guess. Either way this swings, Metzger isn't going to be happy. I wouldn't even dream of questioning Reubens without concrete physical evidence linking him to one of the crimes."

Ellie opened her door and slipped out, standing facing west, her face into the breeze. She could hear her partner talking but her attention was entirely elsewhere suddenly. It felt like the world went eerily silent. "What is that?"

He ended the call and got out. "He's going to—"

"Santiago," she interrupted, her voice a low hiss. "That." She pointed again at a jolt of color between the trees, the scent sharp in her nostrils, the hair on her arms lifting. "Do you smell smoke? I know I do."

"I see it." He let his car door drift closed, his hand measuring the movement, keeping it from slamming, obviously still thinking, still reacting.

Good for him. She was fairly sure she about stopped breathing.

The insects were loud in the trees and the humidity made her shirt cling to her body. She shook her head. " can't believe I'm saying this but I think we have a fire I can even see the occasional flare of the flames."

"Ah, shit. I'm sick of that smell. I think I've been shifted into an alternate reality. Damn, Ellie, this world is one fucking strange place." Santiago took out his gun and checked the clip. "He might be here and we know he has a gun. I'll go first."

She peered through the trees, wishing the dark wasn' descending so quickly, but the country was like this. No lights, and once that sun went down, it was over. " don't see a car."

"Maybe he's already gone."

She'd taken out her weapon also and began to walk cautiously. "You willing to bank on that?"

True to character, he said, "Fuck no."

Chapter 27

figured if it was going to be, it just was, and I think since I was a child, I have always felt a fatalistic sense of resignation. A pragmatic approach to be sure, but I was born with that gene that has allowed me to adapt to different circumstances.

I didn't always like the changes, obviously, but I always adapted.

I'd killed her the day before. I really didn't prefer that, but this wasn't negotiable and logistics being what they were, I also switched venues.

That was no problem. Somehow it seemed fitting that it should end here where it started when I thought it over.

Marjorie had been my first encounter with The System. Well-meaning, smiling, and utterly unaware of how much I despised her, hated the interference, and laughed cynically at the assurances that everything was going to be just fine.

Or maybe she wasn't unaware. Maybe we were all the same. None of us believed.

It wasn't fine. Life had never been fine. I'd once

watched as my father hit my mother so hard she crashed
into the counter and went down like a load of wet sand.
There was something wrong with him—and with her—
for letting it be that way. For as sure as the sun was going to come up the next morning, that was not the last
time he would raise his hand to her. She stayed, he went
on with the abuse, and it was never going to change.

Unless someone did something about it.

I don't think I really wanted to kill them. Maybe a
little. Maybe I wanted to kill them a little—no, him for
sure, but her too in a way—but mostly what I wanted
was to eradicate the place of my childhood. Desecrate it.
Wipe it from the face of the earth.

And I'd liked doing it, watching the flames begin to
feed as I watched in fascination, their hunger gnawing
at the dry, old siding, swallowing the roof, roaring in
pleasure. By the time the fire trucks arrived, it had been
hopeless, an inferno.

It had changed my life.

Marjorie had been in her kitchen and I'd knocked on
the door. She opened it, and I think she might even have
recognized me after a few seconds when I introduced
myself and produced my credentials. She let me in. Even
offered coffee. In this blistering heat.

Gracious of her.

But she didn't know the creature.

I'm not all that convinced I know the creature either.
It is possible he's got the best of me.

The air felt like a moist, hot lick.

That was what his father always called it and it somehow stuck in his brain.

Jason wanted the lead but Ellie was ahead of him already, Glock drawn, both of them walking through the

crisp grass, knee deep in places. At least the snakes were probably down their holes or near water of some kind, or he sure hoped so. He knew there were copperheads and moccasins around and he couldn't see just what he might be stepping on.

What they were stalking was a lot more deadly anyway.

The fire was in the remains of what must have been the basement of the house, the flames casting a lurid light on the dirt walls, the open square dark otherwise. It was a little like seeing a human sacrifice and Jason heard Ellie make a muffled sound at just the same moment he spotted the platform and the shape on it down deep in the hole.

Human sacrifice.

It felt wrong to not rush to put out the flames, but no one could survive that conflagration, and if the pattern held, that unmoving form represented someone who was already dead anyway.

"My God," Ellie said, her voice holding a hint of horror, edging down beneath a bush.

He didn't disagree with her muttered sentiment, crouching behind her. "Where is he?"

"I'm sure he heard the car as we drove up the lane."

That was probably true. "Look, let me go in front."

"Why? Because you're male?"

"Exactly."

"Makes you a bigger target." Ellie's hair reflected the reddish light of the flames but otherwise it was pretty dead black around them from his angle. No streetlights here, no help coming anytime soon if the local officer was an indication, and Grasso was in Milwaukee, as was most everyone else they could call. State police response maybe, county sheriff's department if necessary,

but someone needed to tell them just what they were
dealing with, and finding them was going to be a bitch.
They'd missed the turn twice.

And as for him being male, absurdly enough, that was
it. She was half a foot shorter and in the garish light, her
slender frame looked even less substantial, especially
when she crouched by the edge of the foundation to peer
into the cave of the old cellar. But she held the Glock
with the businesslike comfort of someone who knew
how to handle it.

Woman or not, he was glad of Ellie MacIntosh because he sure as hell had never been in this position before and she had. As a police officer when he was on
patrol, he'd chased his share of suspects into some questionable places, and drawn his weapon more than once.
But he'd never hunted a serial killer with a burning body
just a few feet away.

To make matters worse there was a full moon rising
now, cresting the tree line, flooding light everywhere,
distorting the shadows.

Not helpful.

"Fine, go first," he said in a barely audible voice.
"Prove you have a bigger dick than I do."

She ignored him—it had been pretty crude, even for
him. "I don't see anyone."

"Fucking Reubens," he murmured, inching forward,
stepping through the long grass with an inward prayer.
"By the way, he drives a black Mercedes, not new, but
not that old either, so that fits like a glove right there.
Where is he?"

A now familiar unsettling smell wafted upward with
the smoke and it looked to Jason like someone had piled
timber of some kind under the table, like a funeral pyre
because the flames shot up over the grotesque suggges

tion of a human form. Paramedics would definitely be a waste of the taxpayers' dollars.

"On the way to his tropical vacation? I wonder if we have extradition where he's headed." Her whisper was quiet, but so close he caught it.

Jason swore softly but vehemently. "I forgot about that. Son of a bitch. He warned us. Told us flat out he was leaving the country."

"Let's go check the barn," she said.

"I'll go, you call this in. Get Grasso on that angle so Reubens doesn't get away. They can check the airports. He can't be gone yet. Look at the fire. He's got maybe an hour on us at the most. We need backup, and for all we know he's checking his bags right now and about to board his flight."

"Good point." Her features washed to bleached bone by the moonlight, she already had out her phone and was punching in numbers, her hair a pale halo around her face.

The yard had long since disappeared under the invasion of weeds and Jason barely avoided catastrophe as he came across an old cistern, the cover askew and broken. If he'd gone down into it he might have easily broken a leg, which didn't sound like a whole lot of fun, and besides, who knew what form of animal life might hide there, and he wasn't anxious to find out either.

The barn was dilapidated, listing sideways like a broken old man on a cane, part of the roof gone, the doors completely torn off either by storms or for wood, and even the smell of manure was faint after so many years of disuse.

However, he knew Reubens had driven up here because he could smell crushed vegetation, earthy and fresh, and sure enough, when he stepped carefully over the tracks through the weeds, it did look like a car had been through very recently and might have been parked on the other side of the structure.

An owl called close by, probably from the rafters; he jumped and then swore softly.

Then he caught a gleam of something around the corner . . . metal?

Correction. The car was *still* parked there.

Black, solid in the moonlight, but definitely Reubens' vehicle.

Holy shit. Not at the airport, but right here and he would have heard them . . .

Something moved inside the barn. He only caught it out of the corner of his eye and swiveled on the pads of his feet.

Motherfuck . . .

The first bullet hit him in the chest. Solid. He felt the penetration, the tearing flesh, the crush of bone. The second got him lower, but he was already going down, down, weapon half raised . . .

Down.

The gunshot reports echoed and it was as if the night stopped dead.

What just happened?

Ellie almost fell into the dark pit of the basement with the burning corpse and she could think of nothing she would like less. On the other end of the line, Grasso said, "What was that?"

"Forget the airports, we've got shots fired here." She crouched down, desperately clutching her phone, sweat prickling over her body, searching for cover, but the weeds were about the best she could do. "I need backup right now."

"I heard it. It's fifty miles for me, but I'll call the locals."

She flipped her phone shut and tried to figure out how to approach the barn without running in the open. The moonlight wasn't helpful, pouring down with an almost surreal brilliance.

Where are you?

Her first impulse was to call out, but she knew better. A June bug blundered past her face, the startling sound loud, making her jerk backward. Her heart was going about a hundred miles an hour.

Barn. Santiago had been checking out the barn . . . but there wasn't a good direct approach, and if she had to call it, given that Jason hadn't yelled out to her, he was either trying to stay undercover, or maybe he just couldn't yell at all.

The old orchard on one side of the drive might provide a way to approach, but getting there was still a problem and she scanned the perimeter, not seeing any movement, but not liking the silence.

Fine, she'd break it.

"Dr. Reubens!" she shouted, still crouched down, sweat trickling down her back. "This is the end of it. There are sheriff's deputies on their way and I've alerted the MPD. Why not surrender?"

Now he would know exactly where she was, but she wasn't certain he didn't already. Luckily, the waist-high vegetation provided some measure of obscurity, but unfortunately no protection, and she was pretty sure what she'd heard was rifle fire, not her partner's .45.

The fact that Santiago wasn't communicating was ominous.

He was profane, opinionated, and a pain in her ass, but still her stomach twisted in apprehension and concern.

Something rustled. She swiveled, on her haunches, her weapon steady, the safety off.

Nothing but the eerie moonlit outline of the barn, the barest brush of a breeze, and then suddenly she caught it. A small flare of light from the corner of the back and she realized the hissing sound was a blow torch.

She sprinted toward the growing flame. All she could think of was that he was burning his last victim and that might just be Jason Santiago. . . .

It hurt like hell.

Jason never lost consciousness completely but he was stunned, gasping, trying to take it in. He knew he was bleeding, and he levered up on an elbow, was grateful he wasn't coughing up blood, registered he might have hit his head when he fell because his face was wet, and then slowly got to his feet.

Not as easy as it sounded.

First of all he was soaked in blood, and unfortunately, all of it was his. He took a moment and tried to assess, and it wasn't a gushing wound, but it was definitely dripping everywhere, off his sleeve, off the hem of his shirt, and there was a slight haze of smoke in the air, and when he wiped his temple, his hand came away dark.

You know, he was getting tired of the theme. Blood. Fire. Death.

MacIntosh was out there, hunting Reubens, and when she heard the shots, he was sure she'd kept a cool head and called for help. He told himself that as calmly as possible, because panic right now was the enemy of a good outcome.

Shot, not dead. Look at the bright side. No more shots. Ellie still alive was a good thing.

He wasn't sure he was glad Metzger stuck them together, but he was positive he wasn't getting left out to dry. She was out there, but so was Reubens.

Gun? Where the hell was his gun? He tried to walk, staggered a little, and then heard a noise. It brought him around but it wasn't anything . . . a crackle, and there was a curl of flame in the corner . . .

The barn was on fire.

"Are you fuckin' kidding me?" he muttered and headed for the door, though his progress was hampered by the fact he was shot in the leg and chest, and *shit. It hurt.*

If there was one thing that was not going to happen tonight, he was not going to get roasted by The Burner.

He limped outside, coughed again, happy it seemed to just be because of the smoke, and caught a glimpse of his weapon, lying where he must have fallen. Picking it up was a lesson in torture he didn't care to repeat, but he felt much better with it in his hand.

He eased himself around the edge of the structure, using it for support, his bloody fingers slippery against the old, rough wood.

There was one thing about fire. It was not a secret. The moonlit night showcased the growing inferno at the corner of the barn and it didn't exactly hide Ellie either, crouched by the side of the building, gun extended, her hair pale in the growing illumination from the flames.

"Put your weapon down and come forward," she called. "You know there's no walking out of here."

The hell there wasn't. Trees were everywhere for plenty of cover and while escaping on foot and leaving his car behind might not be ideal, it was possible.

Reubens wasn't going to surrender. Jason knew it. More than that, he understood it. He'd learned it young too, learned how to take care of himself.

To take care of obstacles.

He also knew how to be out of control. But he'd never killed anyone to prove it.

A shadow moved at the edge of the growing flames. It was almost nothing. Ellie, crouched down, didn't see it, and from where she was, he doubted she would, but from his vantage point, upright and behind her, he did.

He might be more old-fashioned than he thought he was because he tensed there as he rested bleeding against that old barn, and that same stupid protective male instinct surfaced.

The shadow moved again on the periphery. From her position Ellie still didn't see it, the fire sending up flickers as it caught and grew.

"Dr. Reubens?" she called. "Come out."

He was coming out all right, with a rifle against her pistol and he wasn't doing it to give himself up. Not this man who burned bodies. Not The Burner.

"MacIntosh, down!" Jason ordered in a rasp.

She turned at the sound of his voice, but stayed low.

The shadow shifted.

But he still saw it. He was swaying on his feet. Infuriating, but true. He stepped out, and there was a sharp blast as Reubens fired and Jason honed in on the flash, took two rapid shots, and then started to fade, the knees going first, in slow motion, and then his shoulder hitting the ground, a grunt making his breath go out.

One way or another, his last thought was, *it was over . . .*

He really hoped he'd wasted him.

Chapter 28

The antiseptic smell of a hospital was not her favorite thing on this planet, and the sitting area outside intensive care reminded Ellie of waiting for news after her father's heart attack, and that had not turned out well.

She hoped this would be different.

Metzger, uncharacteristically rumpled, muttered something under his breath and took another drink of coffee from a Styrofoam cup as he sat down. Out loud, he said, "This is going to go viral. I currently have my phone turned off. Maybe you and Carl need to go over this again for me. I know I'll get reports *this afternoon,*" he said pointedly, "but for now, let's make sure I understand it as much as possible."

"Sir—"

He held up his hand and Ellie closed her mouth.

"Let's see. Our very own medical examiner, the one actually performing the autopsies, was systematically seeking out anyone associated with his former life and killing them? Do I have that right so far?"

Ellie exchanged a brief look with Grasso. "We haven't

confirmed it all yet, but we think he took the bodies to places where he once lived when he was in the foster care system. Unfortunately for us, he was smart enough to not necessarily place the victim in the same place where *they* once lived, but just where *he* once lived before he set their bodies, and the building, on fire. It made it difficult to connect the dots, because *he* really was the only connection."

"Purification by fire, so to speak." Carl Grasso, wearing a faded Harvard T-shirt and worn jeans, sent the chief a level look. "When he was a kid, his parents died in a house fire on the property where Santiago and MacIntosh found him. We've gotten confirmation that when he was sixteen he was finally adopted by two college professors who were impressed with his intellect, I guess, and had never been able to have children of their own, so they took in foster kids. He changed his name to Reubens and the old Randy McNeely went away."

It was Metzger's turn to gift Ellie with his particular steely stare. "The events of last night are a little muddy to me, probably because I am sleep deprived beyond belief due to one of my detectives being shot last night and a series of particularly heinous murders committed by someone in the employ of this city. How did you know he was going to be there, and if you did, I think a team would have been a better decision, don't you, Detective?"

"We had no idea he was there, sir." Ellie could say that honestly to the implied criticism because she knew she'd be raked across the proverbial coals for that fact and was prepared to at least defend what happened. "Santiago was convinced that the old farm might have a connection to the murders. You told me yourself he was an intuitive cop. It just happened. We only went there to check it out."

Not quite. That was too simple. Reubens—she still thought of him that way—must have known they were figuring it all out, and she still believed that Lucy Hamilton was in danger, so if he had heard, and he would have been working closely with the police department, that they were watching her house, he would just relocate and the farm made sense, especially if the initial killings were being done there.

Metzger rubbed a hand over his face. He actually did look exhausted. "Okay, so you arrived, saw there was smoke, realized there was a fire, and still didn't call for backup?"

"You've been in the office for far too long, Chief," Grasso said with a hint of wry amusement in his voice. "They called when they saw the body. It's an old abandoned farm owned by an almost-as-old farmer. He could have been burning anything. Moldy hay, his trash, come on. Both Santiago and MacIntosh are experienced enough to wait to make sure there actually is a crime being committed before screaming for help. Sometimes things go down so fast you don't have the time. They handled it."

Then and there, Ellie started to like Carl Grasso despite her earlier distrust.

"Handled it? Santiago got himself there." The chief pointed at the closed doors to the intensive care unit.

Was that her fault?

It had occurred to her that maybe they should have stayed together, but in retrospect some things were crystal clear, and it really could be this was one of those times. "We had a dead body but no idea where the suspect might be. I called for assistance and he went to look."

If the doctor hadn't come out at that moment, she wasn't sure whether or not Metzger might have pointed out acerbically that procedure wasn't followed precisely, but a weary young man in scrubs came out of the doors, chart in hand, and said, "The family of Jason Santiago?"

Ellie stood. "I'm his"—she searched for the right word—"partner."

"MacIntosh?"

"Right."

"He's asking for you. You have ten minutes."

Well, he'd made it anyway.

Floating out somewhere around Mars, but hey, that wasn't so bad. Painful breathing was a good substitute for the alternative.

Ellie sat down in a chair next to his bed. She looked tired and at some point had pulled her hair back into a no-nonsense ponytail. "Hi."

Without preamble, he asked in a raspy voice, "Did I get him? They won't say anything except to ask if I need another drink of water. I could use a beer, by the way, if you have influence. The nurses seem kind of standoffish."

At least that wrung a laugh out of her. "Your charming attitude needs work."

"I saved your ass."

"Ah, you see? Charm in abundance."

"You might have saved mine too." He adjusted his position in bed and tried to leer, but probably failed. "You took off your shirt. I vaguely remember that."

He didn't remember anything very clearly at all. He'd been losing it, the world blurry around the edges, the sound of that old dry barn crackling as it started to really catch fire, and there was MacIntosh trying to drag him away from the building, her face pale even in the lurid light, and then she was bent over him, ripping her shirt off over her head, asking him to hold on, just hold on . . .

"You were bleeding to death," she said with equanimity. "That's why I took off my shirt. To staunch the blood flow. I was wearing a bra. You've been to the beach. No different."

"A little different. I suspect you've got a nice set of—"

"Santiago." Her voice was full of exasperation.

"Hey, I noticed. Proved to me I was still alive."

"You got him," she interrupted, her face somber. "A round just under the first rib and another just missed the heart but got his lung. In such rapid succession, the deputies who arrived eventually were impressed."

If he wasn't so tired, he'd lift his arm and offer a high-five, but he didn't really think she did that sort of thing, and frankly, there were too many tubes attached to him in various places. "I could see him. You couldn't from your position."

"No, I couldn't," she agreed, her hazel eyes holding his gaze.

One of the machines he was attached to beeped and he ignored it, because he didn't know what the hell the thing was measuring anyway.

He got him.

To be truthful, it helped with the pain of his own wounds, because Reubens had *definitely* shot him.

"I owed him one. Or two, I guess."

"I think you're more than even."

"I take it that means he didn't make it."

"The paramedics worked hard. I'm afraid he's about three doors down on this same floor."

"Still alive? Fuck, I can't tell you how that breaks my heart." He shut his eyes briefly and pushed the little magic button that helped the pain. The relief wasn't quite as instant as he would have liked, but it kept it bearable anyway.

"No shit? You have a heart?" Ellie grinned at him.

"I told you I was rubbing off on you, and you know what, apparently you're rubbing off on me too. I think we've both now shot suspected serial killers during apprehension."

"I suppose that's true. At least I killed mine."

"You win." He was having trouble concentrating on the conversation, some of it no doubt due to the pain meds.

"Let's call it a draw and discontinue the competition."

"Ever been shot?"

"Yes. Thigh."

"That's something I'd like to see. We'll compare scars later."

A nurse came in, said something he didn't quite catch, and Ellie nodded and stood.

She was leaving. That was okay, he was leaving too in a different way, fading out.

But he actually felt good.

He'd got him.

Considering everything, Carl thought that MacIntosh was holding up pretty well. Professional, calm, maybe a little ragged around the edges, but as far as he could tell she'd been up all night as they operated on both their suspect and her partner, and at the end of the day, they had The Burner.

She stood next to him and waited, as did he, as the doctor jotted notes and spoke quietly to a nurse at the station, and then he came over. "I understand you want to talk to my patient."

"If that's possible." MacIntosh held out her badge. "I have no doubt you understand why."

"He's lucid." The doctor flipped the chart shut. "But only in fair condition, though that is a miracle. The surgery went fairly well but there was a lot of damage and I won't bore you with the medical terminology, but he got lucky."

"His victims can't say the same. We need him to answer a few questions. This won't be an interrogation, but please understand, we both know Dr. Reubens fairly well, or we thought we did anyway. We'll keep it brief."

The doctor took a moment. "I'll ask him, how is that? If he refuses, I'm sorry, but you'll have to wait. He's a physician. He can gauge his ability to endure an interview."

A few minutes later Carl followed MacIntosh into a sterile room he preferred to never be one he occupied. Dr. Reubens was attached to so many machines he would feel sorry for him except he was not really deserving of sympathy of any kind.

Pallid and unmoving, he regarded them with a steady gaze. "Detectives."

It was MacIntosh's case in essence, so Carl let her speak first. "What set this off? Why now? Cameron was five years ago."

The sound that came out of his mouth might have been a laugh, but it was so weak it was hard to tell. "Do you really expect me to incriminate myself?"

"As I see it, you have no latitude at all. Metzger is going to push this to consecutive life sentences when he goes to the district attorney, and if you think we won't have enough evidence to convict, I think you know that is unlikely. You're screwed."

"You have been spending entirely too much time with Santiago."

"Thanks to you." Carl said persuasively, "Come on, answer her question. We can prove the crimes, we just don't understand *why*."

"You never will, because I am not sure myself, but . . . Matthew Tobias." Reubens adjusted his position slightly and a strained look of pain crossed his face. "At one time, we were both in the system, shuffled around like a deck of cards, dealt a hand that might be good, and one that might make you fold and wish your life was over. We ran into each other one day . . . a chance meeting and he recognized me. We'd both been with the Camerons at the same time, so we'd gone to the same school, ridden the bus . . . put up with that abusive, sanctimonious man. It was hell."

"And?"

"I'd made the mistake of telling Matthew that one day I planned to kill him." For a moment Reubens let his eyes close. "It didn't matter at the time, though I meant it. However, when Matthew realized I was in Milwaukee after my residency and fellowship were done, and that Cameron really had been murdered, he started to blackmail me. All he wanted was prescriptions for pain medications, which I am licensed to write. I'd told him back when we were friends a few things I regret. I set his home on fire with a clear message. It seems he understood. I got to do his autopsy. How ironic is that?"

Very. Carl understood irony fully. He asked, "Then why kill the others? Were they like Cameron?"

"No. Some were better than others, of course. I don't know if you can understand this, but I wanted to get rid of Randy McNeely. Tobias reminded me that he still existed in other people's minds . . . that someone might remember him, when I was doing my best to forget him. I had."

Not entirely, Carl thought.

A nurse came into the room and looked pointedly at a clock on the wall. "I'm sorry, but the doctor put a time limit on this visit."

"Why did you dismember one of them and not the others?"

"I'm adaptive. She was a little too heavy for me to carry all in one piece."

Carl wasn't squeamish, he'd gotten over that a long time ago, but the pragmatic explanation and lack of remorse was disturbing to a level he hadn't experienced before.

"I'm sorry, but—" the nurse started to say again.

Ellie nodded, looking more tired than ever, and interrupted. "We're done." She walked out of the room, following the young woman.

"Carl."

He stopped, turning back. He had to admit Reubens looked like hell, but his eyes were still alive and intelligent.

"What?"

"You've killed before."

Good God. "Not quite the same thing."

"Doesn't matter. Dead is dead and self-defense is an abstract concept that has a multitude of interpretations. I have something to ask of you."

"Like what?" He stared at the man on the bed.

"I know hospitals in and out. I killed Cameron the year I graduated from medical school and spent three years in residency out of state, and then had a fellowship for two. There, I just gave you the reason for the five-year gap. Could you get something for me? I can tell you exactly where it is."

Epilogue

Ellie took a breath and decided that life was too short to ignore the crucial issues. Breakfast, coffee, Santiago doing well, or so she was told, Reubens in custody . . .

Well, crucial was always a debatable point, but in her life, *she* got to make that decision so she asked, "Did you ever *really* consider it?"

Bryce looked up from across the table, his gaze inquiring, cup poised halfway to his mouth as if he'd caught her tone. "Consider what?"

"Having a baby with Suzanne."

His mouth curved just a little. "That's what you want to talk about right *now*? You had one hell of a day yesterday and I feel sure the fallout is going to be huge."

It was. Metzger was besieged by the press, she had reports to write, and The Burner was in custody, but they still had some things to figure out.

"Yes. This is what I want to talk about right now." She set aside her coffee.

"I thought I already said I wasn't interested in giving my ex-wife a child."

He always looked delicious first thing in the morning, with a slight hint of a beard and tousled hair. She was pretty sure he'd worn that shirt the day before, but someone like Bryce could get away with it.

"*Did* you consider it?"

"No. Ellie, we've been through this."

"Not even for a minute?"

Bryce gazed at her calmly—he had the ability to do it like no one else. "I don't think so. I was startled, I was even a little angry she would ask, but I do not want to have a child that way. I can say very honestly I wasn't interested. At all."

"I'm glad to hear it." It startled her how much she meant that statement. "I really . . ."

What stupid thing was she about to say? Like you? She did, but that was inadequate. Love you? They weren't quite there yet, or she wasn't. It was still about the romance between them, the physical attraction, the differences in their personalities, and she didn't trust quite yet that she saw the situation with the necessary clarity.

"You really . . . ?" he prompted, looking at her in inquiry.

"I'm a homicide detective."

"I know. That's how we met." His smile just hovered on his lips. "So I've noticed that about you. Point taken. You *are* a homicide detective. I believe you just apprehended a serial killer and he is your second. You are definitely a homicide detective."

"Don't try and be funny."

"I wasn't."

She believed him, but . . . "Bad things happen. If they don't, I'm out of a job."

"Bad things do seem to happen. Case in point, recent events." The smile deepened and truly, she wanted to just go over, put her arms around him, and forget the rest of her day.

But he really needed to understand.

Or maybe *she* needed it.

This would never be simple. If he thought so, he should find someone else.

That was what held her back. That he would tire of her job.

"How did this occur in the first place?"

"I think you just lost me again. This?" His dark eyes were direct.

"He had conquered it all, dammit." She took in a long breath, filling her lungs. "Look, Reubens defied all the odds dictated by his disrupted childhood. A nice family adopted him finally, he went to college, got into medical school, which is not easy. Worked hard and ended up with the job he wanted." Very true, considering his fascination with the dead, according to Ms. Hamilton's macabre story about the young boy who visited funeral homes. "Why would he . . . I don't know . . . risk it? That's it. Why would he *ever* risk it?"

"I understand computers a lot more than I do people, but babies to bad guys? Come on, Ellie, admit this is quite a leap. Mind letting me in on the segue?"

"I don't know." Her voice was a soft sigh. "No one understands bad guys. And I don't know how I feel about babies."

He laughed. Slight, but there. "There is a huge list of things I don't understand. My parents, politics usually, women—"

"Definitely not women." Her smile softened the criticism.

Maybe she *was* entirely too involved.

"I'll never pressure you."

He wouldn't, but it was too late. She knew where he stood. Children, permanence; it was abstract to her, like a life meant for someone else, but maybe she was wrong. She could picture it, with him, and that was definitely a first.

"You already have," she said frankly. "I know how you feel and—"

Her phone rang, disrupting the conversation. She glanced at the number. "Metzger."

"You'd better answer."

She listened to the chief's brief message, and then hung up without saying much. Bryce waited in his understated way, not asking. She was the one who said, "It's over. Reubens didn't make it. The chief was fuzzy on the details but it sounds like he committed suicide. No one knows how he got ahold of a scalpel."

"I'm afraid I am not going to shed any tears over that. Whatever happened to the Hippocratic oath? Do no harm. He just ignored that part."

"It seems to me you are exactly right."

"At least, with what you have, you should be able to identify the victims now."

She picked up her coffee. "True."

"That will help the families."

"True again."

"And not everything needs to be decided today, Ellie."

"Metzger told me Santiago will be out for a few months so he assigned Carl Grasso as my partner in the interim."

Bryce took a moment, then asked simply, "How do you feel about that?"

"He killed two people and it was intentional. I don't care that they couldn't really prove it. My impression is that he just got away with it."

"He sounds great, let's have him over for dinner."

"*Bryce.*" She gave an exasperated laugh, but at least it was a laugh. "I'm not sure he should even still be on the force, but it isn't like I have a choice. I guess I'm going to look at it this way, it should be . . . interesting."